Logan turned to his little girl again. Hallie's hand twitched. Tiny fingers latched on to his thumb. Oh, man! A lump formed in his throat. "Hal, it's Daddy. Wake up, sweetheart. Please wake up."

Her eyes popped open.

A great surge of relief flooded through him.

She stared at him, unblinking. "Hal? Hallie, sweetheart, Daddy's here." He smiled, clutching her hand tightly, his heart in his throat.

Instantly Dana was at his side, her eyes glistening with tears.

"Hey, kiddo," Logan said, running a finger down Hallie's cheek. "How're ya doing?"

Her eyes looked like large coals in her little face, and as she stared at her mom, he felt her grip tighten, pulling him closer. He leaned in and she whispered, "D-Daddy?"

"Yes, honey. What is it?"

Hallie pointed a wary finger at Dana. "Daddy... who—who is that lady?"

Dear Reader,

How many of us think, if we could only reach our goal, get that job or find that one perfect person, we'd be happy? How many of us, in pursuit of our goals, have made a few mistakes along the way—or wonder if we made the right choices? Probably most of us, because that's human nature. We don't always get things right the first time around.

Fortunately, life is full of second chances, and when they come, each of us must decide the course of action we'll take. Our decisions will be based on our past experiences, our values and our beliefs. Some of us will try again; others will turn away because we might make the wrong choice or we fear we'll fail a second time.

Daddy in the House is a story about second chances. Logan Wakefield and Dana Marlowe are two dynamic yet fallible people who know exactly what they want out of life. They want their careers and they want each other. A beautiful little girl completes the picture. Then life throws them a devastating curve—but it also gives them another chance at love. The question is: What will they do with it?

I believe in love and in second chances. That's why Dana and Logan's story touched my heart, and I'm delighted to have the opportunity to share it with you. I hope it will touch your heart, too.

Happy reading!

Linda Style

P.S. I'd love to hear from you. You can write me at P.O. Box 2292, Mesa, AZ 85202 or e-mail me through my Web site at www.LindaStyle.com or at LindaStyle@lindastyle.com.

Daddy in the House
Linda Style

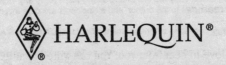

HARLEQUIN®

TORONTO • NEW YORK • LONDON
AMSTERDAM • PARIS • SYDNEY • HAMBURG
STOCKHOLM • ATHENS • TOKYO • MILAN • MADRID
PRAGUE • WARSAW • BUDAPEST • AUCKLAND

ISBN 0-373-70977-3

DADDY IN THE HOUSE

Printed in U.S.A.

To my dear friend and mentor, author Connie Flynn
To my editor, Paula Eykelhof
To my agent, Richard Curtis
Who believed in me and my work, and who gave me
support, encouragement and expert guidance.
My heartfelt thanks and everlasting gratitude to you all.

Acknowledgments

My deep appreciation to Karen McArdle,
Director of Chicago Youth in Aviation and former Chicago
trial attorney, Dr. Jay Style, physician, and Todd Sheridan,
Attorney at Law, for their help with research. Thanks to the
many professionals who were willing to answer questions
related to amnesia, matters of the law and investigations.
Since this is a work of fiction, I have taken liberties in some
areas. Any errors are mine, not theirs. My thanks
to my entire family for your love and support.

CHAPTER ONE

DANA MARLOWE MADE him crazy.

A year since he'd seen her, and she still made him crazy.

That was Logan Wakefield's primary thought as he picked up the telephone this crisp autumn morning to return a call to his ex-wife in Chicago.

Dana was a lot like the city where she grew up. Turbulent. Intense. Charged with energy. Like a stoked fire, she crackled and snapped, and if someone jacked up the heat, she'd blaze into action and, likely as not, scorch the hell out of anything in her way.

If she didn't burn down the town in the process.

No answer. He cradled the phone and glanced at his watch.

What could be so important for her to call him? He'd talked to Hallie just last night to wish her good luck with the school play. Dana couldn't be calling about their daughter.

But there was nothing else in Dana's life important enough to make her call him when he was on a job. He leaned a shoulder against the wall and stared out the cracked window of the seedy hotel room in yet another Third World country, exhaling on a note of regret. Not seeing his daughter as much as he'd like was the one drawback to a job he loved.

A job at which he excelled.

"Yo." Remy DeMarco barreled into the room. "Let's wind it up. We're goin' home."

A sense of relief settled in Logan's bones as he snatched his bomber jacket from the couch and shrugged it on, adjusting the smooth worn leather to cover his gun. "That's music to my ears, buddy."

He'd call Dana from the airport. Whatever she'd called about couldn't be too important if she wasn't even there.

Yet deep down, he knew better. Dana Marlowe Wakefield would undergo a fingernail extraction before she'd call him. It had to be damn important. Still, there was nothing he could do right now—not from halfway around the world.

Logan pinched the bridge of his nose, a bone-deep weariness seeping through him. "I'm gonna need a local assignment after this one," he told Remy.

"You got problems?"

"Nope. Just missing my kid." If anyone would understand, his partner, Remington DeMarco, would. He and his wife were about to have a child of their own.

Friends since fifth grade when Logan had stayed with his grandparents for the summer, he and his business partner went way back. They'd bonded that year in South Philly and renewed the friendship every summer after that. And now, after his own stint in the CIA, and Remy's with the FBI, they were together again—partners in their own Chicago-based investigations firm, Security International Surveillance Inc. SISI for short.

Partners with a growing staff of former elite and special ops agents, they dealt in undercover investigations, top-secret high-tech cases, the stuff most people see only in the movies. Like the case they'd just wound up, an international executive kidnapping in which they'd negotiated a covert payoff for the victim's release.

Remy's craggy face lit up. "You're in luck. We got one. Government contract. Cook County State's Attorney's Office. It's yours."

Logan pinned his friend with a narrowed gaze. Remy's droll sense of humor was working overtime. Remy *knew* Dana worked in the prosecutor's office.

"Right! My masochistic tendencies know no bounds." No way was he going to put himself in the path of destruction. Once was enough. "That's it? That's all we've got?"

Remy nodded as he stuffed his dirty clothes into a plastic bag. "On the local scene, yeah, that's it so far. Hey, it's a perfect cover for you. They need an attorney."

"They'd need an armed guard to keep me from an act of homicide, is what they'd need. I can't be around that woman for more than five minutes before I start thinking murder," Logan said. "And then you'd be visiting me in jail and the job would be down the tubes."

"Can't be that bad, can it?" Remy said on his way into the john.

Yeah, it could. Dana would freak if he turned up in her office. He could almost see her horrified expression, then that laser-quick shifting of emotions to hide what she really felt.

A flash of memory invaded his brain. HLS. Harvard Law School and the day he'd met Dana.

"Ms. Marlowe. Stand and state the case," Professor Karpinsky had demanded.

Logan had watched her rise, slowly, as if accused of a crime and she was facing the jury that would seal her fate. He couldn't blame her. After Karpinsky's brutal inquisition the day before, most of their first-year law class quaked at the prospect of being singled out by the toughest professor on campus.

She cleared her throat. "*Masters v. Woodcliff.* A tort suit," Dana said, addressing their one-hundred and forty peers. Her voice quavered ever so slightly, but enough that the words ran together, making *tort suit* sound a little like *tart soup.*

Professor Karpinsky, an angry-faced man with an electrified shock of gray hair, shouted from across the room, "What does *that* mean?" He barreled down the aisle toward Dana. "Tart soup?" His voice was shrill. "What is that? A dessert?" He stopped a few feet short of her and swung around, his gaze scouring the class for his next victim even before he finished with the first. "Is this a cooking class, Ms. Marlowe? And you're the Gurgling Gourmet?"

A low titter of laughter filtered through the room. Marlowe's face took on a pinkish hue, and oddly, Logan felt her embarrassment as acutely as if it was his own. Karpinsky's reputation as a bully and a tyrant was well-known, and though it was only their second day, Logan had come prepared.

It was obvious his classmate hadn't.

Unless she was plain scared. Out of her element. Which could be, judging by the way she was dressed. Wearing a loose-fitting black jumper over a white turtleneck shirt and black leggings, she looked more like she belonged in a Catholic girl's school than first-year law at Harvard.

She ducked her chin, reminding him of a baby bird he'd rescued once, a defenseless creature that had fallen from its nest and needed protection until it could learn to fly. Well, hell, he could easily state the case, maybe take the pressure off his classmate. He raised his hand.

Karpinsky ignored Logan. And Marlowe, whom he'd thought would appreciate his help, glared at him. Then she hauled in a deep breath, squared her shoulders and addressed her peers. This time when she spoke, her voice was solid, confident.

"It means the plaintiff is seeking a monetary payment to compensate for harms done to him by the defendant." A beat later she added, "Sir."

She went on, her explanation of the case clear, precise and to the point, possibly much better than Logan could've done.

Rocking back on his heels, Karpinsky threw up his hands and sneered. "Well. I guess that's it, then." His lips stretched tight across his face in a grimace of a smile. "We might as well dismiss for the day since you've summed it up so succinctly."

A few snickers erupted before the man whirled around to face another terrified student. "Mr. Beaufort. Perhaps you can expand on that?"

Logan hardly heard the next exchange and would've been sorely pressed to answer if he'd been called on at that moment. He was too busy watching Dana Marlowe settle herself with infinite aplomb. Somehow she'd managed to come out of that exchange unscathed and made Karpinsky look like the jerk that he was.

Logan wasn't sure he would've had as much grace under fire and was impressed by her quick thinking. On the way out, he caught up with Dana, dropping into stride with her. "Hey, congratulations," he said. "You did great."

She looked up at him, her wide-set green eyes full of fire—a combination of anger and embarrassment. And then he saw something else. Determination. He saw it in the firm, slightly tilted set of her jaw. Yeah, that was it. Fierce determination.

"No thanks to you," she said, swinging a cascade of long auburn hair behind her shoulders.

Logan stopped in his tracks. *What the hell...?* She charged ahead, purposeful, arms clamped over the books she hugged against her chest. "Wait." He bolted past her, then turned, walking backward so he could face her.

"What're you talking about? What did *I* do?"

She halted abruptly and so did he, facing off on the sidewalk right in front of the Pound Building. "You made Karpinsky and everyone else in class think I couldn't state the case."

"I did what...?" Logan sputtered.

"You butted in. You raised your hand."

"So?" He shrugged, palms up. He couldn't tell if she was kidding or not. "I was trying to take the pressure off. Trying to save you from humiliation."

A trace of a righteous smile formed on her full, pink lips. She wore no lipstick, unlike most of his women friends. In fact, on closer inspection, he noticed she wore no makeup at all. She didn't need to.

"See?" she said, one eyebrow raised as if he'd proved her point. "Who made you my savior? I didn't need someone to take the pressure off, Mr. Wakefield. I could've handled it just fine. But once you inserted yourself, it was all over. No one even listened."

Logan smiled. He didn't know why he smiled, except that she knew his name, and he hadn't told her. Another thing he noticed was that she spoke her mind, said what she thought.

He liked that. He liked her firm stance, liked that she

wasn't wishy-washy—even when she was wrong. Which she was. People *had* listened.

He'd realized then and there that she wasn't a person to back down.

And he was strangely aroused by the whole exchange.

"Okay," he said. "I apologize. I will never come to your rescue again." Smiling even wider, he raised a hand and saluted. "Scout's honor."

Her smile started with her eyes and worked its way down to her mouth. An inviting mouth with even white teeth and pouty lips. And he had the craziest urge to kiss her. He suddenly felt sixteen instead of twenty-two—at least according to the zing in his vital parts.

Then her expression went all serious. "I don't believe you."

He crossed his arms, shifted his weight from one foot to the other. "Why not?"

"Because that wasn't a real Scout's salute," she said crisply, with authority—and a hint of mischief. Green cat eyes raked over him, then settled on his hair. "I doubt you were ever a Scout. Yacht club, maybe."

A crowd of students rushed by and someone bumped into her, shoving her against him. Thick shiny hair grazed his cheek and he noticed how silky it felt, how it smelled like vanilla, and he inhaled deeply before remembering they were still standing in the middle of the sidewalk.

He pulled her aside, happy she wasn't really serious, because he liked her. And he wanted her to like him, too.

"Okay, so I wasn't a Boy Scout. But I'm sincere. How about I buy you a cup of coffee to prove it?"

A blush had erupted, obliterating the light smattering

of freckles that dusted the bridge of her nose and the tops of both cheeks.

Yeah. Logan sucked in a deep breath. He remembered that scent even now. He remembered exactly how she'd looked that first time he saw her—all shiny and milk-maid fresh. A poster child for wholesome Midwestern life.

He shrugged off the unwanted thoughts, willing his mind to focus on the present. But along with the memory came a rush of regret that caught unexpectedly in his throat. Because all the things that had so excited him back then were the very things that had torn their marriage apart.

But that was eons ago. Life on another planet. Three years of law school, seven married to the woman, and one since the divorce. One year—and it felt like ten.

"C'mon buddy." Remy's voice sounded far off. "You with me here?"

Logan raked a hand through his shoulder-length hair. Hair he'd get whacked off the minute he hit U.S. streets. He hoisted his duffel over one shoulder and squinted at his partner. "Yeah. I'm with you. Let's go home."

"I DON'T UNDERSTAND, Dr. Fleming," Dana said, struggling to keep her voice low and steady. "It was only a little bump. You said she's okay, that there's nothing physically wrong with her, and yet…she's still asleep."

Dana slipped a hand over her daughter's and stared at the slight figure, all but swallowed up in the hospital bed. Her heart wrenched as she ran a thumb over Hallie's baby-smooth skin, so cool and lifeless it sent a shiver of fear crawling up Dana's spine. *Wake up, sweetie. Please, please, please wake up.*

All she needed to know was that her little girl would be okay. But what if she wasn't? What if she wasn't simply sleeping, but was instead in a coma, destined to live in a dark void where needles pierced her tender flesh and plastic bottles supplied her life support? She squeezed her eyes shut, unable to bear such an awful thought.

If she'd only left work right away, instead of working that extra fif—

"Give it a little time, Mrs. Wakefield."

"It's Marlowe. Dana Marlowe. Wakefield is her father's name." She'd given *that* explanation so many times since the divorce it now came by rote.

"Sorry."

Oh, jeez. His apology made her realize how tense she was, how sharp she must've sounded. "No, no…" she said, shaking her head, stabbing stiff fingers through her hair. "It's not important."

Nothing was important except her daughter. Dana took a deep, calming breath. "Back to my question. Why is she still asleep? And please, tell me in layman's terms."

Fear welled in Dana's chest as her patience rapidly slipped away. Her only child was in Chicago General after an accident at school, and the physician, a noted neurologist, a specialist in his field, can only say, "Give it time."

Right!

She glanced briefly at the silver-haired man, not wanting to take her gaze off Hallie for even a heartbeat. If Hal opened her eyes, if she saw her mommy right away, she'd know she was safe and wouldn't be frightened by the strange surroundings.

Dana inched closer, shooting a quick glance to the

clock on the wall. 8 p.m. Her daughter had been asleep for four hours.

"It's not uncommon for children to sleep longer than usual when they've had a traumatic experience, Ms. Marlowe."

"She's been asleep since before I arrived. And it *isn't* usual for her to go to sleep at four in the afternoon. You said she was awake when they brought her in and that there's no concussion, no trauma…" Dana's voice wavered, her nerves drawing tight under her skin.

"No physical trauma. But the whole experience can be stressful for a child—the ambulance, the emergency room, strangers hovering over her. And we don't know what happened before her fall."

Dana gently stroked her daughter's arm as the man's cautious words hit home. The experience *would* be traumatic for Hallie. She'd never been in a hospital, not since her birth.

Despite the divorce, Dana had done everything in her power to ensure her daughter's seven years of life had been comfortable, safe and secure. She'd protected Hallie and made absolutely certain she felt loved and wanted. She'd even left a message for Logan, because he was her father, after all; he had a right to know his daughter was in the hospital.

Poor kid must've been frightened beyond belief when they brought her here in an ambulance. "I assume the hospital staff are experienced and that they acted accordingly."

"Of course," the doctor said, turning to go. "All vital signs are good. She's had a little medication for any aches she might experience, and I'm sure she'll be fine, Ms. Marlowe. I'll check back with you before I leave for the evening."

Dana's stomach bunched. "What if…" *What if she doesn't wake up?* "What if Hallie requires something?"

"One of the nurses can page me. I'll be here for a few more hours," he said with an understanding glance. "Perhaps you should go home and get some rest yourself. Your daughter won't be released tonight, anyway."

She shook her head. She wasn't going anywhere till she knew Hallie was okay.

The next time Dana looked at the clock it was almost midnight—or was it noon? Hard to tell because her eyes were so dry her lids felt like sandpaper each time she blinked. She was so tired her vision was blurry, and it didn't help that the only light came from the night-light off to the side.

Everything was morgue quiet, so quiet she could hear Hallie breathing the low, steady sounds of a deep sleep. Even the busy nurses' station outside the door was mute. And in the wretched white-roomed silence, a hollow, helpless feeling seeped through her, settling in the very marrow of her tired bones.

She couldn't do a thing for her daughter. She was helpless, a feeling to which she was not accustomed. If Hallie was fine, why on earth didn't she wake up?

Sitting on a chair next to the bed, her hand still cupping her little girl's, Dana rested her forehead against her own outstretched arm. If she closed her eyes for just a few minutes…maybe she'd feel better. And if Hallie moved even a muscle, she would feel it.

She drifted into a groggy state in which she was neither fully awake nor asleep. In that strange and fuzzy fugue, the hospital's antiseptic scents faded, and she had but a vague awareness of time passing. And then, somewhere in the conscious part of her mind, she sensed someone watching her.

With her head still resting on her arm, her eyelids snapped open.

Logan.

She felt his presence as vividly as if he'd dropped a hand on her shoulder. Slowly, unsure if she was dreaming or awake, Dana sat up, waited a second and turned.

He stood in the doorway, his tall, broad-shouldered body backlit and thrown into silhouette. He strode toward her, and though she couldn't see his eyes, she could feel their heat—questioning, accusing. Blaming.

Of course he would blame her. She blamed herself. She hadn't been at the school when her daughter fell, but if she'd gotten there earlier to pick her up...

"Hello, Dana."

It wasn't a dream.

His voice was the same. Deep and smooth. Sensual.

"Hello, Logan. Glad you could make it," she stated flatly, squashing a sudden, overwhelming need to seek the familiar comfort of his arms.

"I came as soon as I could—right after I got your last message telling me where to go. What happened? Is she okay?" Though his words were spoken in a hush, his tone was needle sharp. Her need for his comfort dissolved in an instant.

He pulled a chair up beside her and lowered his six-feet-plus of well-honed muscle into it. He'd come from a job, she could tell. Because his normally short chestnut hair was long, practically to his shoulders, a dark shadow of stubble covered his jaw, his jeans were wrinkled and looked as if he'd slept in them, and his boots were scuffed and dirty.

Logan Wakefield, Boston society born and bred, didn't know from wrinkled clothes. Even when he wore jeans, he looked like he'd stepped from the pages of *GQ*.

But when he was undercover, he could become almost anyone, and right now, dressed as he was, the man was the epitome of danger. The familiar scent of leather and faint oriental spice made her far too aware of his masculinity—and of its effect on her. The man was dangerous, all right—to her emotional well-being.

"I don't know what happened," she whispered so as not to disturb Hallie, which was ridiculous because what she wanted most right this minute was for her daughter to wake up.

"I was at work when I received a call from the school that there'd been an accident. No one seemed to know what happened, except that she'd fallen or something and had been taken to the hospital. I came immediately, and when I got here, she was asleep. Aside from a small bump on her head, the doctor said there's no sign of physical injury."

Logan covered Hallie's hand with his. "And?" He turned to face Dana again. "What else? How long has she been asleep?" His dark amber eyes flashed with questions.

Dana cleared her throat, suddenly feeling as if she was under cross-examination. "I don't know. What time is it?" She glanced at the clock. 3 a.m.

"It's been about twelve hours," she continued. "But the doctor said to wait and see. There's no concussion. He said she'll probably be fine."

He waited, nodded for her to go on.

"He said sleeping wasn't unusual. In fact the medications can cause her to sleep longer than normal."

"Medications? What for if there's nothing wrong?

Where is the doctor? I'd like to talk with him.'' Logan pushed to his feet.

''I told you what he said. And the medication was only Children's Tylenol in case she had any aches from the fall.''

Without further response, he crossed the room and was out the door.

Dana's stomach churned. What did Logan think? That she didn't understand what the physician had said? That she was keeping something from him? Or did he think she hadn't been vigilant in caring for their daughter?

Well, she didn't care *what* he thought. Her only concern was Hallie.

But no matter what she told herself, she knew if she hadn't been late, if she'd arrived on time to pick Hallie up after school, her little girl wouldn't be lying in the hospital right now.

She leaned in, studying Hal's sweet face, wanting desperately for her to open her eyes—eyes so like her father's it made Dana's heart lurch. Hallie didn't look like Logan as much as she had his mannerisms, his easy nature and personality. Both Logan and Hallie's defining feature was soft amber-brown eyes that could switch in an instant from playful to so intense they seemed to see directly into a person's soul.

Even though Logan had left her side, his evocative scent lingered, threatening to suck her into a swirl of memories. Memories like that first exhilarating moment when he'd held her in his arms and asked her to have coffee.

The moment when she'd realized she wanted him.

How odd that she'd think about that now. Because in the year since their divorce, she'd done everything she could to forget him and get on with her life. She'd succeeded, or thought she had—until this very moment when she remembered how desperately she'd once loved him.

Once was the operative word. Her once-upon-a-time feeling for Logan Wakefield was ancient history and she wasn't about to let herself get caught up in something over which she had no control. When Hallie awoke, the two of them would go home and everything would be back to normal.

Logan could go. He could go back to the precious freedom he'd always wanted.

"According to the nurse, Dr. Fleming will be back in the morning," Logan said, coming up behind her. He sat again at her side. "She couldn't tell me anything because she'd just come on duty."

Dana's spine went rigid. "I could've told you that if you'd waited. And I already told you what the doctor said."

"I had to do something. I feel helpless sitting here." He drew in a deep breath and reached out again, covering Hallie's hand with his.

Feeling helpless would bother Logan, Dana knew. He always had to be the one to fix everything. He had to solve the problem. Even when there was none.

Still holding his daughter's hand, he turned to look at Dana. "You okay? You look really tired."

"I'm fine," she answered, steeling herself against the concern in his voice. "I'll be better once Hal wakes up and we can go home."

"Business as usual, huh? And just how *is* business these days?"

On the surface, the question was perfunctory, like any friend would ask. Yet *she* knew it went deeper, knew what strong feelings he'd had about her career. Still had, apparently.

He didn't understand, and she doubted he ever would. He'd never understand because everything in his life had come easy.

In fact, if Logan Wakefield had wanted the state's attorney's job as badly as she did, he'd have had it by now. Some influential person somewhere would've been put on notice, all the right strings would've been pulled, and voilà! He'd have the job he wanted.

"Fine. And yours?"

"No complaints."

She shifted in her chair. He shouldn't have any complaints. He was now doing exactly what he wanted. What he'd always wanted.

"Except for missing Hal." He gently massaged Hal's small fingers. "C'mon sunshine. Wake up. Daddy's here to see you."

Dana's heart squeezed. He loved his little girl; there'd never been any question about that. And Hal loved her daddy equally—perhaps even more now that he'd gone. The bond between father and daughter was strong. The kind of bond Dana had always longed for with her own family—and with Logan.

The hardest thing in the world for Hal had been trying to understand why her daddy had to leave, why they couldn't be a family anymore.

She doubted the child would ever understand. At least not until she was old enough to know what it means to be married to someone who doesn't want to be married.

Someone who doesn't love you.

Dana had known what that was like from day one.

Logan had married her out of a sense of duty and obligation. She'd married him, not because she was pregnant, but because she'd loved him so much. Naively she'd thought that maybe he could learn to love her as much as she loved him.

Dana stole another glance at Logan. How would she ever manage to get through the night with him sitting next to her, when his very presence conjured up all kinds of emotions?

She drew another deep breath. She'd deal with it. Just as she'd dealt with everything else in her life. Hell, her whole life had been a challenge.

In school, she'd had to cram till her brains nearly exploded to do as well as her sister. She'd had to fight for a spot on the cheerleading squad because she wasn't pretty or popular enough. Her parents couldn't afford college for her, so she'd scrounged up scholarship funds and worked nights as a waitress to finally reach her goal.

Harvard Law School, where she'd met and eventually married Logan—against his family's wishes.

Though the marriage had failed, the rest of her work would soon pay off. The state's attorney's job was finally within her grasp. If she could do all that she'd done so far and still come out on top, she could deal with sitting for a few hours next to the man she'd once loved.

Sure she could.

CHAPTER TWO

"How's MY PATIENT this morning?" Dr. Fleming strode into the room.

Nervous and riddled with questions, Dana bolted from her chair. The doctor stopped at the end of the bed to read Hallie's chart, so she waited, tapping her fingers against her thigh.

When she couldn't stand it a second longer, Dana rushed to his side. "She's still asleep. We've been sitting here all night and she hasn't blinked an eyelash."

The physician glanced from Dana to Logan, who rose to greet him, hand outstretched. "I'm Hallie's father," Logan said, shaking the doctor's hand. "We're concerned. Really concerned."

"I understand." Dr. Fleming nodded as he thumbed through the chart. "Yesterday we ran a number of tests on your daughter—X rays, CAT scan, the works. We haven't been able to identify any physical trauma, so I'm confident she'll be fine."

Logan had a way about him that said he'd never had a moment of self-doubt, a quality that made people respond to him in a positive way. "And the fact that she's been asleep for so long...?" he asked.

"That," the doctor hedged, "is a little baffling." He walked over to take Hallie's pulse.

Baffling? Dana drew closer, her frustration mounting. That wasn't good enough. "Dr. Fleming, if you don't know what's wrong with her, then I'd like a second opinion. I'd like you to call in another physician, someone who *can* tell me what's wrong.''

Logan reached out to touch Dana's shoulder as he addressed the doctor. "There must be something wrong, otherwise why would Hal still be aslee—''

"The doctor and I have already been through this, Logan," Dana interrupted in a hushed voice. She shrugged from under his hand and turned to face the physician. "Hal's been like this for nearly eighteen hours, and that's not normal. I think we *need* a second opinion.''

"Of course, Ms. Marlowe. In fact, I've already alerted another colleague for consult.'' Dr. Fleming walked to the door, stopped and turned to them. "This is hard on you, I know. It might be better for everyone, including your daughter, if you took a break, maybe get some rest yourself.''

After the physician left, Logan faced Dana. "I think he's right. I know how you feel, but—''

"Do you?" she shot back, still keeping her voice low. All her fears and anger suddenly twisted into one huge knot in her gut. She didn't need rest. She needed to know what was wrong with her little girl and that she'd be okay!

Tears welled in her eyes. No one knew how she felt, least of all her ex-husband, who'd spent half their marriage on the road. "If you knew how I felt, you'd know that you can't just waltz in and start making assumptions and decisions about what I need or don't need to do.''

She watched Logan grind his teeth, holding himself in check. A habit she remembered well.

Finally he drew in some air and said evenly, "Sorry.

But I don't think you're going to help anyone by wearing yourself to a frazzle. Fighting with me isn't going to do any good, either.''

He stopped pacing, then swung around to face her. ''And frankly, right now my daughter is my only concern.''

Dana recoiled a little. She wasn't thinking of anything or anyone but Hallie, either. Certainly not herself as he implied.

She went to her daughter's side and sat on the edge of the bed. ''She's my only concern, too. And I can't go anywhere, not until I know she's okay.''

Logan stalked over to stand beside her. He cleared his throat. ''Okay. That I can understand,'' he said, looking for all the world as if he wanted to strangle her. He snatched the chair closest to the bed, swung it around and settled himself in it. Then he crossed his arms.

They sat in silence for what seemed eons, and when the phone rang, they both jumped, their edgy gazes darting from one to the other. Dana plucked up the receiver on the second ring.

It was her sister, Elizabeth, wanting to know how Hal was doing. ''She's still asleep, but we're getting another opinion soon.'' Dana explained briefly what the doctor had said, then told Liz she'd let her know more as soon as *she* did.

''Sure. I'll be here.'' Dana glanced at Logan. ''For as long as necessary.''

She hung up, feeling no compunction to explain. Logan had never liked her sister, anyway.

''You tell your mom and dad?''

Pausing a moment before she answered, Dana said,

"Yes. Or rather, Liz did. They're on vacation and won't be back until late next week."

"That explains it."

"Explains what?"

"Why they're not here." His disdain for her parents was thinly disguised. Another of the many reasons things hadn't worked out between them. Logan would never understand what he didn't know. But she couldn't deal with that now.

"I didn't see much point in upsetting them when I didn't know anything myself. They weren't there when I called, so I left a message saying the doctor had assured me Hallie would be fine once she awakened. Liz has kept them updated."

He acknowledged her explanation with a curt nod, and then another awkward silence descended. Finally she asked, more out of politeness than anything, "And how are your parents?"

"Fine. They're still in Boston. Dad's running the firm, and Mom...well, you know what Mom does. All that charity stuff." He shrugged. "I'd planned to take Hal to visit them next weekend."

Dana shifted position, crossing one leg over the other. Even if Hal had been capable of going with him, Logan hadn't asked if it was okay, hadn't asked if he could take her on an off weekend. Did he think that just because he'd missed his regular visits, he could take Hallie wherever he wanted, whenever he wanted?

She bit back a retort that would serve no good purpose. Hal wasn't going anywhere right now. And before long, Logan would be off on another job, and she wouldn't have to worry about him taking the child anywhere.

She watched Logan rub his little girl's fingers, saying

over and over, "C'mon, kiddo. Time to rise and shine. Daddy's here."

And for the next hour, he continued saying those words, intermittently singing to Hal in a voice so soft it was almost a whisper. "'You are my sunshine, my only sunshine...'"

Dana closed her eyes for a second. He'd sung that song to Hallie the very first time he'd held her in his arms.

She bit her bottom lip. What good would it do to remember any of that now?

Gripped with an urgent desire to put some distance between them, Dana headed to the bathroom. She hated to leave Hallie's side for even a moment, but she desperately needed space.

Logan heard the door shut, then the water running. He continued to stroke Hal's forehead, her arms and her fingers. He wanted her to know he was there, that he'd always be there.

But he hadn't been. He regretted that and had told her so in their last conversation when he couldn't make her school play. "I'll be with you in spirit, sunshine," he'd said.

"I know, Daddy. I'm always in your heart," Hal had replied, repeating the words he'd said to her every time he went away on a job—the words he'd said when he and Dana had separated.

Only that time Hal had said, "I know why you're leaving, Daddy. You don't have to explain." Sometimes Hal reminded him of an adult, instead of a seven-year-old. She'd had a vocabulary the size of a teenager's by the time she was five.

He supposed having a pair of attorneys for parents

might've contributed to that. Dana never lacked for words, that was sure.

And sometimes Hal sounded so much like her mother it was uncanny. She looked like her, too. Both had the same oval face and perfect smile. Oh, yeah, that smile—one that lit his little girl's happy face most of the time.

He loved the way Hallie smiled—the way Dana smiled. Hal was a miniature of her mother, even down to the smattering of freckles across her slightly upturned nose.

Except that Hal's hair was lighter, the color of burnished wheat. Reaching up, he brushed a wispy curl from his little girl's cheek. "C'mon, sweetie. It's time to go home. Pooka's waiting for you."

He sighed, wondering briefly if having her favorite flop-eared stuffed rabbit at her side would help. The thing had been so ratty and frayed from use that Dana had been reluctant to even wash it. But then, maybe Hal didn't drag Pooka around with her anymore as she once had.

The thought brought home the painful message that he'd been away from his little girl for too long.

Because of his job, he hadn't had much say over Hal's custody during the divorce. But he intended to change all that.

He was not going to be an estranged parent. Not anymore, dammit. Not anymore.

"Hey, kiddo. It's Daddy. Time to wake up."

I'M TRYING TO WAKE UP. I really am. Yet no matter how hard she worked at it, her eyes wouldn't open.

At first when she'd heard the man's voice, he sounded far away. Then pretty soon it seemed like he was coming closer and closer, and she knew he was talking to her. After hearing his nice voice, she *wanted* to wake up, only she got really really tired again and started to feel like she was floating.

"It's Daddy. Time to wake up, Hallie."

There. That was the man's nice voice again, and she wished she could do what he said. But it didn't work. No matter how hard she tried, she couldn't get her eyes to open.

Maybe she'd done something really bad and that was why she couldn't tell where she was. Maybe that was why everything was dark. The dark scared her. Scared her bad.

She heard the voice again, heard him say he was her daddy and he must've been really close to her because she could smell something spicy...like...like... Oh, rats, she didn't know what it was like, except that she knew a man smelled that way and not a lady.

He said everything was okay, so she didn't know why she was scared. Then she heard him singing that pretty song, so she tried hard again to open her eyes to see him, but nothing happened.

"There, did you see it?"

That was the lady's voice again.

"Call the doctor. Please, call the doctor."

A lady voice was different from a man's. That much she knew, too. But this lady sounded all whispery, like something was wrong. She didn't want the lady to call a doctor.

Doctors gave people pills and poked in their ears and things when people were sick. Doctors gave people shots that hurt. That's what she knew about doctors.

If she went to sleep again, she wouldn't hear about doctors anymore, and she wouldn't have to get a shot or something.

"SEE? DID YOU SEE THAT?" Dana asked as she scooted her chair closer to the bed. Logan sat at Hal's bedside, watching her with equal intensity.

"Her eyelids fluttered. I think she's waking up." Dana's excitement surged at the minutest flicker of movement. Hal *would* wake up and everything would be fine. She'd been silly to fear the worst.

Yet fearing the worst was something she'd lived with since the divorce. She was Hallie's mainstay, her protector, her source of stability. It was her job to keep her daughter healthy, happy—and safe.

Another flutter of Hal's eyelids sent Dana to her feet. "There. Did you see that?"

Logan pinned her with one of those understanding expressions that set her teeth on edge. It was the kind of look that told her to settle down, everything's under control in Logan Wakefield's capable hands.

"I saw it," he said. "C'mon, sit here." He patted the chair. "Pacing the floor isn't going to help."

"It helps me," she returned. How could he know what it was like for her? He hadn't been here as long as she, without sleep, on tenterhooks, worrying, wondering, not knowing what to expect next.

All she wanted was to know her little girl was going to be okay, that she hadn't sustained an injury the tests couldn't find. She didn't know what she'd do if—

She caught her breath. Yes, she did know what she'd do. She'd never forgive herself. And it was a foregone conclusion Logan never would. He'd warned her on more than one occasion when they were together that she shouldn't get so engrossed in her work that she forgot everything else.

But what Logan thought didn't matter anymore.

Hal's eyelids fluttered again as if she was struggling to open them.

"I'm getting the doctor. I want him here when she awakes. I want him to look at her immediately." Dana dashed out and down the hall to the nurses' station.

"Get me Dr. Fleming," she demanded of the girl behind one of the two half-moon counters that served as the medical staff's work area. From there, several hallways fanned out like tentacles from all sides of the desk where, supposedly, the nurses could keep a watchful eye on their patients.

The nurse was engaged in animated conversation on the phone, and no other staff were in sight. The usual hum of activity at the station had ceased and Dana had to assume the other nurses were busy. "Please see that Dr. Fleming comes to Hallie Wakefield's room immediately. Room 322."

The girl looked at Dana with a blank expression. A second later, Dana realized she wasn't a nurse at all, but an aide.

"Please, can you get in touch with Dr. Fleming, or find someone who can? My daughter needs him ASAP."

The aide gave a nod, and as she did, Dana whirled on her heel and headed back to Hallie's room, hoping they wouldn't have to get another opinion, after all.

Logan was on the phone when Dana came in. "It's for you." He held out the receiver.

Coming forward, Dana gestured toward Hallie. "Anything…?"

Hope flickered in his gaze. "She opened her eyes for a second. And I think she smiled at me. Did you get the doctor?"

Dana shook her head as a burst of excitement coursed

through her. She perched on the edge of the bed and leaned close. "Hal, it's Mommy. Can you hear me?"

Nothing.

Dana looked at Logan, suddenly desperate for support. Lord, she was a mess, and her emotions threatened to spill all over the place. Which wouldn't help.

Chastising herself for the lapse, she nearly jerked the phone from his hand. The last thing she wanted was to talk to anyone.

"Hello," she said sharply, then sighed with relief when she heard her friend Jillian ask about Hal. "No, there aren't any new developments, though we're getting a second opinion very shortly."

"We?" Jilly asked.

"Logan's here. Hal's father."

Her friend went silent for a moment. Jillian had moved in next door the week after Dana and Logan had split. The two women had connected immediately, felt as if they'd been best friends forever. Jillian was a single mom, widowed, with a daughter, Chloe, the same age as Hal, and the two little girls had become fast friends as quickly as their moms had.

Dana had her new friend to thank for helping her through some of the toughest times right after Logan had gone, and later when the divorce became final.

"You okay with him there?"

Turning her back to Logan, Dana lowered her voice so he couldn't hear her. "I'm fine. Besides, he won't be around for long. He never is," she added with a tinge of bitterness, even as she hated her own weakness of character for feeling that way.

Bitterness wasn't a logical emotion. Not in this case. She'd known going into the marriage what she was up against, known full well that Logan's world and hers were incompatible. But she'd been young and so in love nothing else had mattered.

Perhaps their differences had been the challenge. She was a fighter; she'd always been a fighter. It was the only way she knew to make it in a world where the best of the best were the chosen ones. She'd learned that early on. And perhaps she'd viewed their marriage in the same way.

She should've known what marriage to Logan Wakefield would be like and not had unrealistic expectations. It was the one time she'd fought for something when she never should've even dreamed it could work.

"Okay...and remember I'm here if you need me."

"Thanks, Jilly. I'll let you know what's going on as soon as I can."

When she hung up, Dana saw the aide standing in the doorway and went over to her. The girl whispered, "I told the nurse you needed the doctor right away. She said she'd let Dr. Fleming know when he's out of surgery."

Great. Another wait. While she was used to the legal system being slow, she never expected a hospital to be the same. Lives could be in jeopardy. "And what if there's an emergency, what happens then?" Dana held her voice to a stage whisper, but felt her ire rising, right along with her words.

The aide pulled back. "I—I'm pretty sure there's a doctor on call, ma'am. M-Maybe you can check with the nurse."

Oh, dear. Dana realized she was taking out her anxiety on the poor girl, who was only doing her job. "Sorry," she murmured, watching the aide leave. Lord, she really *was* falling apart at the seams.

She leaned against the door and gulped some air. *Get*

a grip, Marlowe. Because you won't be good for any-
thing if you don't.

Okay, she'd check back with the desk, see when the
other doctor might arrive to give them a second opinion—and then pray that Dr. Fleming was right and that
everything would be fine.

After that, she and Hal would go home and get on
with their lives as planned.

LOGAN WATCHED DANA take off down the hallway,
purposeful, arms pumping. Even without sleep and in
rumpled clothes, she was every inch the professional.
And if she'd worn pants with that navy business suit,
instead of a sexy short skirt, he might not have had a
twinge of desire looking at her shapely legs.

He had to admit, she looked damn good, even though
he'd never seen her quite so agitated.

Which was saying a lot because Dana Marlowe
Wakefield was the most fired-up person he knew, always spinning into action without a thought to the con-
sequences. She'd decide what was needed and then
she'd do it.

An unexpected ache of nostalgia grew in his chest at
the thought. That part of her personality had been frus-
trating at times, but it was also one of the qualities he'd
loved about her.

The woman had no fear of failure.

He'd learned that the moment she'd joined his seven-
member study group—all first-year law students who'd
banded together to ensure they'd get through the next
hellish nine months.

The first-year dropout rate at HLS was devastating,
and everyone knew if you made it through one-L, there

was a good chance you'd make it through the next three years.

Apparently *not* making it had never entered Dana's head. After only a week, she'd already decided she'd make *Review,* something *he* hadn't even considered. Hell, that was for the top of the class, the crème de la crème. People like his buddy, Henry Baker, the Einstein who'd aced the LSATs, attaining near-perfect scores.

Okay, Logan had aced the LSATs, too, just not as neatly as Baker. Even so, two weeks into the year most students were still wondering if they'd make it through the next month, not whether they'd make the *Harvard Law Review,* the oldest and most respected student-run law journal in the country. The publication included articles by professors, judges, recognized experts and selected students, usually in their third year. But selection was tough; only the top five percent made it.

Sure, he'd known in the far reaches of his brain that it was a plum to make *Review,* sort of like sitting on the Supreme Court, an honor that stayed with you for the rest of your life. It had been the last thing on Logan's mind.

All *he* needed to do was learn enough about the law to pass the bar, then segue into his father's business and eventually take over. It had been his parents' plan since the day he was born.

"We'll have to finish up by nine," Dana had announced on her grand entrance into Harkness Commons. "I need a good seven hours of sleep every night if I'm going to make *Review.*"

Hell, it was only her second time with the group, and she was already trying to run the show. And seven hours' sleep? Hah! He was lucky if he got four or five.

"You mind telling me how two weeks into the year

you plan on doing that? D'you know how tough it is to make *Review?*"

She paused, looking insulted that he'd even asked the question.

Logan added, "Only the top five percent make it. Maybe five or six in each section."

She raised her chin. "I know that. And I intend to be one of them."

He leaned back, balancing on the rear legs of his chair, almost laughing out loud at her naivety.

"Yeah? It's a lot of extra work. Forty or fifty hours a week. And that's besides class."

She looked unimpressed. Either she didn't know that making *Review* meant a truckload of extra work and was covering her butt, or she did know and wouldn't admit it.

"I know that, too." She whizzed around him, slung her canvas backpack on the table and dropped into the chair next to him.

She wore a baggy Chicago Cubs sweatshirt and faded jeans that molded tightly to her nicely curved bottom. And the way she sat, casually with her firm thighs the tiniest bit apart, with all that springy energy evident in the tap, tap, tap of her toe and the bounce in her legs. Man, just watching her sent a jolt of testosterone through him.

Then when she pinned him with a challenging gaze and flicked that long hair behind her shoulders, he was sure everyone in the group saw the current that zapped between them.

"Many prominent judges and lawyers rely substantially on the opinions in the *Review*," she declared. "And if I make it, I could get a faculty contract, maybe even a Supreme Court clerkship." She settled back in her chair, her expression as determined as her words. "That's my plan."

Her plan. Dana had always had a plan, he remembered as he covered Hal's baby-smooth hand with his. It was one of the things he'd immediately liked about Dana, and even way back when, he'd had no doubt she'd pull it off.

Stop it, Wakefield! He massaged the tiny fingers curled in his palm. None of that mattered now. Nothing about their former relationship mattered.

It was done. Over. Finished.

He looked up to see Dana standing at the end of the bed, her eyes filled with despair.

It was a look with which he'd become all too familiar in his work—despair and the awful fear that things were going to turn out badly. Seeing that haunted look in Dana's eyes and knowing it was about *their* child made the situation infinitely harder to bear. He wanted to go to her, pull her into his arms and assure her everything would be fine.

She'd not accept it, of course. She never did. Unlike him she remembered every little detail of what had gone wrong between them. Yeah, she was totally unlike him. Hell, he was hard-pressed right now to even remember why they'd gotten divorced.

But then, the *why* didn't much matter anymore. Divorce or no, he was Hal's father, and as soon as she was better and out of here, he intended to exercise that right. In spades.

His nerves went taut with resolve. Before he left this hospital, he would let Dana know his plans, no matter how much his presence bothered her.

He turned to his little girl again. "Hal, c'mon, wake up."

Nothing.

Her skin seemed cold, and she was so pitifully still, almost seeming to fade before his very eyes. His heart sank a little deeper each time he looked at her. A dark dread settled in his chest.

Suddenly panicked, he wanted to shake her, to make her respond. With his other hand, he groped for the nurses' emergency button and jabbed at it.

Hal's hand twitched. Tiny fingers latched onto his thumb. Oh, man! A baseball-size lump formed in his throat. "Hal. It's Daddy. Wake up, sweetheart. Please wake up."

Her eyes popped open.

Oh, God! A great surge of relief flooded through him. She stared at him, unblinking. "Hal? Hallie, sweetheart. Daddy's here." He smiled, clutching her hand tightly, his heart in his throat.

Instantly Dana was at his side, her eyes glistening with tears.

"Hey, kiddo," Logan said, running a finger down Hal's cheek. "How're ya doing?"

Her eyes looked like large dark coals in her little face, and as she looked at her mom, he felt her grip tighten, pulling him closer.

He leaned in, and she whispered, "D-Daddy?"

"Yes, honey. What is it?"

Hallie pointed a wary finger at Dana.

"Daddy...wh-who is that lady?"

CHAPTER THREE

DANA LEANED FORWARD eagerly. Hal had said something to Logan, but she couldn't make it out. Barely able to contain her happiness, she reached out to hug her little girl. "Oh, honey. We were so worried about you."

Hallie visibly stiffened and turned her face away.

What on earth? Dana froze, then looked to Logan in silent question.

He shrugged and nestled Hallie in his arms. "It's okay, honey. Daddy's here. Mommy's here, too. Everything's fine. You're okay and we're here with you."

Hal's wary gaze darted between them as she literally shrank deeper into Logan's embrace, her small fingers clutched at his shirt sleeve. She started sniffling.

"Honey, Mommy's here. It's okay." Dana reached out again, but Hallie shut her eyes.

Horrified, Dana whispered, "Honey, what's wrong? It's Mommy. Don't you know me?"

A terrible silence fell as Dana waited, her heart hammering at the base of her throat, ticking off the long seconds.

Hallie shook her head, small jerky movements from side to side.

Oh…dear…God. Panic seized in Dana's chest. Hallie didn't know her? Her own daughter didn't know her?

"Maybe you better get the doctor." Logan's words

were a gentle command, to which Dana nodded numbly, turned and fled the room, silently swallowing the sobs clogging her throat. In her haste, she nearly plowed down the nurse outside the door.

"What's wrong? The emergency light went on."

Stumbling back, Dana waved her hands and shook her head. She couldn't speak because she'd fall apart for sure.

She inhaled deeply, closed her eyes, then slowly let out the lungful of air, hoping to calm herself. "Hallie's awake," she finally managed. "And something is horribly wrong. Please get the doctor."

The nurse frowned, her expression puzzled. "If she's awake, that's wonderful."

"No, something's wrong," Dana croaked out, trying to keep her voice down so Hallie couldn't hear her. "She doesn't know who I am."

"There, there." The older woman put her arm around Dana. "She's probably a bit confused, that's all. I'm sure everything is fine."

Dana shook her head violently. "Everything isn't fine. Now *please* get the doctor."

"Dr. Fleming is on his way. He called just a few minutes ago. Now let's go see. Your daughter's probably just a little disoriented after waking up in the hospital, that's all."

Oh! That could be! Dana latched onto the explanation like a lifeline. Yes, that could be it. Hallie was disoriented. Yes, she'd go back in and talk to Hal and everything would be fine.

Disoriented. That was all. God, she hoped that was all.

As they walked in, she saw Logan angle his head

closer to talk to Hallie. When he heard the nurse cough, he looked up, then gestured for them to go back out.

No way. She had to be there. Even if Hal was confused, her little girl needed her. She strode to the side of the bed, but the nurse sidled in front of her.

"Good morning," the woman said cheerily. "You took quite a nap there, young lady."

Hal poked her head around Logan's arm, her eyes widening when she saw Dana.

"Hi, sweetie." Dana leaned forward, poised to hug her daughter.

As she did, Hal ducked her chin and turned her face toward her dad's chest, thwarting her mother's attempt to get close. Dana's stomach pitched at the rejection, and it took a moment to collect herself, pull back and stand up straight.

Then Hal whispered something to Logan. He turned to them and said under his breath, "She says she's… uh…scared of all the strangers. She wants…" He cleared his throat. "Uh…she wants everyone to go out and let her rest and…she wants me to stay."

Stunned, Dana stood there, mouth agape. She couldn't believe it. Hallie would never ask her to leave. They were too close. Hallie needed her mom.

A tug on her arm brought Dana around. The nurse urged her to go. Dazed, she moved mechanically toward the door and out into the hallway. Dana heard the nurse talking with Logan but couldn't make out the conversation.

Seconds later, the older woman came out. "I'll make sure Dr. Fleming's on his way. And maybe," she said sympathetically, "maybe it'll be better if you sit out here and relax for a bit—until the doctor comes."

Dana's head began to swim, and her legs felt about

to buckle. She propped a shoulder against the wall and crossed her arms over her stomach. "Sure," she whispered, but the woman had already gone.

Before she had a chance to collect herself, Dr. Fleming appeared. He directed her to sit on the chair near the door, said he'd check on Hallie and return.

Time passed slowly, and it seemed as if the doctor was in Hal's room forever. Unable to sit still any longer, Dana got up and paced the hallway until Dr. Fleming finally came out. Logan was with him.

"What's going on?" She moved to within inches of the physician's face. Then with a sudden realization, she headed toward the room. "She's alone. You shouldn't have left her alone. She'll be scared."

As she brushed past Logan, he grabbed her arm. "It's okay. She's asleep again. She's had a sedative."

A sedative. "What on earth for? She's slept long enough." Panic ripped through Dana as she looked to the doctor for an answer.

"She was a little agitated and afraid. I thought it best under the circumstances."

"And exactly what are those circumstances?"

"I'm not certain what the problem is, Ms. Marlowe. Your daughter appears to have a memory deficit. However, withou—"

"Memory deficit? You mean like...like she doesn't remember what happened?"

The doctor frowned, clearly puzzled himself. He cupped an elbow in one hand and rubbed the other hand across his chin. "Right now she's not remembering certain things. That happens sometimes in situations like this. But I hesitate to draw conclusions without further tests."

"I don't understand," Dana uttered. "What *things*

doesn't she remember? She knows Logan. She remembers him.''

"I'm sorry. I wish I could give you a definitive answer, but without further evaluation, I'd only be guessing. My colleague will be here any time now. He'll take a look at her, and we'll schedule additional tests if necessary. It might be that after a little rest, she'll be fine and remember everything. It's quite common for patients not to remember what happened immediately prior to an accident.''

That was true, she knew from representing clients in personal injury suits early in her career. People who'd been in serious car accidents rarely remembered the actual accident or what preceded it. Even though Hallie hadn't had a serious injury, Dana had to believe that's all it was.

Dr. Fleming reached out and placed a hand on her arm. "It might be better for everyone if you take a break, Ms. Marlowe. Get a little rest yourself.''

Nodding numbly as the doctor left, Dana felt totally disoriented, and when she heard a faint ringing sound, it took a moment before she realized it was her cell phone. She patted both pockets of her jacket, then fished it out.

"Hello.''

It was Cheryl from the office. "Jeez.'' Dana looked at her watch. "I'm sorry, time got away from me. I should've called.''

Dana filled her lungs with air, trying to wrap her mind around something solid. Her job. That was solid. But it was 10 a.m., two hours past when she should've been at the office.

"I'm at the hospital, and...'' She fought to clear her

head. "My daughter's here and I don't know when I can get there. Tell David, will you?"

Damn. David was going to be really upset when he heard she wouldn't be there. She couldn't blame him. She had the biggest case of her career sitting on her desk, a case that could cement David's bid for attorney general—and hers for his job as state's attorney.

"Your daughter okay, Ms. Marlowe? You don't sound too good."

Dana closed her eyes, feeling the burn behind her eyelids. She'd been up all night, her daughter had been in a comalike sleep, her ex-husband, whom she'd avoided as much as possible for the past year because she wanted to forget the pain of their broken marriage, was there larger than life—and her daughter didn't know who she was.

Yeah, she probably didn't sound too good.

Now on top of all that, she could easily screw up everything she'd worked for.

"Hallie's…she's okay. We have to wait for a few tests, though, and I'm a little tired because I've been up all night. Tell David I'll call him later."

She said goodbye, clicked off the phone and pocketed it again.

LOGAN WAITED OUTSIDE Hallie's room with Dana, only going inside occasionally to check on her. Three hours later, the consulting physician, Dr. Nero, showed up, introduced himself and then said it would take a couple of hours to examine Hallie and consult with Dr. Fleming. The blond doctor looked so young it was hard to believe he'd graduated college, much less med school.

Logan decided that as long as he had to wait, he'd

take a cab to his office to clean up. It wasn't far and he'd be back long before the tests were done.

He hadn't been able to get Dana to leave, but did convince her to lie down on the couch in the hospital's family waiting room.

Later at his office, Logan wiped the steam off the mirror and peered at the nearly unrecognizable image of himself. No wonder Hal had given him such a strange look when she saw him.

In the past, when he'd completed an undercover job, he'd always managed to get a haircut, shower, shave and change clothes before going home. This time had been an exception. Not knowing why Hal was in the hospital, he hadn't wanted to waste one second.

Thank God she was okay—for the most part. If there had to be something wrong, a little temporary memory lapse was not a big deal. Of course Dana wouldn't feel that way, considering. He couldn't blame her.

He lathered up with menthol-scented shaving cream, the odor of which seemed to clear his head. He'd had little sleep in the past two days and it was catching up with him. He scraped the straightedge razor across the dark, three-day growth on his chin, glad he'd thought to keep a couple of sets of clothing on hand at the office.

Since the divorce he'd been a nomad, going from one undercover job to another, staying in hotels and motels, at Remy's when he was in Chicago, and in the carriage house at the family estate outside Boston when he was there.

Dana and Hallie had stayed in their home in the quiet Beverly neighborhood and he hadn't had the heart to settle anywhere else. A huge mistake. Because while he was having his own little pity party, he'd distanced himself from his daughter.

He hadn't intended for that to happen. He'd hardly seen Hal in the past year, but he hadn't even realized it till he got the call from Dana.

Well, all that was going to change.

On the flight to O'Hare, he'd called an old friend, a real estate broker, and set him on a course to find a condo, town home or a house. He didn't care which as long as it was a permanent place to live and was near his daughter.

"Yo, buddy. You in there?" Remy sounded breathless.

"Yeah." Logan cracked the door and peered out. "Can't stay long, though. I've got to get back to the hospital. What're you huffing and puffing about?"

Remy bent at the waist, hands on his knees and then stood up again. "Took the stairs." He sucked in a deep breath. "I forgot what eleven floors can do to a guy who hasn't stayed in shape."

Logan laughed. "You? Not in shape? Give me a break. Did you miss your 5 a.m. workout at the gym?"

Remy drew in some more air. "Yeah. After the last job took so long, Crystal wants some quality time." He set a deli bag on the table outside the door and pointed to it. "The sandwiches you ordered."

"Thanks." Logan shoved the door wide and went back to the ultramodern pedestal sink to finish shaving. "Can't say how long I'll be gone. Once we get a handle on what's wrong with Hal, I'll give you a call."

"Fine." Remy swaggered in and leaned against the door. He wore wrinkled jeans, a faded blue T-shirt that was a little snug across his broad shoulders, white sneakers and a baseball cap. Since they'd returned, Remy had already gotten his usual military haircut, shaved the beard he'd worn for the job and shucked his fatigues. He'd gone from a Third World guerilla to all-American mother's son in a flash.

"You clean up pretty good, boy," Logan teased as he toweled the remaining froth from his face. Remy was one of those guys who didn't give much thought to the clothes he wore or how he looked.

"I'm really sorry about the kid," Remy said. "Man, that's gotta be tough. How's Dana doing?"

Logan shook his head. How could she be doing? Her only child didn't know her, was afraid of her almost. Knowing how close Dana and Hal were, he knew she had to be devastated. "She's holding up. She always does."

"Yeah, I suppose. She's tough."

Too tough for her own good. "So, tell me about the job," Logan said, changing the subject. He didn't want to think about Dana. He got too damn twisted up inside when he did.

And since he and Remy had taken separate routes home, they hadn't had time to catch up. "I'm guessing internal corruption, or the state wouldn't need an independent investigation. Right?"

Remy nodded. "Feds made the call, and since signing our new contract with them, it's a done deal. File's in the safe when you've got time, but I'm thinking you might want to stay out of it." His expression turned thoughtful. "Considering."

"Who's on it?" Logan asked, ignoring the comment because Remy was right. The less Logan was involved, the better. As a partner, he needed to know about the job, but because of the location, Remy should handle the rest.

"Gideon Armstrong. It's a good cover. Yale Law School, state barred. He knows the territory, and since he's new in the company, there's no chance he'll be recognized.''

Logan nodded his agreement. ''Anything local for me?''

''Not yet, but something will open, and if not, you can do scut work from headquarters for a while, once you get settled.''

Remy picked up a thirty-pound weight from the floor and tossed it from hand to hand. ''For me, I've got a couple jobs on the line and haven't decided which to take. Crystal is pushing for me to stay put a while, too. Can't be gone too long with a baby on the way, ya know. Besides, she's been feeling like hell.''

''Right.'' Logan felt a twinge of guilt over his own travels. When Hal was born, he'd barely made it to the hospital in time. His job with the CIA wasn't one in which he'd had any say about where he went or for how long, which was why he'd finally chucked it all and gone into business with his buddy. Never mind that it was already too late for his marriage. He doubted it would've mattered, anyway.

After Remy left the office, Logan dressed in tan Dockers and a black turtleneck sweater, his only other choice besides a custom-made Armani suit. Wishing he'd had time for a haircut, he combed his damp hair straight back, shoved on a pair of loafers, donned his other leather jacket and was out the door.

At the hospital, he juggled the deli sandwiches and the coffee he'd picked up from the cafeteria, then nudged the elevator button with his elbow. Dana had refused to leave, not even to go out for coffee or food, but she'd been grateful when Logan said he'd bring something back for her.

On the third floor, the doors slid open with a dull

thud. He got off, took a right and walked toward the room, the scent of disinfectant strong in the back of his throat. He hated hospitals, hated the sterile atmosphere, the responses that seemed both caring and impersonal at once.

Sure, the people who worked in health care had to be competent and skilled, or they wouldn't be in the profession, but they were strangers, nonetheless. And he hated for his little girl to be in the hands of strangers.

Man, he hoped he'd hear good news.

Dana was sitting on a chair outside Hal's room. She looked up when she heard him, and for a fraction of a second, he thought he saw her eyes light up, like maybe she was glad to see him. By the time he reached her, he realized it was his imagination.

"Both doctors are with her now, doing some tests," she explained.

Dana looked awful. Faint purple smudges colored the delicate skin under her eyes, and her hands shook when he gave her the cups of coffee. She set the cups on the floor near her feet as he rounded up another chair and pulled it next to hers, sitting close enough for their shoulders to touch. He pulled a sandwich from the bag and gave it to her.

"What tests?"

"Some kind of memory testing, I think."

She inhaled the aroma before unwrapping the sandwich. "Mmm. Goldberg's pastrami on rye?"

"Still your favorite?"

She glanced up. Their eyes met and held. In that microsecond, a deep sense of intimacy infused him—the intimacy of knowing another so well that thoughts and feelings were transmitted without a word being said. He felt as if he'd been gut-punched.

She looked away, started unwrapping the paper. "Sure. One of them. Thanks."

They ate in silence, and he wondered if she'd remembered their post-sex, late-night sandwich runs, too.

Forget that. He tore into his own sandwich, his mouth suddenly so dry the pastrami tasted like cardboard. He took a gulp of the scalding-hot coffee and burned his tastebuds all to hell.

They finished in silence, after which Logan bagged their empty cups and chucked the remnants into the trash. As he did, Dr. Fleming came out of Hal's room. Logan went to stand next to Dana, dread and hope fighting for supremacy inside him. He imagined Dana felt the same and placed a hand on her elbow for support.

"Dr. Nero will be out shortly." The silver-haired man motioned toward the waiting room. "When he finishes, we'll come in and talk with both of you."

Logan directed Dana to the waiting room, thankful that it was empty now. He had a strange foreboding that whatever the doctor had to say, it wasn't going to be what they wanted to hear. Otherwise, why put it off?

Why not tell them everything's fine?

Only five minutes had passed, yet it seemed like hours to Dana. She couldn't sit, so she stood. She couldn't stand still, so she paced from one side of the claustrophobic room to the other.

Logan's effort to lend support had only exacerbated her raw emotions. God, her own daughter didn't know who she was!

Dana remembered Logan's touch, his solid hand on her arm. Lord, it would be so easy to seek comfort in his arms, even though all he was offering was support for the mother of his child.

But another emotion had risen full-blown like the

mythical Phoenix bird inside her. An ugly emotion. As much as she hated to admit it, Dana realized her hurt about Hal not recognizing her was magnified by the fact that Hal *had* known Logan.

How could Hal not recognize her, the one person who'd been there for her since birth? She hadn't been away from Hal, not even for a weekend. She hadn't gone undercover and disappeared for weeks and months at a time.

She'd been there, stayed there, done everything in her power to ensure her daughter felt secure in her love, knew that her mother would always be there, no matter what.

In the next instant, she felt even worse. That she'd allowed those thoughts to form was unthinkable. It wasn't Hal's fault whom she remembered or whom she didn't. It wasn't something the child had arbitrarily decided.

How could any mother be so selfish and petty as to think of herself in a moment like this? Neither Logan nor Hal had control over any of it. The only person to blame was herself for not being at the school when she should've been.

That small window of time, that lousy fifteen minutes might've made the difference.

Dana closed her eyes and leaned her head against the door frame. Where were the doctors? Why weren't they here to explain? What was taking them so damn long?

The door suddenly opened, and she jumped, her nerves snapping like rubber bands. She stepped back, allowing Dr. Nero and Dr. Fleming to enter. Logan rose, but Dr. Nero gestured for them both to sit.

Obeying, Dana's heart raced. Her mouth went dry, her hands clammy. "Is Hal okay?"

"Physically she's fine."

Logan and Dana glanced at each other, relief, hope and a thousand unspoken questions passing between them. In unison, they asked, "And?"

"There are no injuries," the physician said, repeating what they already knew. "She has, however, lost some recent memory."

Dana glanced from one doctor to the other. "You mean like...amnesia?"

"Yes. Though in cases like this, the likelihood is that it's temporary."

She reached for Logan's arm and felt his hand close over hers. "Amnesia? I...I don't understand. She knows her father. How could she have amnesia?"

The doctor cleared his throat. "It happens sometimes directly after an accident. In this case, we don't know what triggered it. She may have had a scare, a shock, she may have fainted, or fallen and hit her head. The contusion is minor and the important thing is that physically she's as healthy as any seven-year-old."

"You said this memory-loss thing is probably temporary," Logan injected. "What does that mean, exactly?"

Dr. Nero became thoughtful, as if choosing his words. "It means her memory may return at any time. Or it may take a while...or she may have to relearn some things."

Relearn? Dana's heart plummeted. Did that mean...

"Are you saying she may never remember?" Logan finished the thought Dana couldn't vocalize, and his confused expression matched the emotions raging through her like a flashfire.

The doctor nodded. "That's a possibility. And another possibility is that she could remember everything an hour from now.''

"I simply don't understand," Dana interrupted. "What would cause this…this kind of thing?"

The doctor shook his head. "There's much we don't know in cases like this. But when there's no evidence to support any organic or neurological damage, we assume the cause is shock, possibly an emotional blockage. A psychological repression, if you will. In medical terms, dissociative amnesia, or hysterical amnesia of a dissociative type."

"She remembered her father! Why would she remember him and nothing else?" Lord, she felt on the verge of hysteria herself. "Or—" she clutched at a thread of hope, "—or does she remember other things?"

"I can't be sure until we talk further, but it appears she remembers some learned things. That's common in cases like this. She remembers things like how to brush her teeth, how to ride a bike and so on. Other than those learned behaviors, she seems only to remember who her father is. She doesn't appear to remember anything else about her life and family."

Dana slumped onto the couch at her side as if she'd been poleaxed. Logan settled a hand on her shoulder.

"What can we do?" Logan asked.

"Oh, yes. What?" Dana chimed in. She needed to *do* something, not sit and wait—and wonder if her daughter would ever remember her own mother.

"The best thing you can do now is to act like everything is normal," Dr. Nero said. "We'll keep her here for observation for the rest of the day and overnight. If there's no change in her condition, she'll be discharged in the morning. If she hasn't remembered anything by then, my advice would be to take it one day at a time.

Take her home, get back into your regular routine. It may be that normal activities will help her more than anything. Being in familiar surroundings, even going back to school could help.''

Dana looked at Logan only to see a multitude of questions swirling in his eyes. The whole thing boggled her mind. It was a bad dream. No…it was a nightmare.

''If nothing changes in a week or so, I recommend counseling.''

''Counseling? What on earth for?'' Her little girl didn't need counseling. How ridiculous!

''If her memory doesn't return, you'll all need help in learning to cope with this,'' Dr. Nero answered. ''You'll have to make adjustments. That's down the road, of course. Right now, let's give it a little time, see if she doesn't come around in a week or so.''

He patted his pockets. ''I don't seem to have a pen, but if we reach that point, I'll get you the name of a colleague. In the meantime, act as you would any other time. Don't rush it or treat her differently than before. Go about your business, do the things she's always enjoyed, get her involved with her friends and relatives. That's probably the best medicine you can give her right now.''

Of course, Dana thought. Surely that would help. She'd take Hallie home, and in familiar surroundings, in her own room, seeing Chloe and Jillian and Pooka and maybe even her aunt, Liz, that would certainly help.

But what if… Dana's excitement diminished as quickly as it had come. What if Hal didn't want to go with her?

''Until then…while she's still here in the hospital, what should we do, how should we act?''

If Hallie didn't remember her, how could she act normally? How could she act as if nothing was wrong?

"Just be yourselves. She's a pretty scared little girl right now."

Oh. Dana's heart wrenched. Of course she's scared. Poor little thing, she must be frightened to death not knowing anyone—except Logan.

She should be grateful that at least Hallie remembered something, and that she only had partial amnesia. That was better than remembering nothing at all.

What the doctor said made sense. If she could spend time with Hallie, bring her home and let her be in familiar, comfortable surroundings, her little girl would probably remember everything. She'd had a scare, that was all. Maybe it was the fall, or the ride in the ambulance all alone. Whatever it was, she was certain things would be better once she and Hallie went home.

"No doubt, you'll want to spend time with her today, but don't force anything," Dr. Nero went on. "Let her get a good night's sleep and I'll be back tomorrow morning. If everything is fine, we'll talk about her release and what to do afterward."

All Dana could do was hope, she realized. When they went home, everything would work out. It just had to.

After both doctors left, Logan said, "It won't take long for it all to come back to her. I'm sure it's only a matter of time."

His words were meant to reassure, yet somehow they brought home the reality of it all. What would happen when they went back into her room? Hallie was afraid, she'd said, afraid of the strangers. And her own mother was one of them?

If Hal was afraid of her, Dana didn't know how she

could possibly handle that. How would she ever manage without giving away how much her heart ached?

"C'mon. Let's go sit with her. I picked up one of those *Little House* books on the way back. Hal likes those stories, doesn't she?"

The pain in Dana's chest was so great she felt as if her body would split in half. She nodded, raised her quivering chin, squared her shoulders and started for the door. "Yes, she does. We used to read them all the time. Maybe it'll spark a memory."

"Hey, sunshine," Logan said on the way into the room. "It's storytime."

A few hours later, after reading the book twice through, after eating dinner and two desserts, Hal and her daddy read the book one more time before she said she was tired and wanted to sleep. She climbed under the covers and Logan tucked her in.

"No problem, sweetheart," Logan said. "We all should get a good night's sleep, and maybe the doctor will let you go home in the morning."

Hal glanced at Dana, who was sitting in a chair at her bedside where she'd been the whole time. The child, biting her lower lip, glanced down and self-consciously picked at the thin flannel blanket.

"It'll be great to get home and see all your own things," Dana said to her. "And your best friend, Chloe. You'll feel much better about everything then. I know you will."

Hallie gave a barely discernible nod and reached for Logan's hand like a life preserver.

"Mom's right, kiddo. We'll be back in the morning, and if we don't get the warden's okay, we'll have to break outta this joint."

Hal cracked a tiny smile. The first smile Dana had seen from her daughter in two days.

After Logan had said his goodbyes, Dana leaned down and pressed a kiss to her little girl's forehead. Then it took every shred of her willpower to turn and walk out the door.

Passing the reception desk on their way out, Logan asked, "Can I hitch a ride to the office? I'm without wheels at the moment." He swiped a hand across his chin, his amber eyes piercing hers.

She drew her gaze away. If she gave him a ride, it would delay going home to an empty house for a little while longer. "Sure, it's on the way.

They rode in silence, passing the Hancock Tower, until they neared the building where Security International was headquartered. Logan's presence loomed large, and her midsize van suddenly felt like the smallest compact. Finally, when she pulled to the curb, she said, "Would you like me to call in the morning to let you know what the doctor says…or do you have other plans?"

She couldn't blame him if he wanted to be there, too, even though if she had her druthers, he wouldn't be there. Because if he wasn't, maybe Hal would remember some little thing about her mom, maybe remember that it was her mom she lived with, her mom who took care of her and didn't disappear without notice to save the world from the bad guys.

Logan gave her an incredulous look. "I *plan* to be there. I'm the only person she knows. She'd feel abandoned if I didn't come."

He paused, shoved the door open and got out. He waited, holding the door ajar. "Besides, Hal thinks she's going home with her mom *and* her dad. She thinks we're *all* going home together."

His eyes narrowed. A beat later, he said, "So plan on having a house guest for a while."

CHAPTER FOUR

"I DON'T THINK I can do it, Jillian, I just don't." Dana sagged into the soft corduroy chair, combed stiff fingers through the tangles in her hair and toed off her shoes. In the past twenty-four hours, she'd had almost no sleep and barely enough nourishment for a gnat. She couldn't think coherently about anything, much less how she was going to handle this new development.

All she wanted to do right now was go to bed and sleep. She wanted to sleep, get up in the morning, go to the hospital and bring her daughter home. Alone.

"And he just *told* me I should plan on him staying for a while. He didn't even ask!"

"And if he had?" Jilly asked as she made her way to the couch. She plucked a mint from the candy dish on the buffet, popped it into her mouth, then sat in the matching chair facing Dana and leaned forward, elbows on her knees. "You know darn well you wouldn't have agreed."

Dana drew a deep breath. "Yeah, you're right about that. Logan probably knew it, too."

"So maybe he can help you get Hal settled in. Once she's back home and sees Chloe, maybe everything will kinda come together for her."

Dana scanned her comfortable family room, her gaze landing on the brick fireplace with the charred remains of the last toasty fire she and Hallie had had just last weekend. She took in the fawn-brown, supple leather couch and matching love seat that still held the indentation where she and Hal had snuggled to watch the fire snap and crackle as it consumed the dry timber. The scent of pine and cedar still hung in the air.

Yes, once Hal was around familiar things, she'd surely remember everything. And seeing Chloe? How could she not remember her best friend?

"I guess you're right, but then, you usually are." She smiled affectionately at her friend. Jillian Sullivan hadn't gone past high school, yet she knew more about people than anyone Dana had ever known. "Besides, Hallie told the nurse she's going home with her mom and dad, and I sure don't want to be the bad guy by telling her the one person she recognizes won't be staying."

Dana sighed. "It's probably best, at least until she gets settled in. Which means I'll *have* to handle being around Logan for a while."

Her friend's blue eyes widened, blond eyebrows shot up.

"What? What's the matter?"

"Does that mean what I think it means?" Jillian asked.

"Which is…?"

"Which is…that Hallie thinks you two are still married."

"Whoa." Dana jumped to her feet and jammed her fingers through her hair again. "I hadn't thought of that. Oh, wow, she probably does." She whirled around. "Unless Logan told her differently, and I doubt he would've, because now certainly isn't the time for that." Dana's pulse quickened at the thought. "She'll learn the truth about that soon enough. On the plus side, since she doesn't remember me, she won't remember how crushed she'd felt about her daddy leaving, either.''

Time and again she'd assured Hallie that her mommy and daddy's breakup had nothing to do with her. Still, no matter what, Hal kept coming back to that one thing, thinking the divorce was her fault.

Hal's reaction was a common one, Dana knew. Children of divorce frequently thought they were somehow to blame.

"Well then," Jilly said, "you've got more than one problem to solve."

"*That*, my friend, is the understatement of the year. I think I need a drink. You want something?" Dana padded in her stocking feet toward the kitchen.

"Nope, gotta get back. My mother-in-law and Chloe will be home in a few minutes and I should be there. If I'm not, Harriet'll get on her child-neglect rant again."

Dana stopped in the archway between the family room and the kitchen. "That's ridiculous."

Jilly gave a full-bodied laugh. "Yeah, I know it and you know it. But the woman can't understand that I have a life, too. To her that amounts to child neglect."

"You want me to tell her to butt out or we'll sue for slander? I'll represent you." Dana said, only half joking. No one messed with the people she loved!

"That'd only prove her point that I'm a heartless slut. Which she thinks I am because I'm not wearing black for the rest of my life. Nah, I'd much rather report her to the IRS and keep her so busy she won't have time to stick her nose into what I'm doing."

Dana laughed for the first time in two days. But because Jilly made jokes about everything, she didn't know if her friend was serious or not. "Do you know something you can report?"

"No, but it sure would keep her busy trying to deny it." She headed for the door, giving Dana a hug on her way out. "Or I could hire a hit man."

Dana followed, bolted the heavy door and stood for a second with her hand pressed against the smooth stained oak. Though her friend was kidding, a chill had run up Dana's spine. She was prosecuting a man for doing just that.

Joey Lombard, a small-time hood with mob connections, had been arrested for murder. Word on the street was that he'd been hired to take out Bruno Altoona, a big-time threat to Sal Leonetti, the Mafia boss who controlled the major crime syndicate in Chicago. David thought it the perfect vehicle to nail the elusive Leonetti. Unfortunately Lombard had blown the job and killed a woman who'd apparently stepped into the line of fire. Consequently it would be tough to prove Leonetti hired him to do Altoona. Their only hope was getting Lombard to rat on his boss.

That was if the guy didn't jump bail. Though she'd tried every tactic she'd ever learned to keep Lombard from making bond, he'd hired one of the most prominent trial attorneys in Chicago. Where he got the money for that was obvious.

All of which reminded her that she had to call David and tell him she wouldn't be in tomorrow. She didn't usually go into the office on Saturdays, but had been doing it recently to stay on top of things, Lombard's case in particular. There was a lot of work to be done if they wanted to get Leonetti, too. But the case, even though it might be the most important of her career, wasn't as important as her daughter.

Tomorrow morning she would to go to the hospital and bring her little girl home. With or without Logan.

After a phone call to her parents and one to Liz to report that Hallie was coming home tomorrow, Dana left a message for David, then climbed the stairs to her bedroom. On the way down the hall, she stopped briefly before the closed door to the master bedroom.

The room she and Logan had shared for nearly five years. Squelching the urge to open the door, she kept on walking to the guest room, where she'd taken to sleeping after Logan had gone. It wasn't long before she'd started sleeping there permanently. There were no memories in the guest room.

As she entered the room, her anxiety about bringing Hallie home multiplied. What if Hal didn't want to come home with her mother? What if she wanted to go with Logan when she found out her parents were no longer married? And what kind of trick was she, Dana, going to pull out of her hat to manage any sort of normalcy with Logan in the house?

Technically they still owned the house together. Logan hadn't wanted to disrupt Hallie's life more than necessary and neither had she. He'd said he'd deed it over to her. Just as well—he'd never wanted to live there in the first place. If he'd had his way, they'd be living on some huge estate near Boston, instead of the comfortable hundred-year-old colonial in Chicago's South Side.

Yet somehow, they'd never gotten around to transferring the home into her name only, and now, she preferred it that way. If Logan had deeded it to her, she would've felt beholden to him.

Jilly and Dana's sister, Liz, both found her attitude hard to understand. Liz thought that because Logan was wealthy, Dana should've taken him for every penny she could get. Jilly thought that living in the house without getting the deed in her name alone put Dana in a vulnerable position—that Logan could order her out at any time.

As an attorney, Dana knew all the legal ramifications. But personally, she knew Logan.

Crossing the bedroom to the closet, she shrugged off her blazer. In the end, it wasn't important what anyone thought. She knew Logan would never do anything to disrupt his daughter's life.

So why was she dredging up the past? It served no purpose. She wasn't a young girl in love. She was a single mom with a daughter and a career to take care of. And that's what she would do.

She would *not* let her ex-husband's presence disrupt her life. There were many things to deal with. Wondering if she was still in love with Logan Wakefield wasn't one of them.

IN THE MORNING, Dana called the nurses' station as soon as she arose and learned that Hal was still asleep. She showered quickly, threw on a pair of khaki Dockers, a white turtleneck and a black blazer. She was out of the house by six-thirty and hoped to get to the hospital before Hallie awoke.

On the way through the doors and up the elevator at Chicago General, she mulled over all the things she needed to do and prayed that everything went smoothly with Hal's discharge. But the main reason for getting there early was to see if Hallie's condition had changed during the night.

To see if Hallie remembered her.

Outside the room, she peeked through the open door.

Still asleep, Hal looked so peaceful it was hard to believe anything was different.

Dana wanted to go in. She wanted to be the first person her little girl saw when she opened her eyes, yet she wasn't sure how she'd be received. Indecision gripped her.

What if Hallie was afraid when she saw her? As much as she wanted to be with her daughter, she decided to wait until Logan arrived. She just hoped to hell he hadn't had to dash off on another assignme—

A warm hand landed on her shoulder. She whirled around. "Logan. You surprised me."

He stood so close she could smell the scent of fresh air, as if he'd been outside awhile.

"I'm glad you're here," she said.

Logan looked surprised. "Really? Well, that's a new development."

Heat warmed her cheeks. "Not at all. I simply didn't want to go in without you."

He paused, locking her gaze with his. "Like I said, that's a new development."

"I was afraid Hallie might wake up and be scared. Don't read anything more into it, Wakefield."

Logan, she noticed, had gotten a haircut—casually short, longer on top and stylish as always. He wore jeans and a newer lightweight, black leather jacket that looked so buttery smooth she was tempted to reach out and run her hands over it.

"She won't be scared. You're her mother. And if she still doesn't remember and is a tiny bit wary, I'm sure she'll get over it quickly."

Dana gave him a wobbly grin. "I wish I was as sure of that as you. Look at what's happened already. I don't want to do anything to make this any harder for her than it is.'' She paused to pull in a deep breath. ''I want her to come home, that's all.''

He reached out, gently stroked her arm. ''C'mon, let's go in so we're there when she wakes up.''

They tiptoed into the darkened room, quietly sitting in the same chairs they'd sat in the day before. Logan was much better at waiting than she, Dana thought, remembering another time that they'd waited together, she impatiently, he totally relaxed.

It was the night before the *Harvard Law Review* results were to be posted. She'd been so nervous she couldn't eat or sleep and had called Logan in the middle of the night to ask him to come over. She'd called him because she believed he was the only person who might understand how important making *Review* was to her.

The fact that he hadn't cared about it for himself really hadn't mattered. His knowledge of the law was intrinsic and his grades showed it. He was, in fact, brilliant, and what a shame it was that he wasn't practicing law anymore.

She, on the other hand, had had to sometimes study all night to get the grades that would allow her to be in the top five percent of the class. Logan knew her struggle and had helped her.

The waiting had been hell, and she couldn't have even imagined what she'd do if she didn't make it. Making *Review* had been part and parcel of her plan. Her plan was her life. It defined who she was. Failure was not an option.

As they'd waited together for the rankings, Logan had said, ''If I make it and you don't, I'll give up my spot so you can have it.''

Something inside her snapped. ''Don't joke around, Logan. You know how important this is to me, and it galls me that you can take it all so lightly. This is the most important thing in my life right now and the fact that you can blow it off like... like nothing really bothers me.''

The light dimmed a little in his eyes. He seemed hurt, and she wished she could retract her words. He was being supportive in the only way he knew how, because he knew he'd make it. No wonder he was relaxed about it. That he'd give up his spot for her should've made her feel good, but it didn't. This was something she needed to do on her own.

In the end, she squeaked in under the wire, but she'd made it, all the same. Logan came out on top as she suspected, and though she'd expected him not to take on the job, he had. If she was going to work on the *Review*, he'd told her, so was he. ''How else will I get to see you?'' he'd said.

A quick nudge in the ribs brought her to the present. Logan motioned toward the bed. Hallie's eyelids fluttered a hair. Dana's stomach flipped.

''Hi, sunshine. Daddy and Mommy are here.'' Logan reached for his daughter's hand, and at his touch, Hal's eyelids flickered a couple of times, then slowly opened.

Her small fingers curled around Logan's as she struggled to come awake, and when she saw him, the tiniest trace of a smile curved her lips. Dana waited, her stomach churning, half in anticipation, half in dread. She prayed Hal would have the same reaction when she saw *her*.

But when Hal turned to Dana, her expression went blank.

Dana's heart dropped. The blood drained from her limbs. A tense silence enveloped the room. Nothing had changed.

Dana grappled with logic. Hal *had* been through a trying ordeal, it would be natural for her to feel out of sorts. Good Lord, she couldn't even *imagine* what it would be like to wake up without a memory.

It wasn't long before Dr. Fleming arrived and directed Dana to the desk to complete the necessary discharge papers. "I'll be right back, you two," Dana said with forced enthusiasm. She would *not* let Hallie know how awful she felt.

On the way out she heard Logan say, "Looks like we won't have to break outta this joint, after all." She resisted the urge to turn to see if his joking had made Hallie smile again. She hoped it did. God, how she hoped it did.

A little girl needed to smile.

When Dana came back, Hallie was sitting in a wheelchair, waiting to go home.

"Hospital procedure," the nurse explained as she escorted them to the elevator. On the way to the lobby, Dana searched for something to say, something that would sound natural and not give away the awful anxiety that invaded every cell in her body.

Normally, the doctor had said. Just act normally. How the hell would she ever be able to do that? She was a stranger to her own daughter, and her ex-husband was going to be living in the same house with her, pretending they were still married.

At the hospital door Logan announced he'd get his car and bring it around because their Indian summer had suddenly turned cold and rainy. Okay. That meant she'd either have to drive home alone, or she'd have to leave her van and come back later to get it. She decided on the latter because she wasn't planning to let Hallie out of her sight for even a minute.

Hal sat in the back by choice, and when Dana offered to sit with her, Hal shook her head no. It took all of Dana's energy to manage even the tiniest smile. The ride was interminable. Logan drove slowly, as if too much jostling might hurt Hal, and when they finally arrived at the house, Logan pressed the garage-door opener and drove inside as if he'd never left.

"C'mon, twinkle toes," Logan said, reaching out a hand to help Hal out of the car. She looked a little unsteady, so Dana reached out, too.

Hallie clasped Logan's hand first, then reluctantly, hers, almost as if she couldn't touch Dana without Logan's support.

Once inside, Dana hesitated, searching Hal's face for some sign of recognition, uncertain about what to do next. Finally she decided to take Hallie upstairs to her room on the off chance that she would remember something there.

Hallie's gaze darted about as they walked down the hall. She looked as if she was seeing a strange new world. Which, it seemed, she was. Upon entering her bedroom, Hal glanced from the dresser on the left where she kept her collection of music boxes, to the white four-poster bed in the center of the room, to the bookshelf on the right that held her *Little House* books, her American Girl doll collection and the books that went with each of them.

Dana had promised Hallie that on her next birthday, she'd take her to the American Girl Museum and she could pick out another historical doll, or she could get the Girl of Today doll, which, if she wanted, could be made to look like her. Hallie probably didn't remember that either.

Pooka, her favorite stuffed animal since she was a

baby, lay ragged and limp on a chair. Hallie gave it no more than a cursory glance.

Dana bit back her growing alarm. "Why don't you get comfy?" Dana said. "Take all the time you want to look around, and while you do that, I'll make some lunch."

Eyeing the dolls, Hal walked over and reached out for Kirsten, the doll dressed like a girl growing up on the American frontier. Before touching it, Hal pulled her hand back, then looked at Dana. "Is it okay to take them down?"

Dana nodded, fighting an urge to give her daughter a reassuring hug. But she might scare her if she got too close, too fast. "Sure, sweetheart. Everything in here is yours. This is your private space, and you can do whatever you want."

Forgetting the doll, Hallie inched toward the bed, then looked up, eyes rounded in question. "Do I sleep here?"

Whether she liked the idea or thought it was a bad thing, Dana couldn't tell. "Yes, you do sweetheart. This is the bed you picked out for yourself last year. And then you helped me decorate the room—exactly the way you wanted it—with all the things that you love."

Dana walked to the window and motioned toward the dollhouse next to it. "We made this together, and we had a lot of fun doing it." Logan, she noticed, stood in the doorway taking it all in.

Hallie stared at the dollhouse, her eyes not registering a single emotion. "Why did we have to make it? Couldn't we afford to buy one?"

While Dana stood in stunned silence, Logan quickly strode over and reached down to pick up one of the miniature dollhouse chairs.

"I suspect you and mommy made it because that would be more fun than just going out and buying one. When you do it yourself, you can make it look exactly how you want."

He crouched next to the structure so he was at Hal's eye level. "See, look here, the little bedroom is blue, like yours. I bet you and mommy decided on blue because it's your favorite color."

Hallie peeked inside the dollhouse, then glanced around the room. "I didn't know that I like blue so much. But now I'll remember that I do."

Dana felt like an intruder. "While you two are getting acquainted with things, I'll rustle up some lunch. I'll make your favorite, Hallie. Macaroni and cheese." She edged toward the door, feeling a need to escape so she could gain some semblance of control over her erratic emotions.

Again Hallie looked at Dana with blank eyes. "I had macaroni and cheese in the hospital and it tasted kinda yucky. I had that red wiggly stuff there. I liked that a lot."

What the…? Hallie had always hated Jello. She'd never liked the consistency of it and now she loved the stuff? Dana opened her mouth to speak, then thought better of it. She felt as if she was talking with a stranger. Maybe she was.

"Sounds like a great idea to me," Logan said. "I love macaroni and cheese." He shot Dana a look and it took only a fraction of a second for her to realize what that gleam in his eyes was all about. The infamous macaroni-and-cheese fight that had led to more than a bath; it had been the first time they'd made love. Her first time ever.

Her heart skipped a beat. How could he think of *that*

at a time like this? "If I remember correctly, you love anything you don't have to cook," and with that she turned and headed to the stairs, taking them two at a time on the way down.

Between her daughter not knowing her, and an ex-husband who knew her entirely too well, she just might lose her mind.

Don't frighten Hallie. Don't let her see how hurt— or how scared you are. Don't be weak. Don't let Logan get to you. Don't fall prey to his charms. Above all, don't let him know you still care.

Reaching the sanctuary of the kitchen, she braced her palms on the counter of the island in the center of the room and stood for a minute willing herself back to that unfeeling place she'd found so comfortable for the past year.

She had to keep a clear head. Nothing mattered except helping Hallie get better. If that meant putting up with Logan, she'd do it—no matter how long it took.

She straightened and, shoulders back, brushed the hair from her eyes. She dragged out a pot and ran water in it. She could do it. Yes, she could. She could do almost anything for her little girl.

WHEN LOGAN WENT downstairs, steam was billowing from a pot on the stove, and Dana was nowhere to be found. Odd. It wasn't like Dana to leave something unattended on the stove. Maybe she'd gone upstairs to change clothes?

Not likely, though. She'd always been careful about things like that. Too careful. Annoyingly so at times.

He picked up a wooden spoon on the counter next to the stove and stirred the bubbling water and macaroni. Hal had wanted to be alone for a while, he guessed to look things over, maybe even see if anything in her room seemed familiar.

"It'll be ready in about fifteen minutes," Dana's voice called from behind him.

He turned. She'd changed shirts and now wore a white sweatshirt with her jeans and had pulled the top part of her hair into a ponytail, leaving the rest hanging. Her hair looked a lot shorter than before.

When they'd first met, her silky auburn hair had hung midway down her back. But each year she'd cut it shorter and shorter. He'd liked her hair long, and no matter what style she wore, it looked great. One of the things he liked to remember when he was away on a job was how her hair fell against his face when they made love, how the scent always produced a primal reaction in him, even when he was just thinking about it.

His blood surged. They'd been good together that way. Really good. They'd—

"Something wrong?" she asked, fingering the hair at her neck.

Realizing he was staring, he moved away from the stove and pulled out a stool at the island. "I noticed your hair is shorter, that's all."

She frowned. "It's been this way for a while." Her expression said she had no patience for small talk right now, especially about herself.

Talking about herself had always made her self-conscious, and damn if he didn't love to do it. He liked to see her hand flutter to her neck, the pink rise to her cheeks.

Yeah, he liked to do it, and he knew why. It meant she wasn't in total control. The only other time that happened was when they made love.

Dana went about draining the water from the pot and dumping the macaroni into a sieve. Avoiding his gaze, she asked, ''Did Hallie say anything when you were with her?''

Her movements were apprehensive. She was hurting. Badly. He knew how she'd feel if he told her the truth—that Hallie had said she was scared. ''Yes, she said she liked the dollhouse, but she wished she could remember.''

Dana gave a wry laugh. ''She's not the only one who wishes that.''

''Yeah, it's tough on everyone.''

He studied the way she stood at the sink running water over the macaroni, her back rigid, her muscles tensed.

''Sorry, I shouldn't have said that,'' Dana murmured.

''Why not?'' He came up behind her. ''I can only imagine how I'd feel if it were me.''

''What either one of us feels isn't important. I have no business feeling sorry for myself.''

Her words were filled with resolve. A phenomenon he admired, but found difficult to understand. She'd make up her mind about something and that was it.

He, on the other hand, could no more tell himself not to feel something than he could stop breathing in the seductive scent of her. A scent that even now infused him with memories of urgent kisses and the pounding desire that had sent two young law students into the back seat of his BMW more than once.

Memories of young love and lust washed over him like a tsunami. Back then, his need for her had been so strong, so intense, he'd literally ached with it. And the best part was that her passion had equaled his every step of the way. They couldn't get enough of each other, and the memory lived deep within him.

She turned to face him, leaned the side of a hip against the counter. He wanted to kiss her. Just like he'd wanted to kiss her when they'd stood on the sidewalk in front of the Pound Building so many years before.

He raised his hand to touch her cheek, then thinking better of it, pulled back. "You're right. The only thing that matters is doing whatever we can to help Hal. We need to talk about it, figure out how to provide a united front—under the...uh...circumstances."

She eyed him warily. "Meaning?"

"Meaning—" he raised a brow and lowered his voice as he moved closer, until his mouth was near her ear "—if Hallie thinks we're still married, we're going to have to act like it."

Dana flipped the macaroni back into the pan with a splat. She ripped open the cheese packet and emptied it into the pot with the rest of the ingredients. Then she grabbed the wooden spoon and began beating the mixture, each stroke harder and faster than the last, until he was sure there'd be nothing left in the pan but yellow paste.

Finally she said, "Forget it, Wakefield. Because if we're going to act like we did when we were married, you'd have to leave for parts unknown in about five minutes. Now make yourself useful and set the table."

Right on target. He'd unnerved her. Avoidance was her stock in trade and if confronted with an unwanted emotion, she'd counterattack.

"Sure," he said softly, teasingly. "I'll set the table." He winked. "Just like old times." Pausing, he added, "And you gotta admit, some of them were pretty damn good."

A noise on the stairway made them both turn. Hallie stood there, eyes wide and full of questions.

"Hey, sunshine." Logan motioned her over. "C'mon and help your dad. I can never remember where mom keeps everything. Sometimes I think she changes things around just to keep me on my toes."

Hallie smiled at the joke, then looked at Dana as if to ask if it was okay for her to help.

"It works for me." That her daughter seemed even the least bit eager to help ignited a spark of hope within Dana. "You can get the napkins from the counter over there and put them on the table."

The meal went well, and despite what she'd said earlier, Hallie seemed to enjoy the macaroni and cheese. As she ate she listened raptly as Logan described the many foreign countries he'd visited on his job.

The rest of the day passed slowly. Dana tried to talk with Hal while Logan made a few business calls. She should've been happy to have Hal all to herself for a while, but the conversation was so stilted and unnatural that Dana wanted to cry. Instead, she bit her lip and asked if Hal wanted to play checkers, which they did until Logan returned and regaled them with more adventure stories. At last, when Hallie announced she wanted to go to bed early, relief flooded Dana. She hoped the tension would be further eased in the morning after they'd all had a good night's sleep. When Logan said he'd head out in his car to pick up the groceries she needed, she felt as if another weight had been lifted from her shoulders.

Jilly called and they discussed when would be a good time to get Chloe and Hallie together, finally deciding to feel it out in the morning if Hallie seemed receptive.

After she hung up the phone, Dana mulled over the

options on their sleeping arrangements. With Logan staying there and Hallie thinking they were married…Lordy, it was a scenario she didn't even want to think about.

She fixed a hot cocoa and went into the family room where she flopped onto the couch and punched on the television remote, hoping for a little mindless entertainment and a respite from her problems. She flipped through the channels. Nothing kept her attention.

Her gaze drifted to the bookcases that Logan had built to hold her collection of first-edition books. He'd built another set of bookcases in their office for her journals, law books and state statutes.

Everywhere she looked, something reminded her of Logan. The gold-framed photos on the oak library table, photos of the three of them that she couldn't bring herself to remove, the cocoa-brown stressed-leather chair and ottoman that he'd wanted because it looked squishy and comfortable, the music box he'd bought her as a birthday present the year they'd begun dating—all reminders of Logan and the love she'd longed for, the family she'd wanted.

Girlish, unrealistic dreams that couldn't be fulfilled.

In the past year, she'd managed to come to grips with that—and the failure of their marriage.

So why did everything come back in a rush? Logan was there for one reason and one reason only, the same reason he'd married her in the first place.

His child. His daughter.

Never had the point been made so clearly.

CHAPTER FIVE

AS LOGAN PULLED into the driveway after his run to the store, he thought how the house didn't look any different than it had a year ago—at least not on the outside. The Colonial Revival-style home was still the same, even down to the taupe trim on the windows and doors. The Beverly Hills neighborhood, appropriately named for its California counterpart, had once been a haven for the elite.

The area had gone into disfavor for a period of time, but a few years later became popular again and was subsequently populated by young professionals who liked the old mansions and the convenience of being close to work.

Unlike Dana, his preference had been to buy or build a place in the country, where their children would have the freedom to run and play, and where it was safer. But Dana had insisted that Beverly Hills was as safe as anywhere, and near all the action that made Chicago the vibrant city it was.

They'd finally reached an agreement—a trial year—and if it didn't work out, they'd move. Luckily, he'd come to love Chicago nearly as much as she.

He pulled into the garage, hit the remote to close the door and sat for a minute with ten-year-old memories of his ex-wife's strong-willed nature filling his head. One night in particular—it was in their second year after an Ames Moot Court Competition, and their team of four had briefed the issues in an advanced hypothetical appellate case and conducted arguments before panels of faculty, attorneys and student judges. Dana was practically spinning with excitement as she waited for the results. Only two teams would advance to the semifinals in the Ames Competition, and many students considered it the highlight of the academic year.

The final round would be held in their third year before a Moot Court that included a state Supreme Court judge and involved issues currently before the Supreme Court. Dana was beside herself waiting to hear. He didn't know then that it meant more than prize money to her—that she considered it the springboard to success—to reaching her goal. He couldn't understand it because nothing had ever meant that much to him— then.

In his naiveté, as they stood in the hall waiting, he'd assured her it wasn't the end of the world if she didn't make it. "After all, a hundred years from now, who'll remember any of this?"

She'd sighed heavily, then flicked her long hair behind her shoulders. "You couldn't possibly know what it's like to want something so badly you'd do anything to get it," she said. "I doubt you've ever wanted anything you couldn't have, not for more than an hour—a minute maybe."

"It wasn't *quite* like that," he protested, standing as close to her as he could get in public without getting aroused. "I wanted a Corvette on my sixteenth birthday and got a big, ugly four-door Mercedes, instead." He sighed wistfully. "I wanted that Corvette pretty damn bad."

"Just as I suspected. And I bet you rushed right out

and got a job at the local hamburger joint so you could buy one on your own.''

''Aha! See, that's where you're always going wrong. You make far too many assumptions. Or you really do have a twisted opinion of me.''

''Convince me I'm wrong.'' She jutted her chin, her green eyes flashing in challenge.

He wanted to kiss her. Damn! He always wanted to kiss her. But he doubted that would convince her of anything except that he was like every other guy who only wanted to score. Which might've even been true at first.

''Okay. How's this. During high school I worked for a month every summer at my dad's firm in Boston.''

She snorted. ''Yeah. That's really working the salt mines, Wakefield. I can hear the violins. Pardon me, but I think I'm gonna hurl.''

''What?'' He punched her arm playfully. ''You think working for my father isn't grueling? It's torture of the worst kind.''

Yeah, Logan remembered, he and Dana had spent lots of time together, in study group and with the rest of their gang. Seven of them in total. But most of the time, he'd wanted to be alone with her. He wanted to make a connection that would allow her to open up— at least enough to let him into her heart. But she'd always remained a fingertip out of reach.

He'd never had trouble with girls before. On the contrary, they usually hung all over him, acting helpless and needy. In his whole life, she was the first girl he'd known who wasn't impressed by his looks or his family's money.

And he just knew that if she liked him, she liked

him—for who he was and not for any other reason. That was the way Dana Marlowe was.

Back then, she was filled with energy and ideas, ready to suck up every microcosm of life that she could, and it was stimulating just to be around her. In lots of other ways, too. His twenty-two-year-old hormones had been put to the acid test.

For the first time in his life, he'd really wanted something he couldn't have. And because he'd wanted her so badly, he would've done just about anything to make it happen.

But she'd made up her mind that she was there to learn. She had no time or inclination to socialize she'd said. Study, making *Review,* being the best at everything, that was what she was all about. Still was, as far as he could tell.

Logan exited the car, grabbed the groceries and headed into the house. In ten years nothing had changed. She'd never opened that inner door, not completely. She never let him know what drove her so hard, and there seemed nothing he could do about it.

The lights inside were low when he went in. All was quiet. He popped open a beer, put the groceries away, then went into the family room. Dana was sleeping on the couch and for a while, he just stood over her, watching her sleep.

A low fire burned in the fireplace, giving the room a soft umber glow that made her face look almost angelic. She didn't look her thirty-two years, and he guessed it was the freckles across her nose, the wholesome freshness that made her look so young.

He rounded the couch and sat on the chair opposite her, grabbed a news magazine from the coffee table and started to read about microchips.

"We have to make plans." Dana's voice startled him.

He looked up from the magazine as she pulled herself to a sitting position. Her hair had that messy tangled look it always had after a night of lovemaking.

"What kind of plans?"

Dana smoothed her hair, not wanting to acknowledge the invitation in his tone. "For starters, where you're going to sleep and store your clothes, assuming you have some." She'd waited up for him so they could clear the air.

"I do. They're in the car."

"We also need to discuss the ground rules and how we're going to handle things with Hallie."

He snapped a military salute. "Aye, aye, Cap'n." Then he grinned. That slow, slightly off-center Harrison Ford grin that let her know she was taking things way too seriously.

"Be a duck," he used to tease. *"Let it roll off your back."* Logan believed being unhappy never changed a thing, and served only to make a person crankier and more disgruntled.

"Okay," she said. "But I do want to make sure we're on the same page. It's going to be hard enough for Hallie as it is without problems between us, too."

His expression switched from teasing to puzzled. "Problems? I thought we solved all those by getting divorced." His tone, while teasing, was tinged with challenge. "What problems could we possibly have now? We both want what's best for Hallie. Right?"

"Right." She gave a jerky little nod. She wasn't going to buy into his challenge. Because she knew that could lead to other things. Two other things to be exact—an argument or making love. She didn't want either one. Not anymore. "Let's talk about the sleeping arrangements."

"Sure. That's easy." He sank back in the leather chair, his jeans-clad legs stretched in front of him. She couldn't help staring.

She knew the taut muscles that rippled beneath the fabric, and she didn't like how the knowledge unnerved her, made her think of other, sensual things.

"You know my preference," he drawled, "and I think in ten years, I got a pretty good handle on yours." There was that grin again. Teasing, baiting her.

Dana shifted her position to sit bolt upright, her blood pulsing hotter by the second. "Smart-ass. You know what I mean."

He scrubbed a hand over his chin. "Yeah, unfortunately I do."

Now, what the heck did *that* mean? Well, whatever he meant didn't matter, not one iota. "Hallie thinks we're still married," she said quickly to get it over with. "So I guess that means we have to share a room. I'm sleeping in the guest room now and there's a couch in there you can sleep on."

Logan arched a brow. "You're sleeping in the guest room?"

"It's cozier," she shot back. "Closer to Hallie's room. I wanted to be closer because I sleep so soundly." The look on his face said he didn't believe a word, not for a second.

"Okay," he finally said. "We can work that out. What's next?"

"I spoke with Jillian. If Hal's feeling better tomorrow, we thought maybe we'd get the girls together. It's a Sunday and if it's nice outside, we'll have a picnic or something."

His eyes lit up. "Sure, we can do that. I think you're right. The sooner she gets involved, the better it'll be for her. So, yeah. I'm game."

We? She hadn't contemplated the *we* part of it. It hadn't occurred to her that he'd want to go along with two women and two little girls—on a picnic, no less. Granted, they'd had a few picnics of their own in the past, but that'd usually been when they went to the cabin they owned on Rainbow Lake. The cabin they still owned.

"Okay," he said. "It's settled. Right now I've got a little business to take care of. Mind if I use the phone in the kitchen?"

She waved a hand. "Be my guest. I'm going to go to bed. I'll put some sheets out, and I think you can manage the rest."

He nodded. "I can manage."

Yeah, she was sure he could. But she wasn't sure about herself. Fact was, she wasn't sure about much of anything these days—except that life with Logan had never been boring.

"HEY, KIDDO. HOW'S it going? Have a good sleep?" Logan's voice reverberated from outside the bedroom door. Dana heard Hallie's voice, too, but it sounded like they were walking away, and she couldn't make out the conversation.

She stretched languidly, pulled the quilt up and then drew in a long breath. She'd heard Logan come into the room late last night and had pretended to be asleep. Then she'd listened to him breathe, her senses assaulted by the faint scent of his cologne, a scent that wafted toward her like a potent aphrodisiac until her stomach ached with desire.

She'd spent half the night like that, her awareness of him so acute she couldn't deny the physical need he'd awakened in her. Finally in the wee hours she'd dropped off.

She stretched again, still tired and wishing she could yank the covers over her head and go back to sleep. Instead, she pushed herself upright, then swung her legs over the edge of the mattress and touched her feet to the polished hardwood floor. She stood and stretched once more to get the blood circulating and her mind functioning.

The doctor had said to do familiar things with Hallie and that's what she would do, if her daughter was up for it.

She glanced at the window and noticed sunlight sifting through the gauzy sheers. It looked like a good day for a picnic. Hal had always loved picnics.

Dana's spirits felt buoyed. Even if Logan went along, Jillian and Chloe would be there. And if the girls went to play, she wouldn't have to sit there alone with Logan. That was, if he still insisted on going along.

The thought of Chloe and Hallie together sent a burst of hope through Dana. The girls had formed a close bond, and there was every chance that Hallie might remember her best friend.

And maybe then, she'd remember other things.

After throwing on a pair of jeans and a turtleneck sweater, Dana hustled downstairs. She'd make breakfast, call Jilly, pack some picnic supplies and they'd be off.

Halfway down the stairs, she smelled bacon frying, and when she reached the kitchen, she stopped, dropjawed at seeing Logan at the stove. Barefoot, wearing jeans, a white shirt, unbuttoned, his hair still tousled from sleep, he looked sexier than ever. Hal stood next to him.

Dana dragged her gaze away and toward the table that held three place settings, each with a glass of orange juice. Her insides went all mushy and nostalgic—though she wasn't sure why.

Logan had never been one to fix a meal of any kind. In fact, he'd so rarely been there in the mornings, the scene shouldn't call up any emotions at all.

Maybe it was because they were together now, the way their family should've been all along. Just then, Dana's stomach growled loudly enough to be heard across the room. Both Logan and Hallie turned to look at her.

She cleared her throat. "What're you doing?"

"We're making breakfast, of course," Hallie piped up.

Dana's heart did a tiny flip. Hearing her daughter say something without fear in her voice wasn't the same as getting a big hug, but it was progress.

Dana walked forward, stopped next to Hal, then peered into the pan. "And exactly what is it you two are cooking up?"

Logan gave her an insulted look. "Pancakes and bacon. Can't you tell?"

She glanced into the pan again, then looked at Hal and winked. "Sure. I...uh... I guess I just haven't seen pancakes look quite that...that special before. I thought maybe you were giving Hal a geography lesson."

Dana angled her head to the side, scrutinizing the free-form mass in the skillet. "Yeah," she said, "I'd recognize the state of Texas anywhere."

Hallie covered her mouth and giggled.

Logan frowned. "You ladies want to cut me a little slack? It *is* my first time at this, you know."

Dana opened her mouth, ready to offer to finish the job, when Logan barked an order. "Make yourself useful, you two. Dana, you can pour the coffee, and you, stretch—" this to Hal "—you can get the milk from the fridge. This feast will be ready in another minute or two."

"Okay, okay." Dana held up a hand. *An interesting development for sure.* Logan had never made of pot of coffee in his life. At least not that she was aware of. "It's going to take me a minute to get used to all this."

Hal stood at the open refrigerator, her eyes searching.

"It's on the door, honey," Dana answered the unspoken question. Then she helped Hal with the milk and they pulled their chairs to the table before she said, "I noticed how nice it is today, so I guess a picnic is in order. What do you think?"

Hal shot Logan a pleading look.

"I thought we could ask Chloe to come along," Dana said, "and we'd go to that little park at the nature center. It's your favorite place to picnic," she added to make Hal feel a little better.

Hal was silent, but panic shone in her eyes. A second later Logan brought the pancakes and bacon to the table.

"Chloe's your best friend in the whole world, honey," Dana tried again. "You two are like this." She held up two entwined fingers, but her daughter's expression still registered wariness.

"Syrup?" Logan asked. "Still in the fridge?"

Hal's eyes widened even more, then the uncertainty that was there switched to a quick flash of relief. "You don't remember where the syrup is, Daddy?"

Dana and Logan exchanged fast glances.

"Yep. That happens sometimes to us old geezers," Logan said. "But it's no big deal. Actually it happens to everyone now and then. And just so you know, no one will know or care if you don't remember something, either."

Dana pressed her fingertips to her lips. Hal was scared. Scared to meet her best friend because she didn't remember her. How had she missed that?

"Besides, Mom and I will always be right there with you. Got that, squirt?" Logan slapped a couple of pancakes onto Hal's plate and then did the same with Dana's.

Hal gave him a wobbly nod and seemed to relax a little. Then she dived hungrily into the state of Texas.

After a reasonably relaxed meal, Dana told them that since they'd made breakfast, she'd clean up. She was happily wiping off the table when the phone jangled. She picked it up with a cheery hello.

"Hi," her friend said with surprise in her voice.

"Hey, Jillian. I was about to call you."

"Well, I guess things are improving? You're sounding pretty chipper."

"Chipper, huh? I've never been accused of that before. How about relaxed and excited because it looks like a good day to get the girls together? Are you and Chloe free for a few hours later on, maybe around lunchtime?

"Drat. Sorry, I forgot. I had company last night and it slipped my mind. Hold on while I check."

Waiting, Dana peered out the kitchen window, wondering where Logan and Hallie had gone.

"Just as I thought," Jilly said, coming back on the phone. "I can't today. I've got to work. If it was just a couple haircuts, I'd be done by noon, but I have a color job and a perm. Gotta keep the place open on weekends for my working clients, ya know."

"Darn." Dana couldn't squelch her disappointment. The sooner she got Hal back to doing normal things, the sooner she'd remember. "How about Chloe? Can she come?"

"I planned to take her to the shop with me. But hey, if you want her to come without me, I'm sure she'd love to go."

"How do you think she'll feel about Hal not remembering? Will it bother her?"

"Nope, I already told her. It won't be any big deal. Kids are more adaptable than we are."

"Yeah. Guess you're right. Sure wish I had some of that resilience right now."

"Me, too. Harriet's getting harder to deal with."

"Something happen?"

A long pause was Dana's answer, but finally Jilly said, "Nothing you need to worry about. You've got enough on your plate as it is."

"Hey, now wait a minute. Are you saying it's okay for me to cry on your shoulder, but not vice versa?"

"Of course not. But this is different. Besides, I've got other things to think about."

"Like that guy who keeps coming in to get a haircut and asks you out for coffee?" Dana heard a long sigh on the other end of the phone.

"Couldn't even if I wanted to. You know that."

"No, I don't. You *could,* but you won't. And that old battle-ax of a mother-in-law of yours is part of the problem."

"Can't argue that. But it's not the whole reason—

and we're not going to talk about my problems right this minute. One of these days, we'll do it over a bottle of wine.''

"Promise?"

"Yeah. Promise."

"Good. When are you going to work? We can pick Chloe up there, or she can come over now."

They made arrangements to pick up Chloe at the beauty shop at eleven-thirty. When she hung up, Dana wished to heck Jillian would tell her what was wrong. Jillian had been her main support after Logan had left, and she'd do the same for her best friend—if only she'd open up.

At least enough to tell Dana what really happened between Jillian and Chloe's father—or why her ex-mother-in-law had such a hold on her. For the life of her, Dana didn't understand why Jillian didn't tell the old crone to stuff a sock in it.

"Mother?"

Dana whirled around. Hal was right behind her. Hal had never called her "Mother" before, and it sounded so formal, so detached and unfeeling. She'd always been Mommy. On the brighter side, it was the first time Hal had voluntarily addressed Dana or called her anything since they'd arrived home.

"Yes, sweetheart. What is it?"

"Daddy told me to tell you he was going to shower and then he'll be right down." With that said, Hal turned and headed for the stairs, presumably to wait in her room.

Dana sucked in a deep breath, trying desperately to fill the empty spot in the middle of her chest.

Mother. It wasn't much, but it was a start.

"YOU WANT TO CLIMB on the gorilla bars for a while?" Chloe danced around Hallie as she waited for an answer.

Hallie sat atop the slide ready to go down. "Sure. But I thought they were monkey bars." It didn't matter to Hallie what they did. Whatever it was had to be better than hanging around with her mom and dad watching and waiting for her to remember something. Maybe she should just say she remembered something so they'd quit looking at her like she had a big ugly nose.

"They used to be called monkey bars," Chloe said. "But I heard the *real* name is gorilla bars." She squinted at Hallie. "Do you believe me?"

"Sure, why wouldn't I?" Hal slid to the bottom of the slide and dropped on her butt. She got up, brushed off her red pants and the matching sweater her mom had put out for her. She started to follow Chloe, then stopped. Her parents might get mad if she ran off without saying anything. She waved to get their attention because they were sitting on a blanket talking. "Can I go to the bars?"

"Sure thing," her dad said with a big smile, but her mom looked worried. "I'll be careful," Hallie added. Maybe that would make her mother feel better. Her mother smiled then, and Hallie liked that she made her smile. Being careful was good, so she smiled back before she ran off to where Chloe was.

"So why wouldn't I believe you?" Hal asked again when she caught up with her friend.

"Oh, that. Never mind, I was only teasing." Chloe scrambled to the swing set near the bars.

"I think I'll swing first," she hollered. "C'mon. You do it, too."

Hallie followed and selected the seat next to her

friend, who shoved herself off and started pumping her feet like crazy.

"They think you're gonna remember everything if they take you to all the places you used to go and do everything you used to do," Chloe said matter-of-factly.

"I know," Hallie lamented, pointing her toes and pumping her legs in sync with Chloe's. "I wish I could remember, so everyone would stop watching me."

"Well, I don't care if you remember," Chloe said. "We can have fun, anyway."

Hallie grinned. It made her feel good that Chloe didn't care if she remembered anything or not, because then she didn't have to pretend.

"Your mom's probably mad 'cause you don't remember her but you remember your dad. That's all."

Hallie frowned. She didn't want anyone mad at her. She just wanted them to stop watching her every second. "But I can't help it. And besides, she shouldn't be mad 'cause I really don't remember all that much about my dad, either. When I was in that hospital and couldn't get awake, I heard him singing to me, and then when I woke up, I knew that he was my dad and he was really nice. Then everything got all weird, but he was still nice—even when I was all mixed up."

Chloe stopped swinging in the middle of Hallie's sentence, jumped off the seat and landed in the sand with a soft thud. Hallie wished she had hair like Chloe's, all curly and kind of reddish-blond. She didn't like her own hair. It was just plain brown and straight.

"No shit," Chloe said, coming to stand in front of Hallie with her hands on her hips. "That's cool."

Hallie gasped. "You swore!" She frowned at Chloe. "Maybe I don't remember things, but I know it's not nice to swear."

Chloe ignored Hallie's scolding and yanked at the crotch of her faded jeans. Then she pulled at the front of her purple sweater, which had bunched up when she hit the sand. Hal stopped swinging, too. She wished she was wearing old jeans like Chloe so she could fall down and it wouldn't matter.

"Oh, you just forgot. Swearing's okay between us girls. You swear, too, but we only do it when we're together. We don't swear at school or anything. Are you gonna tell your parents you don't remember stuff about your dad, either?"

Hallie shook her head. "Uh-uh. Then I might hafta go back to that hospital again, and maybe they'll keep me there."

"Yeah. You don't hafta tell 'em," Chloe said. "They don't need to know everything. I never told anybody about that man on the playground when you fell, 'cause they'd go all crazy saying we shouldn't be there by ourselves and it was our own fault 'cause we shoulda been in class."

Hal's mouth dropped open. "Did we skip school?" She grinned. "Cool." That meant she wasn't one of those goody-goody kids. Somehow she knew there were kids who were all nice and everything like that, but she figured it wouldn't be much fun. She'd much rather be like Chloe who did whatever she wanted.

"Nah, we didn't ditch. We got bathroom slips before the end of class and went outside early for a minute. But we don't want to tell anyone, 'cause they'll ground us for a long time."

"Wow," Hal breathed. "I guess it doesn't matter 'cause I don't remember it, anyway." They both giggled.

"Hey, high five!" Chloe smacked her hand against Hallie's and they laughed even louder.

"Uh-oh, I think we better talk about something else, 'cause here comes my dad."

Dana watched Logan head toward the girls to tell them it was time to go home. He moved purposefully, and she marveled at how even his carriage exuded self-confidence. Every movement was a statement of decisiveness and power. He was a man who knew who he was and where he stood with the world.

The girls had run over to sit on the whirlybird and when Logan reached them, he sat beside Hal and pushed off, making them spin around like a top. Their laughter rang in the air.

It seemed strange to see a man trained by the CIA, a man who'd spent most of his career undercover in foreign countries, a man who spoke four different languages and probably even knew how to make the perfect kill, having such a great time playing with two little girls.

His natural affinity with children was amazing. Dana had to admit that even though Logan had been away much of the time, when he was there, he'd spent a lot of time with Hallie, taking her swimming, to movies, helping her learn to print the alphabet and count by tens. A child couldn't have asked for a better father.

Logan, she remembered, had wanted another child or two; he'd said so early on in their marriage. Before they'd even gotten involved, he'd talked about joining the CIA and not taking over his father's law firm, but he wasn't sure how that would work if he got married and had children, which he definitely wanted to do. He'd said because he was an only child, he'd always wished he'd had a brother or sister, not only for a playmate, but also so he wouldn't have to bear the sole responsibility of pleasing his parents.

She'd told him he didn't know what he was wishing for. Her own experience was the best testimony in the world for having only one child. It had been awful growing up in her sister's shadow, having to compete for either of her parent's attention, her resentment building, until sometimes she almost hated her sister.

Until the day she realized Liz wasn't the problem. Her parents were.

She'd never told Logan all that, because the one time she'd tried, he'd laughed it off and said her sister was a spoiled brat. She knew then that he would never understand, because he didn't have a frame of reference. She doubted he'd ever had a moment of feeling inadequate in his life.

In fact, Logan was so much like Liz it was scary; he was loved, charming, impossibly attractive, extremely intelligent, and he even had tons of money.

He'd hate the comparison.

"Hey, you two! Get your booties over here," Logan shouted as the girls playfully hid from his view. "I'm gonna count to ten, and if I don't see both of your freckled noses right here in ten seconds, we're heading to the ice cream shop without you."

No sooner had he said it than the girls came running. When they all reached the blanket where Dana sat, Logan said, "Okay, ladies. We're ready to blow this pop stand!" He held out a hand to Dana and pulled her up. "The girls think a visit to the ice cream shop on the way home is in order."

"Yay!" both girls squealed, then ran to the fountain for a drink.

Still holding Dana's hand, Logan trailed his thumb

across the top of her knuckles, pulled her closer and whispered, "Think you can handle one of those peanut buster parfaits?" His breath was warm on her cheek, sending a jolt of electricity right through her.

She smiled. She hadn't had one of those since…

Oh, jeez, forget it! Just forget it, Marlowe, once and for all! Damn. Why did everything have to remind her of something else? And why did she seem to remember only those tiny moments that even when strung together wouldn't amount to more than a few good weeks in a ten-year relationship?

She yanked her hand away. "I lost my taste for those a long time ago," she said, although not as convincingly as she would've liked. "Besides, I don't need the extra calories."

Logan scraped a hand across his chin, tilted his head to study her from the angle he always favored. Then he drawled, "Don't think you have to worry much about calories. And if I remember correctly—" he ran his tongue across his lower lip "—you were always eager for a little self-gratification now and then."

Her face warmed. He wasn't talking about ice cream, and all she could focus on was his mouth, how his lower lip was just a little fuller than the top.

"I'll bet one little taste and you'll be unable to resist the tempta—"

"Uh-uh." She dragged her gaze away, grabbed her jacket and jammed an arm inside. "Forget it, Wakefield. I've learned to control my impulses."

She shoved the other arm into the other sleeve, snatched up Hallie's windbreaker, then looked him directly in the eye. "I've learned that some things aren't good for me—no matter what."

The girls came back on the run. "Do we hafta go?" Chloe asked.

"We'd love to stay longer," Dana answered, turning her full attention to the girls. "But I promised your mom we'd be back by four-thirty. If we don't leave now, we won't make it." She handed Hal her jacket.

Chloe pressed her lips together, obviously disgruntled. She looked a lot like Jillian when she did that, Dana decided. Hal looked as if she was having trouble with the zipper on her jacket, so Dana reached out to her. "Here, let me help you."

Hallie ignored Dana and turned to Logan. "Dad, can you help me with this? I think the zipper is stuck."

Dana's cheeks burned as if she'd just been slapped.

CHAPTER SIX

"I'M GOING TO SEE Jillian for a minute," Dana said as Logan followed the girls into the house.

"And *we're* going up to my room until Chloe's mom tells her to come home," Hal called out on their way up the stairs.

"Sure." Logan watched them go, glad Hallie had taken to Chloe so spontaneously. Whether she remembered anything or not, it was a good sign. He hoped the friendship made Dana feel a little better.

He'd seen Dana's eyes go dark with hurt when Hal had rejected her offer to help with her coat. Then she'd quickly shifted her interest to packing up the picnic supplies and loading the car. She'd been so quiet at the ice cream shop that he'd wanted to reach his arm around her and give her a hug.

He hadn't done it, of course. Instead, they'd left and let the girls polish off their ice cream cones in the car.

In the kitchen, Logan grabbed the coffeepot, rinsed it out and filled the container while glancing out the window. Dana was in the driveway, waving Chloe's mother over with one hand, the other holding her jacket closed after a gust of wind caught her off guard. He couldn't tell what the woman looked like except that she had a wild mane of strawberry-blond hair and was a little taller than average, about the same height as Dana.

He'd always liked that Dana was on the tall side. It made her mouth that much closer to his. Made those full lips easier to kiss. The thought quickly brought other thoughts, of soft skin and slick naked bodies, frantic kisses and heavy breathing, which was probably his own right this very minute. Blood pulsed in his ears as his hormones kicked into gear.

Now where the hell did all that come from, Wakefield? Can't you even think of her without getting worked up? He scooped some coffee into the basket and punched the start button. Then he sat at the kitchen counter to wait for Dana to return.

He wished he knew what to say to help her. He knew what it was like to have the rug pulled out from under him. When the court had awarded Dana sole custody of their daughter, he'd been devastated. Dana's attorney had painted him as a reckless soldier of fortune, and he'd been hard-pressed to dispute it, since most of what he did with the CIA was classified information.

Changing jobs hadn't helped much, either.

Well, he was done with being an absentee father. If working from Chicago didn't pan out, he'd just have to leave the investigation business and do something different. If Dana didn't agree with his plans to see Hal, he'd petition the court for joint custody.

He knew the pitfalls when things were left to chance. He would *not* let that happen again.

Logan heard the door open behind him.

"Jillian's ready for Chloe to come home," Dana said, rounding the counter of the center island. She pulled up a stool on the other side, slid onto it, planted an elbow on the counter and cupped her chin in her hand. Her shoulders sagged.

"They're upstairs. You want me to get Chloe?"

Dana's eyes had the same defeated look he'd seen on the faces of clients when they held no hope.

He'd never seen defeat in her eyes before, and it laid him flat. He wanted to take her in his arms and tell her everything would be okay. He wanted to, but he didn't, because just then she said, "Sure. I'm going into my office for a while."

DINNER WAS QUICK and silent. At first Dana had tried to make small talk, but no matter what came out of her mouth, she'd get no more than a nod or an uh-huh from Hal.

When Hal requested that Logan tuck her in bed for the night and read her a story, Dana wanted to crumple into a heap. Instead, she said good-night, poured a glass of wine and headed for her office to read some briefs.

Anything to take her mind off herself. Self-pity was a wasted emotion and she couldn't afford to indulge in it.

On the way into her office, a knock on the front door startled her. She peered out the peephole, saw her sister and opened the door. Liz flounced in like an actress making a stage entrance. She shrugged off her faux-fur coat, and in an overly dramatic gesture, tossed it onto a chair.

"Can't stay long, darling. I've got a hot date."

Dana followed Liz as she sashayed into the living room.

"Got another one of those, hon?" Liz eyed the glass of wine in Dana's hand.

"Sure, here, have this. I'll get another."

"So the kid's okay?"

"As well as can be expected when one has amnesia," Dana said wryly, then disappeared into the kitchen for another glass of wine. When she returned, Liz was in the family room.

Her sister picked up the conversation where she'd left off. "It's so awful about Hal, Dana. But she's not physically impaired, is she? I mean, except for the amnesia thing, she's okay, isn't she? "

Dana nearly laughed out loud. Her sister was too much. "Yes, aside from that, she's okay. Hal's physician says the amnesia is due to the accident and probably temporary. We're hoping that's the case."

"We?" One of Liz's dark, perfectly defined eyebrows went up.

"Yes, we," Logan's deep voice sounded from the doorway.

Liz spun around. "Well, well. Logan. How nice to see you." She waited a second, then as if deciding, stuck out her hand.

Logan didn't come forward. "I'd say the same, sis, but you know it'd be a lie."

Unaffected by his remark, Liz drew her hand back. "In case you've forgotten, we are no longer related."

"All right! That's enough," Dana muttered. "There's plenty to worry about without you two sniping at each other."

Dana found a book of matches on the mantel, struck one and tossed it into the fireplace atop the logs and kindling she'd placed there a couple days ago. Good grief, had it only been three days since the accident? It seemed like an eternity.

She dropped onto the couch and nodded at Liz to sit.

"Sorry, I can't stay long, sweetie. I was hoping to catch my favorite niece before she went to bed."

"She's sleeping," Logan said, glancing at his watch. "You should've come earlier."

Ignoring Logan, Liz sent Dana a pinched smile. "Oh, I also wanted to tell you the folks won't be back for a few weeks. I told them you said everything would be fine and there was no need for them to rush back."

Dana stared at her sister in disbelief. "But everything isn't fine. I didn't tell you it was. I said the doctors speculated she'd be fine, that the amnesia was temporary."

Liz raised a hand to her throat as if realizing she'd done the wrong thing. "Well…uh…it isn't like a life or death thing. And you can't expect them to come running back from Hawaii when it wouldn't matter, anyway." Liz's eyes darted between them. "I mean, they've saved for this vacation for years, and…well, Hallie wouldn't know them, anyway, would she?"

"No, it wouldn't matter." *But it might be nice if they showed a bit of concern.*

Liz checked her watch and set her unfinished glass of wine of the table. "I've really got to run, sis. Can you give me a call and let me know when I should come back? I'm going out of town in a couple of days because Jerrod won't leave me alone. I think that restraining-order thing you did for me was wasted. But I do so want to see Hallie before I go. You'll let me know, won't you?" she said, but it was more like an order than a question.

"Sure." Dana nodded, and then Liz scooped up her coat and seconds later was gone.

"Nice to see you, too," Logan said as the front door slammed shut. His sarcasm wasn't wasted on Dana. She felt much the same right now. He rolled his eyes skyward, then came around the couch and sat next to her.

"Don't say a word," Dana warned.

He shrugged. "About what? And what difference would it make if I did?"

"Liz means well."

"Yeah, sure. What's all that stuff about Jerrod and the restraining order?"

"Nothing really. He's upset about their divorce and Liz said he'd tried to break into their house one night. She stayed with me a couple times because she was worried. But she always worries, and—" Dana waved a hand in the air "—you know Jerrod."

"Yeah. Casper Milquetoast."

"And Liz does tend to exaggerate. The order is more for her peace of mind."

"And your parents? What was that all about?"

"That's nothing, either. I'd already told the folks not to cut their vacation short." Dana defended her parents even though she wished they'd made an effort.

"Sure, whatever you say."

Dana reached for her glass, annoyed that he knew the truth. "Well, your parents haven't exactly been calling on the hour to see how Hal is, either," she added as some sort of vindication, then tossed back the rest of her drink.

"They'll be here late tomorrow."

She choked midswallow. "Here?" she sputtered, one hand at her throat. She hadn't seen Logan's parents since the divorce. Although they'd seen Hallie a few times, they'd always made arrangements through their personal secretary, for which Dana was glad.

"Yeah," Logan clarified. "At the Four Seasons."

"Of course." *Where else?* "Look, I'm going to get a little more wine, and then d'you mind if we figure out how all this is going to work so I can get some sleep?

I really haven't slept much for a few days." She got up and started for the kitchen.

"Good idea," Logan said. "I'll have one, too. Here, let me do the honors." He took the glass from her hand, walked past her and led the way.

Dana's gaze focused on Logan's back. He moved with sublime grace, muscles flexing almost rhythmically, and she could see at a glance he still took great care of his body.

More to the point, she knew what was under that black knit shirt and tan pants as well as she knew the law: broad shoulders, a powerful chest that narrowed to a trim waist and hips, and strong muscular legs. Because of his job, Logan's body had been honed to sculpted perfection, with nary an ounce of fat on him. He'd been trained to withstand grueling physical effort, pain and even torture. It was hard to believe that finely tuned fighting machine was equally adept in the art of making love. The knowledge did strange things to her reserve.

Apparently not much had changed in the year they'd been apart. She still had the same intense physical awareness of him as she always had. She still loved to look at him, couldn't draw her gaze away any more than she could keep her thoughts from going in another direction. That totally useless other direction.

But there were more important things to focus on than the beauty of Logan's body and her lust for him, a problem likely related to her year of abstinence. Yes, that was it. Her desire had nothing to do with leftover feelings for the man. Nothing whatsoever.

She leaned leisurely against the island, waiting while Logan fetched and poured the wine. "D'you think Hal is really ready to go to school tomorrow?" she asked as she reached out and took the glass he proffered. His fingers brushed against hers, sending a rush of warmth up her arm.

He settled himself next to her against the island, so close she was sure she could feel the blast-furnace heat radiating through her. She concentrated on sipping her wine.

"Hard to say. The doc said it was best that she resume normal activities, and Hal did ask if she could go to school."

Dana took a deep breath. "Yeah. But I don't know. I'm so worried about her."

Every hour, every minute that passed in which Hal didn't remember, seemed worse than the last. If she never remembered, Dana didn't know how she'd ever handle that.

"I know. I'm worried, too," Logan said. "But she's got to do it sometime, and maybe sooner is better than later." He turned, looking into Dana's eyes. "Hey—" his tone was suddenly soft with concern "—are you okay?"

Tears burned in the backs of her eyes. Oh, Lord. She couldn't cry. She just couldn't. Yet no matter what coping mechanism she used, she couldn't make the awful, hopeless feeling go away, couldn't keep the question from escaping her lips.

"What if she never remembers me, Logan? What if I'm always a stranger in her eyes?"

"Hey, you," he said softly, turning to enfold her in his arms. "She'll remember you. Just being here sparks all kinds of memories for me. It *has* to do the same for Hallie."

Dana rested her head against his chest, allowing herself the immense comfort she'd always found in his arms. He held her tightly, as if somehow he could transfer his strength to her.

With his head touching hers, he stroked her hair and whispered soft reassuring words, words that soothed yet sounded jumbled in her brain because all she could think of was how wonderful it felt to be so close to him again. He was warm and strong and, without a doubt, the most compassionate, caring man she'd ever known, and right now, she couldn't remember why she'd ever wanted him to leave.

She heard his breathing quicken, just like her own. Her sorrow gave way to a pulsating physical need. A need so deep and compelling that when he gently touched her cheek, she automatically raised her chin and parted her lips.

Their eyes met and held. His mouth touched, featherlight on hers. Like a starving woman, she pulled him closer, savoring the softness of his lips, his warm moist tongue, the erotic sensations that coursed like hot liquid through her body.

He pressed closer, and she felt the warmth of his hand against her skin under her shirt.

Then her hands were all over him, his all over her. Every cell in her body seemed electrified, and her desire was suddenly so great it blotted out all common sense.

She wanted him. And dammit all to hell, she couldn't remember a time when she hadn't.

But what good had it done? The thought invaded the sensible part of her brain. She mustn't do this. It wouldn't change anything and she'd feel terrible later.

"No," she said with not a whole lot of resolve as she pushed away. "Logan, please." She pushed again, this time with clenched fists.

Instantly he stepped away, hands up in surrender.

Her chest was heaving so violently she couldn't breathe, much less speak. "This," she managed, pulling down her shirt, "is not…a good idea."

Logan stepped to the side. He didn't say a word, just ran his fingertips over the shiny black-marble countertop, his eyelids at half-mast.

"It won't help," she added, her voice still husky with wanting.

His eyelids raised, and the desire she saw there was almost palpable. She'd seen that smoldering, sensual look many times before, and it always had the ability to reduce her resolve to pudding.

"It can't hurt," he said quietly.

She straightened her shoulders, flicked back her hair and smoothed the front of her sweatshirt. She had to be sensible. Having sex wasn't sensible. Fun, maybe, and if she could leave it at that, there wouldn't be a problem.

But she knew herself too well, at least where Logan was concerned. "It'll only confuse things. Really. We need to make a pact."

"You mean like crossing our hearts and swearing we won't do it again, no matter what?"

"The swearing part will suffice."

He grinned, and she had the same weird sensation she'd had the first time she'd seen him do that—as if she'd been air-lifted to a cloud somewhere.

"So," she said, "you really think Hal's okay to go to school?"

He kept eyeing her in that deep soul-piercing way that said he knew what was on her mind. She wanted him, and he knew it.

"That's what she said."

"I suppose… I mean if Chloe can be counted on to

stick with her, and if the teachers keep a real close eye on her and if—''

"Whoa!" Logan raised a hand. "Don't start sticking too many *ifs* in there or she'll never get out of the house. We've got to let her try."

We've got to let her? Why did that sound so strange—and so good? "Okay. Let's see… I'll drop the girls off on my way to the office." She whirled around, clasped her hands. "Sure, that'll work, and I'll ask Jilly if she'll pick them up. She sometimes leaves the shop early."

"That's not necessary." Annoyance edged Logan's words.

Dana glanced at him from the corner of an eye and twirled a lock of hair at the back of her neck around an index finger. "Why not?"

"It isn't necessary because I'm not going anywhere. Someone needs to be here. So, I'll pick the girls up after school and bring them home. In fact, I'll drop them off in the morning if you don't have time to do it before you go to the office."

Dana's jaw dropped. When she realized it, she cleared her throat and said, "I never said I wouldn't have time. I'm trying to figure out what'll work for both of us. I have this important case and I've got to go into the office for—"

"Fine. You take care of your job and don't worry about the girls. I'll take care of them." He yanked a chair away from the kitchen table, swung it around in one hand, then straddled it so his crossed arms rested on the top of the chair back. "You don't have to figure out anything for me."

Damn! He still resented her dedication to her job. She yanked her own chair from the table, scraping it across the ceramic tile, not caring that it sounded like finger-nails scratching a blackboard. She threw herself into the seat and crossed her own arms.

"Fine. But *I* will drop the girls off. If you want to pick them up, that's okay with me. I'll tell Jillian."

He paused, scrubbed a hand across his chin. "Yeah, I do want. I'll be here. I'm not going anywhere."

She frowned. "You're not going to work?"

"Nope. If Hal goes to school and something happens or for some reason she decides she wants to come home, *someone* has to be here. I want her to know I'm here for her, no matter what."

"Not necessary. She can reach me at the office any-time. She knows that. The principal and her teacher know that."

He stared her down. "Fine. But this way, she won't have to wait. I'll be nearby, not halfway across town."

Dana launched to her feet, trying to keep her hands from clenching into tight little balls. "Fine." She counted to ten, then turned and stormed from the room. "Fine."

CHAPTER SEVEN

"JILLIAN?" DANA SHOVED open the heavy oak door a crack. "You here? It's Dana. Chloe?" Dana stepped into the foyer.

Chloe slid around the corner from the hallway to the living room in stocking feet. "I'm almost ready. But I gotta find my shoes, and my mom is helping me look."

Dana smiled and sighed. The apple didn't fall far from the tree. Chloe was just like her mother. Both were hopelessly disorganized and couldn't care less about it. Chloe also seemed nearly as street savvy as her mother, if such a thing could be said about a seven-year-old girl.

"I got 'em!" Jillian came flying around the corner herself. "Omigosh. Is it that time already?"

"Yep," Dana answered. "And we only have fifteen minutes before the girls will be late."

"Here, honey. Take these and put them on in the car," Jilly said as she shoved a pair of sneakers at Chloe's chest. She dusted her hands. "There. Now I've got to get dressed for work, too."

"You need a ride? I can drop you."

Jillian shook her wild mane of curly hair. "Nah. I'll be fine, once this kid gets off."

Dana smiled at Chloe and then at Jillian. "Okay, I gotta run, too. Remember, Logan's going to pick the girls up after school. And I want to talk with Hal's teacher before I go to work to make sure she fully understands.'' She was still uncomfortable sending Hallie off to school, essentially alone.

Jilly nodded. ''Yeah. That's probably best. And you're gonna help, too, aren't ya, Chloe?'' She ruffled her daughter's hair. ''Stick with Hallie like bubble gum. Okay?''

Chloe nodded her okay. With her mom's help, Chloe poked an arm into the sleeve of her jacket and struggled to get the rest on as she followed Dana out the door. ''Bye, Mommy,'' Chloe called as the door slammed behind them.

''Okay, girls.'' Dana pointed at the seat belts. ''Buckle up, and we're outta here.''

After dropping off the girls at school and talking with the principal and with Hal's teacher who promised to call her immediately if anything came up or if Hal got scared and wanted to come home, Dana headed for her office.

Nine o'clock and already the building was filled with people bustling across the marble-floored lobby, or clustered in front of a triple bank of elevators. Security guards positioned themselves by the heavy glass doors in front, and several people hovered around the information desk in the middle of the room.

Dana positioned herself amid the smallest group of people getting ready to storm the next available elevator car going up. She fought for a place close to the door and got off on ten. Her high-heeled shoes clicked down the long hallway to her office where she shouldered open one of the shiny mahogany double doors. Once inside, she shifted her briefcase to the other hand while she wriggled out of her trench coat. On her way past the front desk, she nodded at Cheryl, whose lilac perfume formed a protective barrier around the girl.

"Your daughter okay, Ms. Marlowe?"

"Sure. As okay as she can be right now." Dana continued on to her office. No time for chitchat. She'd missed all day Friday, and hadn't done a thing over the weekend, which was her habit. Cheryl followed Dana into her office.

"You've got a bunch of messages." She waved a hand toward the battered oak desk. "And David said to call him as soon as possible when you came in. He said it's important."

Dana shifted her stance, eyed the stack of messages next to her phone and threaded her fingers through her hair, shoving the wayward strands off her face. All she could think of was how Hal had looked when she'd dropped her at school.

Her little girl had been stoic and brave, but Dana had seen the distress in her eyes. She was scared to death—and Dana couldn't stop thinking about it.

She let out a burst of air. "Sure. I'll get to it," she answered, letting her gaze drift over three mile-high stacks of folders on her desk. The workload suddenly seemed overwhelming. "As soon as I can."

She waved Cheryl out of the room, and for a second, she just stood there, unable to coordinate her thoughts. Prioritize. She had to prioritize. Maybe she should call Logan and tell him her concerns.

No. He'd tell her she should've stayed at home or waited a day or two to see how things went for Hal before she went back to work. She could've. But nothing would be different. Either way the school would have to call her if something happened. It didn't matter where they called as long as she was available, right?

Still she couldn't help thinking maybe she should've waited longer in the school office. She could've done that. No, Hallie might've been frightened going to a strange place, but Dana could tell by the way her little girl pressed her lips tight and stood as tall as she could that she was determined to do it on her own. Which proved that fundamental personality traits don't change, regardless of memory loss.

For the second time she glanced around the sparsely decorated room. A walnut framed photo of Hallie occupied the top right corner of her desk, and the rest of the surface was covered with case folders and whatever else Cheryl had deposited there while she'd been gone.

Sighing, she picked through the messages. The Lombard case was the most important; she couldn't afford to let anything slide on that one. If she did, she could kiss her career plans goodbye.

Think. Focus. David. The case. Joey Lombard.

An update, that was what she needed. She punched Cheryl's extension and then the speaker button. "Get me the Lombard file, will you?"

"I did. It's on your desk."

"Oh. Thanks." She glanced at the mountain of folders, started rifling through them.

The phone chirped, and she jumped, quickly reprimanding herself for being preoccupied and not attending to task.

"Yes."

"You got a minute?"

"David. I was about to call you. What's up?"

"Can you come down?"

"Sure. Give me five, okay?"

"Fine. How's your daughter?"

"I'll fill you in when I get there."

She continued to rummage through the folders, tossing one after the other to the side, grabbed the one she wanted and headed to David's office. As she rounded the corner in the hall, a mountain of a man strolled out of David's office. He nodded and smiled as he went by almost as if he knew her, but he didn't look familiar.

Surely she'd remember if she'd ever met a tall, bald black man the size of a refrigerator who wore what looked to be a thousand-dollar suit and a diamond stud in his left ear.

David stood at the window with his back to her. Lake Michigan was visible from their offices, and she could see Navy Pier. She loved the neon lights and the carnival atmosphere at the pier. It was one of the first places she'd brought Logan when he'd come to Chicago with her to meet her parents.

A lifetime ago, it seemed.

"Looks like rain," she said.

David turned. He was a striking man for his age. His hair was close-cropped and dark with gray feathering near his temples. He stood ramrod straight, as if he'd be perfectly at home in a five-star general's uniform— or the attorney general's office.

And when he made that transition, his position as state's attorney would be open for her. She hoped she'd have his recommendation when the time came to run.

She'd still have to be elected, but her job as the state's chief deputy prosecuting attorney put her in prime position for the job—even though she was a woman, and younger than anyone who'd held the job before. Her Harvard background, clerking with a Supreme Court judge, her work with Narcotics and the Special Prosecutions Bureau, and her high success rate in cases argued, had paved the way. Her pro bono work and her experience and involvement in numerous commissions and committees didn't hurt, either.

If she nailed Leonetti, it'd be a done deal.

She tipped her head toward the door. "Who was that? I haven't seen him around before.

"New P.A. Name's Gideon Armstrong."

"Huh."

"Sit, please," David said. "Would you like some coffee?"

"No thanks." Though she was tempted by the aroma wafting through the office, it would only make her jittery. "I'm fine." She eased into the chair. "I didn't know we had an opening for another prosecuting attorney."

"Assistant P.A. It just came up. Increased workload, new funds." He gave a wave of dismissal. "Cheryl filled me in about your daughter. Is there anything I can do?" He sat in the wingback chair next to her, instead of behind his desk as he always did. He leaned forward, his eyes expressing concern.

"No, but thanks. There's not much anyone can do. We have to take it one day at a time."

"You let me know. Okay? If I can do anything, I will. Just let me know."

She shifted in her chair. He was unusually solicitous, and it made her uncomfortable. They'd always had a professional relationship; he respected her abilities and she his, but it had never gone beyond that. "What about Lombard?" she asked, changing the subject. "Anything new?"

He shrugged. "The court date's set."

That wasn't what she'd hoped for at all. Not right now. They needed extra time to prepare, time to get Lombard to agree to a plea bargain in exchange for information to nail Leonetti. As it was, they had to go for manslaughter because Lombard's bullet had missed his mark and ricocheted off a streetlight, killing an innocent bystander. He'd said his gun had gone off by accident, which meant they had no proof Lombard was trying to take anyone out. No premeditation. If a couple of street cops hadn't been on the scene, they'd never have had a case. But the fact that they had two eye-witnesses was enough to convince Lombard he'd be going away for a long time. She'd make sure he knew that with his reputation as a snitch, he wouldn't last two weeks in a maximum security facility—and she could change that. All he had to do was finger Leonetti. "Who's the judge?" she asked.

He smiled. "You'll like this." He paused, steepling his fingers for maximum effect, obviously drawing out the suspense before he said, "Wellesy."

"Really?" She collapsed against the back of the chair. Judge Wellesy was a good friend, her former mentor. She'd clerked for him way back when, and he'd always given her advice whenever she'd needed it.

"I thought you'd be pleased."

"Pleased? I'm not pleased at all. Someone might see that as a conflict of interest, or it could give the appearance of impropriety. It could hurt our case."

"No," he said quickly, emphatically. "It's the best thing that could've happened."

Obviously they had different points of view on the matter. But David's seemed out of character. "When?"

"Two months."

"Two months? Not exactly a lot of time to prepare, is it?"

"No, but we can do it. I'm counting on you." He paused again, then stroked his chin. Eyes narrowed, he leaned forward and rested his elbows on his knees. "We *need* a conviction on this. We *need* to get Leonetti."

That was the plan. "It's going to be tougher with Lombard on the streets. And if Leonetti decides to protect his interests, Lombard's life won't be worth spit."

David's lips thinned and she saw a muscle twitch in his cheek. He got up and started pacing. "Lombard's a liability to Leonetti. We have to do something."

Dana frowned. Apart from finding a reason to get Lombard off the streets, she didn't know what they could do.

Her boss looked more serious than she'd ever seen him. He cleared his throat. "Uh…you're pretty close to Wellesy, aren't you?"

"Was." She didn't like where this was going. "I haven't had any close contact for a long time. What's your point?"

Hesitating, he reached out and patted the top of her hand. "I think if you had a little talk with your old friend, we might be able to turn things around. Find a reason to revoke bail."

Dana gaped at him. Was he asking her to compromise herself to win a case?

"Off the record, of course," he added quickly. "I'm sure if he knew how important this was to you, to your future…" He shrugged, leaving the rest up to her to figure out.

Disappointment swamped her as she tried to sort it out. He wanted her to talk to Judge Wellesy? To do whatever she could to slant things in their favor? Or was there more? What did he want her to do? Whatever it was, it was obvious he wasn't going to come right out and say it.

"I can't talk to him. And if I did, Wellesy would take himself off the docket."

David rose to his feet, stuffed a hand in one pocket,

the click and jangle of change keeping time as he paced. "Not likely. Not if you do it right. It's important, Dana. More important than you can imagine. It's a way for you to lock in your future."

Lock in her future. What was he saying? That he wouldn't support her bid for his job if she didn't talk to Wellesy? Was he implying her well-planned future was down the tubes if she didn't do as he asked?

She wanted the job so much she could taste it. She'd dreamed about it, planned it for as long as she could remember. And David's recommendation would all but guarantee she'd get it. She never dreamed she'd have to compromise her principles to get that guarantee.

He wanted her to sell out. And if she didn't...she could kiss her future goodbye.

LOGAN DROVE HIS Lexus into the school parking lot, noticing as he pulled into an empty space the odd-looking man loitering around the perimeter of the building. The guy was bundled up in a long winter coat and wore a funny knit hat pulled way down. Logan couldn't see his face.

His internal alarm went off like a siren, and in a split second, he'd cut the ignition and jumped out, fully intending to corner and question the guy. But as he shut the car door, the school bell rang and droves of children streamed out the wide double doors of the building.

A fraction of a second later, when he looked again, the man had disappeared. Logan hurried toward the school entrance, expecting that was where Hallie and Chloe would come out. He scanned for a little girl wearing a red sweater, black tights and black high-top boots. But as the throng thinned, he could see the girls weren't anywhere. His gaze darted to the left and to the right, his adrenaline surging.

He started inside, then saw Chloe's bright hair first, and Hal right next to her as they came around the corner of the building. His heart was still pounding wildly when Hallie ran up and hugged him. In the process, she glanced warily from side to side. "What's wrong, kiddo?"

Hal looked at him with large eyes and said, "I want to go home."

Logan looked to Chloe, who shrugged. He asked, "Everything go okay today? Maybe I should talk with your teacher before we go home."

"Dad! I'm not a baby. You'll embarrass me if you talk to my teacher. All the kids will think I'm a baby!"

"Okay, okay." He raised his hands. "If you say so. You got everything? Homework, too?"

Hal held up her backpack. "Uh-huh. It's right here."

Logan hustled the girls into the car, but the feeling that something wasn't right lingered. Hal was unusually quiet during the ride home, so when they reached the house and Hal went inside, he cornered Chloe.

"Listen, Chloe." He hunkered down to her level. "I don't want you to mention this to Hal, but I want to know if you know why Hal seemed so upset right after school. Did anything happen today?"

Chloe's eyes rounded like moons. She sucked on her bottom lip and shrugged.

Jeez. Kids! He didn't know that much about 'em, but he sure knew when one was withholding information. "It's important, Chloe. Really important in helping Hal remember things. If anything happened, I want you to tell me."

Chloe frowned, then glanced toward the door to the house where Hallie had gone in. She was clearly torn.

"Please, Chloe. I promise I won't say a word to anyone, but I need to know."

The little redhead kicked the toe of one sneaker against the other. "Promise? 'Cause if you tell Hallie, she won't be my friend anymore."

He nodded and raised a hand. "Promise."

"Well, okay. I think she got scared 'cause of the man."

"The man? Today?"

Chloe shook her head. "Nope, not today. I told her about the man who was on the playground when she got hurt. I guess I shouldn't have told her 'cause I think it scared her."

Logan's blood thrummed. "Did someone do something the day she fell?"

"Uh-uh." Chloe shook her head. "Nothing happened. He was just there…and…and he saw us and we were supposed to be in the bathroom, but we went to the playground, instead." She looked at the floor and whispered, "I think he talked to Hallie a little. But then she fell and he went away. We couldn't tell anybody 'cause then we'd get in trouble, big time, for skipping class."

"What did the man look like, Chloe?"

"Uh, he had on this long coat and a hat like the kind you wear in winter."

Logan stood up. "Thanks for telling me. I appreciate it very much."

Chloe started to go, then she turned. "You won't tell on us, will you? You promised."

He couldn't help the smile that formed, thinking

about two seven-year-old girls cutting class. "Not a word. I promise."

But it didn't change the fact that some man had been at the school and had talked to Hal.

"C'MON CHLOE. LET'S GO to your house for a while," Hallie pleaded as she shoved an arm into the sleeve of her sweatshirt. "You're mom's home now, isn't she?"

"Awright. Lemme get my shoes on first or my mom'll brain me."

Hal plunked down on the pink-and-white chair in front of the dressing-table mirror to wait. Turning her face from side to side, she said, "Do you think I look like my mom or my dad?"

Chloe came over to stand at Hal's side and squinted. "I think you look like you and I look like me." She stuck out her tongue and grimaced at her own reflection.

"Do you think my mom is pretty?" Hal asked.

Chloe nodded. "Yeah. D'ya think mine is?"

"Uh-huh."

"Guess we're lucky, huh? 'Cause did you see Brandon's mom at school? She looked really mean! And she's—" Chloe spread her arms wide, then burst into giggles. When she settled, she went back to tying her shoes. "I wouldn't want a mom who looked that mean." Chloe gave her laces one more try, then left them untied.

Hal came over to help her. "Maybe Brandon's mom only looks that way and can't help it 'cause something bad happened."

Chloe shrugged. "Maybe, but she didn't sound nice, either, when she yelled at Brandon."

"I wish my mom laughed a lot, like your mom."

"She laughs. I saw her with your dad and she was

smiling. And she laughs all the time with my mom. You just don't remember.''

''I mean *different* laughing. With me. Then I wouldn't feel like she's mad at me 'cause I don't remember things. Sometimes I even act like I know what they're talking about when I don't.''

Chloe pressed a hand to her hip. ''Maybe you do remember and you just don't know it. I know you remember *me*—even if you don't think so.''

''How come you think I do?'' Hal smiled. She really really wished she could remember stuff, specially Chloe because she was her best friend.

''Because you act like you do, that's why. You just don't remember some stuff, that's all. You remembered how we pretended to be sisters when we went to school and old Mrs. Kronstad believed us.'' She squinted at Hallie. ''Or were you pretending to remember?''

Hallie frowned. ''I don't pretend to you, Chloe. But sometimes it seems like I know some things, and I don't think about if I knew it before or not. But you don't care if I remember or not, do you?''

Chloe shook her head.

Hal smiled. ''I think we shoulda been sisters. Hey, don't you ever wonder if you had a real sister what she'd be like?''

Chloe laughed and threw herself across the bed. ''I'm never gonna have any sisters! Brothers, either, 'cause my mom's not married anymore. Besides, she's too old. I heard when you get too old, you can't have babies. And my mom is *really* old. She's thirty already.''

Hallie went back to the mirror and pulled her hair into a ponytail, craning her neck to see her profile. ''I wish *I* had a baby brother or sister, because then my parents would be busy changing diapers and getting all worried about a baby, instead of me.''

"You could tell 'em you want a sister or brother. Then they'll be too busy *making* babies and won't bother you.''

Chloe started giggling and Hal joined her. She remembered about babies and where they came from and figured her mom and dad must've been together like that so they could have her. She stopped giggling. "I don't know, Chloe. They don't seem to like each other enough to have babies. Maybe I was adopted or something.''

"I don't think so," Chloe said. "But hey, let's get going. My mom can make us some popcorn and we can watch that movie I told you about, the one 'bout those twin girls who got separated at birth.''

DANA PULLED INTO the driveway in time to see the girls slip into Jillian's house. She hit the garage-door opener and drove inside, thinking she'd get Hal to come home right away so they could talk while she made dinner. Maybe she'd ask Hal to help with the cooking the way she used to do. Her doctor had said any little thing might trigger something.

Something at school could've triggered a memory, too. Anxious to see her daughter, Dana quickly exited the van. At the same time, Logan opened the door that led to the kitchen and motioned her inside.

"We need to talk before Hal comes back."

"What's wrong? Is Hal okay?"

"She's fine." He gestured for her to go ahead of him, taking her coat as she claimed a stool at the counter in the kitchen. Logan pulled up a stool next to her. Hal had to be okay or Logan would've called her at work, but something was definitely going on.

"What do you know about the day Hal had the accident?"

"I told you what I know already. Why?"

"When I arrived at the school, I noticed a man hanging around the side of the building."

Shocked, Dana parted her lips to speak, but Logan held up a hand. "The bell rang and kids started pouring out. When I looked for him again, he'd disappeared. Hal came out looking a little uptight, so I asked if anything was bothering her, and she denied it. But I still had this weird feeling that something was, so I took Chloe aside and asked her."

Dana quickly nodded for him to go on, and he told her about the girls' skipping class on the day of the accident and the man on the playground who'd talked to Hal, a man who sounded like the same one he'd seen today. "I didn't ask Hal about it because Chloe said that when she told Hal about the man, Hal got scared."

Anger flooded through Dana. "Are you saying some strange man is hanging out at the school? That he might be a danger to the children? No one at the school has ever mentioned anything like that!"

Logan placed a calming hand on her arm. "I don't know that he was bothering anyone, but it appears he was there on the day Hal fell and he was there today, too."

"Did you get a good look at him? Maybe it was a parent waiting for his kid? That's the most likely scenario." God knows it was what she wanted to believe.

"No, I didn't. But he didn't look like a parent, and the whole thing seemed suspicious."

"But you think everything is suspicious."

"I do *not* think everything is suspicious." Logan stood, tipping the stool back in the process. He deftly caught it before it crashed to the floor. "I'm trained to recognize unusual situations, that's all."

"Did you tell anyone what you saw? The principal? Did you report it to the police?"

He gave her one of his tempered-with-patience looks, then began to pace. "I couldn't do much with two little girls in the car, but yes, I called the school the second I got home. The principal wasn't there, but the admin assistant said she'd have her call me back tonight. Then I decided to ask you about it before alerting the authorities."

"Me? Why?"

"In case you had an explanation. Or information we could give the police."

"Such as?"

"Such as, do you know if someone might have a reason for following Hallie? Do you know of anyone who might be carrying a grudge against you?"

The thought was abhorrent, though not something that hadn't ever crossed her mind. In her line of work, it was wise to be cautious.

She'd always had an unlisted number and never gave her address to anyone. Hell, it was the main reason she used her maiden name in her profession and part of the reason they'd had the house alarm system installed. Yet his prying about her job annoyed her.

"I don't know if anyone is carrying a grudge against me. If this guy were bothering Hallie, and we don't know that's the case, why would it be because of my job? Why wouldn't he follow me, instead?" She shook her head. "I think we should get some facts before we start jumping in and digging for motives."

Logan ran a hand through his hair and continued to pace. "Yeah, I know. I was speculating to save time if and when we get the police involved."

"Okay, speculate on this. What about *your* job? If we're digging for motives, we'd have to look at it, too. Both of your jobs, as a matter of fact." Logan's former job with the CIA was twice as likely to generate that kind of response as hers. It was why he'd always kept that part of his life secret, even from his family. But his new job *could* produce that kind of reaction.

"True. But with the CIA I had a cover. A damn good cover. No one outside my unit knew who I was or anything about my real life. It's not likely anyone could connect the two, and I haven't been with SISI long enough to make many enemies." He spun around, his arms spread. "But in your position, hell, you're right out there."

"True, also. But on the other hand, that makes it pretty ridiculous to think someone I prosecuted would do anything. He'd be the first suspect if something happened to me or to my family."

She thought a bit more. "Maybe we're both overreacting. And besides, Chloe told you this, right?"

He stopped pacing. "Yeah. Is that significant?"

Dana nodded. "Sort of. Chloe's been known to fabricate a story or two. Maybe we ought to get the facts first. Didn't you say the school was going to call? I'd feel really foolish calling the police if the man was a parent waiting for his son or daughter." Abandoning her stool at the counter, she said, "I'll get Hallie for dinner. We can talk about this later."

Logan laid a hand on Dana's shoulder from behind, stopping her before she reached the door. "Children disappear all the time, Dana. Do you think because you work in the state's attorney's office your family is immune?''

She pulled away. ''No. But I think maybe you've been playing cops and robbers for too long.''

''What about the case you're on?'' he pressed. ''Or an old case, someone who might have reason to get even?''

Her nerves tightened, her exasperation suddenly at flash point. ''Please leave it alone, Logan. It's my job and I can handle it!'' With that, she turned and walked out the door.

Yeah, Logan thought. *You can handle it all right. Like you handled that whacked-out guy when we were doing pro bono work.* He remembered it as vividly as if it were yesterday.

The first year they were married, not long after Hal was born, Dana'd volunteered to do pro bono work with the American Civil Liberties Union and was defending a man who'd been arrested for assaulting an officer. They discovered later he'd been diagnosed as paranoid schizophrenic, with a few other serious problems tacked on, including a history of violence.

The man had continually harassed and threatened all the attorneys who tried to help him, and then he'd focused on Dana, said he trusted only her. She'd insisted that was even better reason she should continue working with him—alone.

Logan had accepted many things when it came to Dana's work, because he knew how dedicated she was, how she needed to help people, and because he cared more about her than he'd ever cared about anyone.

She'd worked damn hard to get where she was, so it was difficult to deny her the pleasure she got from it.

Besides which, she was incredibly good at the law. If anyone had been born to the bar, it was Dana.

But that expertise hadn't helped in the ACLU case. Logan knew the guy was dangerous and he hadn't been about to let her be alone with the man.

He'd told her, "I don't care how paranoid he is or that he won't trust you if you bring someone along. I'm not going to let you endanger your life for a cause."

He'd never forgotten her response.

"You won't *let* me?" she'd uttered incredulously. "That's not your choice to make, Logan. I don't want your help to do my job! I don't need you!"

Her words had stunned him. And for the first time, he'd wondered about their future. Because he'd realized right then and there that she really *didn't* need him— for anything. But his response had seemed so petty he'd put it out of his head.

He loved her. He didn't want a clingy dependent wife. He admired Dana's independence and her determination. Those qualities were part and parcel of why he'd fallen in love with her. But somewhere deep inside, he'd felt a void. He knew there was something intrinsically wrong with loving someone who didn't need him at all.

When the client went berserk, destroyed her office and held her hostage for three hours, Logan had almost gone crazy himself. But she still refused to admit she'd been in danger. "I handled it," she'd said proudly, defiantly, even though he'd seen right through her. He'd let it go because, for whatever reason, she needed to think she'd done the right thing.

He knew differently. But the fact that the situation with the client had turned out badly was no consolation to him. He'd wanted to protect her and he couldn't. He loved her, but in the end, it seemed as if she was angry at him for what had happened, as if it was his fault that the man went off the deep end.

Mostly he'd never really forgotten the kick-in-the-gut feeling when she'd uttered those words, *"I don't need you."*

He picked up the phone again to call the school. He damn well wouldn't ignore his instincts this time, no matter what.

CHAPTER EIGHT

"C'MON, LET'S FINISH UP," Logan said to Hal after dinner that night. "I'm ready for a game of crazy eights." He winked at Dana. "After we clean up."

As they began clearing the dinner dishes from the table, Dana felt mollified that the school had called earlier and dispelled their fears. The principal had assured them the man was most likely old Mr. Snyder, who lived across the street and came over frequently to see his great grandson. Unfortunately he sometimes confused other children with his great-grandchild. She also assured them they had a guard at school who was always there when the children were.

They'd both been relieved, and with that settled, they drifted into an easy rapport during dinner. Her only desire was to get through all this in the easiest way possible. She wanted Hal to get better and to resume a normal life.

She couldn't get too used to Logan being around, because all the rapport in the world wasn't going to change who they were.

Despite her resolve, she found it incredibly easy to forget all the problems they'd had. Jilly had come by to pick up Chloe's schoolwork, which the child had forgotten, and Dana could see that her friend was as charmed by Logan as she herself had been when they'd first met. Now she watched Logan as he teased Hallie about her schoolwork. He talked about things they'd done together as a family and regaled Hallie with stories about trips to their cabin and the time they went to Disney World.

Dana studied Hal as she listened to Logan, and every time he told her about silly things she'd done when she was little, her face would light up and she'd giggle.

Dana had a hard time not lighting up a little herself after listening to Logan talk about their marriage as if it was the best thing since man had walked on the moon. For the first time, she realized how different their perceptions of the marriage had been.

Or was he simply painting a brighter picture for Hal's sake? That was probably it. He couldn't really think about their marriage in the way he'd described. How could he? He'd been gone most of the time.

Besides, hearing him talk about their marriage in a positive way didn't make it a fact.

Logan had never wanted to be married, least not to someone so removed from his life in Boston. His parents had had big plans for Logan—before he met her.

If she hadn't gotten pregnant and decided to keep the baby, Logan wouldn't have felt compelled to marry her. How could she blame his parents for thinking what they did?

Today, after only a few days together, he'd slipped right back into that same pattern of questioning her job, her choices and her judgment. It was the reason she'd stopped talking to him about her cases. Because whenever she did, he'd tell her how to do her job—his way.

Still she couldn't stop wondering if their marriage might've worked if their circumstances had been different. Later when Hal had finished her schoolwork and was in bed, Dana headed for her office. She had to put some space between them.

An hour passed, and between thinking about the events of the day with Logan and Hal, and mulling over what David had asked her to do, she'd accomplished nothing. Every time she opened another file and started reading, she ended up staring into space again.

"You don't look like you're working too hard now."

Dana jumped at hearing Logan's voice behind her. She turned to see him standing in the doorway, the planes of his face highlighted by the room's incandescent light. He was a man's man, strong and capable, and yet he was also the kind of man who made women weak in the knees.

Not her, though. Instead, he made her palms itch and her skin go all hot and fiery. She tapped her pen on the desk, keeping time with her pulse. "I'm thinking. Some work requires use of the brain, you know." The tease came naturally.

It was the plane on which the two of them could always connect.

"I'm thinking, too. I'm thinking about how this reminds me of old times." He sauntered toward her.

The tapping quickened. How many times in the past had she gone into the office to work after Hal went to bed, and inevitably Logan would follow? She always had work to do, but as soon as they started talking, sparring and joking, she'd forget the work, and before she knew it, they were on the couch, or on the floor in front of the fireplace.

Her blood rushed just thinking about it. She moistened her lips as he came closer. "Old times." She turned away from him to concentrate on the papers on her desk, on anything but him. "That's exactly what they are. That was then, and this is now."

A second later she felt a hand settle gently against her neck. Deft fingers lifted her hair and she knew what would happen next. Oh, how she knew!

His talented hands would glide over her shoulders and neck, thumbs slowly rotating, fingers gently probing, seeking out all the tension spots. Then he'd apply light pressure and soothing manipulation that could make her so relaxed she'd agree to almost anything.

"That can be easily changed, can't it?" His voice was low and smooth, like rich cream. "We can make it as now as we want."

"Logan, don't," she said softly. She held her spine rigid, but with his fingers plying her shoulder muscles, it was impossible not to enjoy the sweet release of tension. "It won't make any difference, you know."

His warm breath fanned her neck. "No? But it would make us feel good. And we'd both relax a little."

Relax. She didn't need to relax. She needed to be on her guard and not let her stupid emotions get the best of her. She knew darn well what would happen if she didn't stop right now.

They'd have great sex and she'd end up wanting things to be different. She'd start hoping again, and God knows, she couldn't do that. Not anymore.

"A warm bath will do the same thing. In fact—" she wrenched herself from under his hot hands and stood up "—I think I'll take that bath right now. I can't seem to concentrate on work anymore."

She strode purposefully toward the door, stopped and turned to him. "I suggest a cold shower for you, Wakefield."

She was sure she heard him chuckle as she took the stairs two at a time.

DANA TOSSED AND turned, trying desperately to find a way to shut off the thoughts that invaded her mind even when she was sleeping.

She'd told Logan to set the security alarm and had gone to bed before him, promptly dropping off to sleep. The mental strain of the past few days had finally caught up with her. But she'd been woken by a delicious dream, a continuation of the massage, but in the dream, the massage became a seduction, an erotic lesson that brought her to near orgasm and culminated in sybaritic passion on her desk.

And for a few groggy seconds after she awoke, she'd almost thought it was real. Her insides had so ached with wanting that she was ready to find Logan and make the dream a reality.

But she was alone. Alone with her needy pulsating desire.

She pried one eye open. Although the room was dark, enough moonlight filtered through the sheer curtains for her to see he was there, stretched out on his back with a sheet corner barely covering his middle; one long muscular leg was stretched straight out and the other was bent over the side of the couch. His foot rested on the floor, and his athletically sleek body looked bronzed all over.

Blood raced through her veins. A quick self-reprimand followed. They were done! Kaput! Finito!

Proximity, that's all this was. Physical proximity.

With him in her face all the time, not thinking about him was next to impossible.

There had to be a better arrangement. Maybe they

could give Hal an explanation that would solve the problem. They could say her father had a cold and didn't want Dana to get it by sleeping in the same room. Nothing wrong with that. Or maybe he had an allergy to something in the room.

Though she prided herself on her honesty, in this case a little white lie seemed justifiable. Necessary, even. She'd never get a good night's sleep with Logan in the same room, and she couldn't go to work every day looking as if she was hung over.

Something had to give.

For the moment, a glass of milk might help, and afterward she could sleep on the couch in the family room. Deciding, she rolled off the side of the bed opposite from Logan, quietly tiptoed to the door and turned the knob, hoping like crazy the one-hundred-year-old door wouldn't squeak when she opened it.

She turned off the alarm at the top of the stairs and made it to the kitchen without a sound, relieved to put space between them. The kitchen was dark except for a night-light that gave the room an eerie quality.

The air felt chilly, and she shivered. Her skimpy Cub's T-shirt wasn't long enough to keep her warm. While the house had been renovated more than once in its history, it was still drafty when those Chicago winter-on-the-way winds cranked up and roared through.

Wishing she'd grabbed a robe, she padded to the refrigerator and took out the milk carton, got a glass from the cupboard and poured. Her thoughts drifted inexorably to Logan and how they used to forage for cookies and milk on those all-night study sessions when they'd crammed for final exams. When *she'd* crammed, she amended. And Logan had coached her.

On instinct, she reached for the cookie jar, curled an

arm around it, then took a step toward the center island—when a crunching noise outside the kitchen window startled her.

She whirled around. A large dark shadow flicked across the window shade, and she let out a startled cry of surprise. The jar slipped from her grasp and crashed to the floor.

She froze. Someone was out there! Omigod! 911. She had to call 911. She turned to run to the phone but collided with an ''Omphhhh'' against a man's bare chest.

Shaking and about to scream, she caught a whiff of Ralph Lauren cologne, and more by feel than anything, knew it was Logan. She clutched his arms and pulled him closer.

''There's someone outside.''

His hand came up to shush her. Panicked, she whispered, ''I heard a noise, then I saw someone outside the window.''

''Don't move,'' he whispered back. ''You'll cut yourself. I'll be right back.'' Then he was out the door.

She glanced to the floor, and in the dim light, she saw the shattered glass of the cookie jar scattered around her. He was right. If she moved she'd cut herself for sure.

But she still had to call 911. What if whoever it was was still out there? Logan could get hurt. Another kind of panic gripped her.

Quickly deciding, she stuck out a foot to step over the glass when his voice stopped her.

''Stay where you are. I'll get a broom.'' He flicked on the kitchen light.

She did as he said, standing, waiting, feeling her

knees tremble as he swept up around her. She was really cold, shivering cold, unable to shake off her fright.

But Logan didn't seem alarmed. Apparently he'd seen nothing outside. Maybe she was stressed out and overtired, and her imagination was playing tricks on her.

The rationalization didn't help the shaking, and it didn't quell the fear that roiled inside her. "Who was it?" she finally squeaked out in a voice that sounded strangely not her own.

The sweeping stopped. He moved closer and studied her, his gaze so intense she felt as if he'd reached into her and plucked out her soul to examine it.

"No one," he said after a pause. He cleared his throat. "I mean, I saw a guy walking his dog across the street. I think it was the streetlight throwing his shadow."

"The noise—what was that?"

He shrugged. "Probably a stray cat. I didn't see anything suspicious. But I did notice you'd been doing some gardening on the side by the window. I didn't know you had a green thumb."

She gave a weak laugh. "I don't...but I thought I'd give..." Her voice cracked. She couldn't finish the sentence.

"You sure you're okay?"

A sudden tide of emotion threatened to overwhelm her. She couldn't talk, because if she did, she knew all the uncertainties of the past week would rise up and render her a hopeless, emotional wreck. Placing a hand to her lips, she nodded.

As if he'd read her mind, Logan set the broom aside and in one smooth motion pulled her into his arms.

He felt so strong, so solid and secure. She wanted

more than anything to let go, to feel the strength flow from his body into hers. She wanted so much to give in to the longing that had formed inside her.

If only she could take the comfort he offered in the way she knew it was given, if only she could keep herself from expecting it to mean something more, then she could enjoy the sweetness of his embrace.

But she knew herself too well. And she knew him. Giving in to her desire wouldn't change anything. He cared about her, she knew that, but he didn't love her—not in the way she needed him to love her.

No, giving in to her need would only make her ache for something she knew could never be.

"Hey, it's okay," he whispered, rocking her gently in his arms. "It was nothing."

She sniffled, trying desperately to contain herself. "I'm okay." She gave a shaky sigh. But he continued to hold her, and for a moment she couldn't move. She needed his arms around her...for just a little while.

She buried her face against the corded muscles in his neck, and with her cheek resting against his warm skin, she closed her eyes, relishing the here and now.

Logan wasn't absolutely certain of what he'd seen outside, because it was too dark. He'd check again later, maybe first thing in the morning, just to be sure. All he'd seen was that she'd been doing some gardening near the window.

Something inside him wrenched when he heard her sniffle again. "Hey, it's okay to be frightened." But as he said the words, he knew she wouldn't allow herself the luxury. She never had before, at least not so anyone could tell.

She raised her head from his shoulder, and he reached to brush the hair from her face, his fingertips grazing her cheek. Her eyes glistened with unshed tears, and for the first time since he'd known her, he saw a trace of vulnerability. Within seconds, all his protective urges kicked into gear.

Along with those urges came another more primitive one. Instinctively he pulled her closer. Her arms came up around his neck, and he became acutely aware that she had nothing on under the T-shirt. Even through the fabric, he felt her nipples peak against his bare chest.

Her skin was soft and smooth and it would've been so easy to act on his impulses, but that wasn't what she needed. Instead, he held her close, his head resting against hers, relishing the fact that she hadn't pushed him away.

Then he heard a sound from upstairs.

His senses went on alert. He jerked his head up. "Listen, is that Hallie?"

When he heard another sound like a whimper, he grabbed Dana's hand. "C'mon. That's our daughter."

Hand in hand they climbed the stairs. Logan knocked lightly on Hal's door before opening it. "Hey, what's going on? Bad dream?"

Hallie was sitting up rubbing her eyes. Her hair was tousled and in the moonlight he could see tears staining her cheeks. He and Dana parted, then sat on opposite sides of the bed with their daughter between them.

Hal nodded. "A really bad one. And I got scared. Can you stay with me, Daddy?" She reached her arms out to him for a hug.

In his peripheral vision, Logan saw Dana sit up a little straighter and knew she'd felt the sting of rejection again. She and Hal had been so close, closer than Hal and him, yet now Hal acted almost as if her mother didn't exist.

"Sure, sweetheart. Both Mommy and Daddy will stay here with you." Pulling the covers up around Hal's shoulders and tucking her in, he saw Dana's silent thank-you.

He wanted to hug Dana, too, to tell her things would work out. Because he knew right then that whatever they were or weren't to each other, they were Hallie's parents and they'd always do right by their daughter— no matter what.

Filled with that knowledge, Logan laid his head on the pillow next to Hallie and nodded to Dana, who did the same on the other side of the bed. Then he reached across Hallie and found Dana's hand.

HALLIE LOVED THE smell of her daddy. He smelled all spicy and clean, and she snuggled under the covers next to him. She didn't like it when she had bad dreams, but she didn't know how to make them go away.

All she knew was that she felt better with her mommy and daddy there because they were bigger and she knew parents were supposed to protect their children. She didn't remember the dream now, but was glad her mommy and daddy were going to stay with her.

She had a nice mommy and daddy, even if she didn't remember lots of stuff about them. They loved her. She knew that because they said so.

She could've gotten a parent like Brandon's mean mother, who always yelled at him. Hallie didn't understand that. *Her* mom wouldn't yell at *her*. And sometimes she even thought she did remember things, like right now when she could smell her mommy's hair. It smelled like peaches and she knew what peaches smelled like, so maybe she did remember it from before?

Curling closer, she felt good inside and reached up to touch her mommy's hair. Rubbing a strand between her fingers, she closed her eyes and yawned. Maybe she could go back to sleep now. Maybe she wouldn't have any more bad dreams.

CHAPTER NINE

DANA FELT THE familiar tug on her hair and held her breath, hoping it meant what she thought it did. Hallie had picked up the comforting habit as an infant. Whenever the baby was tired but too restless to sleep, Dana had rocked her in the old wooden rocker that had been her grandmother's.

Hallie would snuggle her sweet-smelling little head against Dana's chest, shove one thumb in her mouth and reach up with the other chubby little hand to twirl Dana's hair.

Moisture filled Dana's eyes, and a lump formed in her throat.

Even if it wasn't a conscious thought on Hal's part, it was a start. And right now, she desperately needed that tiny glimmer of hope. That small intimate gesture buoyed her reserves and infused her with longing for the way things had once been.

For the first time since Hal had been hurt, Dana drifted into a peaceful sleep.

Morning came much too soon, and the second Dana realized where she was, she rolled over, hoping to see Hallie and Logan. The bed was empty. They'd already gone down to the kitchen. Dana stretched, still feeling no small amount of satisfaction about the way things had turned out. Except for what had happened between her and Logan last night. What on earth had she been thinking? She'd almost let herself fall into her old mode just because he was being kind.

She and Logan had to talk. It was all well and good to acknowledge her sexual attraction, but that was as far as it could go. They were adults and adults could deal with their urges. Not every desire had to be acted on.

Hell, she should practice what she preached to all those kids when she gave talks at the schools about the prosecutor's office. To get them involved, she always asked, "What kind of world would it be if people always did exactly what they wanted, when they wanted?" *What kind, indeed.*

A slow smile emerged as she rubbed the sleep from her eyes. Stretching lazily, she glanced at her watch. Good grief! She had only twenty minutes to shower, get Hallie in gear, make breakfast and leave for work.

Less than ten minutes later, with her hair still wet, Dana dashed downstairs and into the kitchen, all the while inhaling what smelled like fresh-brewed coffee. So where the heck *had* Logan picked up all his new talents? He'd never known how to boil water, much less brew coffee when they were married.

Of course it wasn't his fault. The Wakefield household staff had always taken care of his every whim.

"Can we do that after school?" Hallie inquired around a mouthful of food. She sat on a stool at the counter, swinging her legs back and forth below her. Logan stood near the sink pouring two cups of coffee.

"We'll see," he said, handing Dana a steaming cup.

He wore blue sweatpants and a loose, white muscle shirt, which she guessed meant he still exercised when he got up.

He smiled. "Good morning. Did you sleep well?"

She reached for the coffee, trying not to notice the way that one lock of dark hair sprang out over his forehead. "Thank you. And yes, I did. Eventually." Setting the cup on the counter, she tipped her head toward the window and asked under her breath, "Did you check outside?"

"First thing. Looks okay to me, but you should check yourself before you leave. See if things look the same."

"Sure," she mouthed so Hal didn't hear her.

"Daddy says we can maybe go to the Pier after school," Hallie piped up, wriggling with eagerness on the stool.

Hal had always eaten breakfast at the table next to the bay window because she liked to watch the birds at the feeders in the backyard, and somehow that little change took part of the pleasure out of Hal's unconscious action during the night.

Dana glanced at Logan. "Didn't you say something about your parents arriving today?"

He pointed to a button she'd missed on her teal silk shirt and nodded. "Yep, I did. But I called earlier and told them to wait until things settle down a little." He sent a look toward Hal from the corner of an eye. "I told them I'd let them know."

Well, that brightened Dana's day—more than it should've. "In that case, the Pier sounds like fun. But I'm guessing you mean after the homework is done, huh?"

With a piece of peanut-buttered toast halfway to her mouth, Hallie looked at Logan for a response.

"Mom's right, kiddo. That's what I meant—I forgot to mention it."

Hal bit into her toast, crinkling her nose in apparent disappointment. Dana got the distinct feeling that even though Logan had supported her, she somehow came out the bad guy on that exchange.

Shrugging into her black blazer, Dana countered, "What your daddy means is that he forgot because he never worried about homework. He was so smart he never had to think about it." She took a gulp of her coffee and ruffled her wet hair to get it dry before leaving.

"Ah, but your mom was the one who taught *me* things. She was a great tutor." A wicked gleam sparkled in Logan's eyes as he handed Dana a plate of toast. "Wheat with honey. That and the geographic pancakes are pretty much the extent of my breakfast expertise."

Dana took the proffered plate and sat next to Hallie. *A great tutor? He'd* been the one to help *her*. She didn't have a clue what he was referring to.

"Okay, kiddo. You got five minutes before Mom's outta here. It's upstairs to finish getting your things together for school."

"Okay, but can we go to the Pier *after* the homework?"

Logan looked to Dana. "Sure. And y'know what? That's even better because Mom should be home by then and she can come, too."

"Yay!" Hallie cried, then jumped off the stool and headed upstairs.

Dana's spirits lifted in the wake of Hallie's exuberance. She hoped the child's excitement was because her mother was going to come, but she wouldn't bet her paycheck on it. After Hal had gone, Dana looked skeptically at Logan. "I tutored you? In what, might I ask?"

He stood silent for a second. "In the ways of the world."

Dana nearly choked on her toast and had to wash it

down with another sip of coffee. "Yeah, right. I guess you mean the other ways of the world. The world you didn't know existed outside your own circle of—" She cut herself off.

No reason to get into that. It wasn't important. Not now.

"Exactly. I was pretty egocentric when we first met."

Dana did a double take. He wasn't kidding on that one. Then she felt a sudden burst of pride that he'd thought *she'd* actually taught *him* things. He'd never said anything like that before.

She cleared her throat. "And you're not now?" she teased, unable to resist. Besides, it was better to joke about their past than get all serious. His remark probably meant nothing, anyway.

"Hal? You ready? We gotta go." She carried her plate to the sink, catching a chagrined look on Logan's face as she did. Or perhaps it was her imagination working overtime.

The feelings she'd had last night were clouding her sensibilities. Something had happened between them that she couldn't define, and the sooner she got away from him the better.

"Okay," Logan said as Hal came back into the room. "Here's the drill. I pick you up, you do your homework, and when Mom comes home we go to the Pier…and maybe we'll get to eat hot dogs for dinner while we're there."

Hal's eyes shone as she skipped over to Logan for a hug before they left.

Jillian had hitched a ride to the salon because her car was in for repair, and after they'd dropped the girls off, they sat in the van and waited for them to reach the school door. While they waited, Dana realized she'd felt a separation from her best friend since Logan had moved in; even though it had only been two days, she sensed that things were changing. She and Jilly used to talk twice a day. Now they talked only when the girls went to school.

"You're looking cheerful this morning," her friend commented after the girls disappeared through the school doors.

"I'm hopeful." Dana smiled, thinking about last night. "Hal seems more accepting of me, and she even seems to remember some of her old habits. Not memories exactly, but she's doing some of the same things she did before. I think it's a good sign."

"What does the doctor say?"

Dana glanced out the window, pulled out of the circle drive and headed toward Jilly's shop. "I've got to call him today." But truth was, Dana wasn't sure she wanted to call, on the off chance the changes in Hal's demeanor didn't mean anything. She needed to hold on to the hope that it did.

"I'll be curious to hear. You know, when the girls were playing at my house, I thought Hal seemed right back in the groove. If I hadn't known she didn't remember things, I'd have thought everything was normal."

Dana sighed, taking the corner to the shop a little sharply. "Kids are like that, aren't they. They meet and within minutes you'd think they'd been friends all their lives."

"I suppose. But y'know, that describes us, too."

Dana turned to look at Jilly. Her friend seemed to know instinctively how she was feeling. "Yeah, it does. So I guess I don't need to tell you it's driving me crazy with Logan there all the time. I can't seem to focus on anything.''

"That's not hard to understand. He's one great-looking guy. Does he have a brother, maybe?"

Dana leaned against the back of the seat and laughed. Her friend also knew how to make a joke at exactly the right moment. "If he did, I doubt you'd want to hang out with him—not unless he divorced his parents."

Jillian let out a whoop. "Like I really need more of that! No thank you. One meddling mother-in-law is enough." Jilly's eyes went serious before she asked, "Is she really that bad? I mean, maybe there's a reason she feels as she does. Maybe you can talk to her about it."

Yeah, right! She'd tried that once, and the result was a disaster. And even if the pregnancy hadn't entered into it, it wasn't likely things would've been different. Dana had grown up in the wrong place. She was "trailer trash" as far as Andrea Wakefield was concerned.

"No, talking with that woman is like talking to a brick. I finally realized she'd never come around, so why waste my time?" She shrugged. "It doesn't matter now, anyway. My ex-in-laws rarely see Hal, and when they do, I don't have to deal with it because Logan takes care of that." She sent her friend a lame smile. "But you know all that—I've been on that rant before."

"Yeah, me, too." A note of wistfulness tinged Jilly's words.

Jilly had adored her husband, still did. Dana knew her friend's casual joking manner was her defense against the unfairness of it all. Her husband had been a young virile man, cut down in the prime of life by a sniper taking potshots at cars on the Santa Monica Freeway. One of those freaky things you hear about on the news but somehow think only happens to other people.

Jilly dealt with his death in the only way she knew how. She'd even moved to Chicago so Chloe could be near her paternal grandmother. Jilly's own parents were dead.

"What a pair we are," Jilly lamented as Dana pulled up to the Mane Show, the shop she'd purchased with the insurance money from her husband's death a year and a half ago. "Well, I don't know about you, but I'm going to go to work and forget all this frivolity and fun."

Jillian exited, then stood with the door open for a moment. "Why don't you come over tonight after the girls are in bed and we'll have a glass of wine?"

The offer had never sounded better. Another night with Logan might be her undoing.

"You got it!"

After dropping Jilly off, Dana reached her office on a high note. Nothing had really changed, so why did she feel such a lift? And why was she questioning it? It had been way too long since she'd felt this good.

When she caught the elevator and headed for the prosecutor's domain, her spirits were as springy as her walk. "Morning Cheryl," she chirped, plucking her mail from the assistant's hand on the way down the hall to her office.

First she'd work the Davis Case, do the two scheduled interrogatories, and the rest of the day she'd work on Lombard. On the way home she'd pick up a bottle of wine, go to the Pier with Logan and Hallie, and when Hal was asleep, she'd join Jilly for an hour or so. A perfectly planned day.

She liked that. She worked best when things were planned and ordered. Making decisions, setting goals, that was what had gotten her where she was today. Placing her briefcase on the floor next to her chair, Dana settled in to read the mail and return the high-priority phone calls before she started on anything else.

Her daily routine had been set from the moment she'd opened the door to the P.A.'s office some four years ago.

Aside from the curve David had thrown her the other day, her job was the one part of her life of which she was certain, and she intended to do everything in her power to keep it that way.

She'd figure out a way to deal with David's request, but the thing that really nagged at her was why he'd asked her to do it in the first place. She had utmost respect for David, and the more she thought about it, the more she thought she'd misinterpreted his meaning. That had to be it.

Her gaze drifted to the plaques on the wall. Some were for work-related accomplishments, others for community service and her pro bono work, as well as sitting on the board of directors for the children's shelter. All were commendations for her skills and her expertise.

She should be proud. She *was* proud. But all the commendations in the world couldn't compare with the feeling she'd had last night when Hal had curled her fingers into her hair.

Hallie was the only person in the whole world who had loved Dana for no reason other than that she was her mommy. It didn't matter to Hal if Dana was successful or smart. Her little girl loved her just because— The thought gave her sudden pause. If Hal didn't remember her, how could she love her? Dana let out a whoosh of breath, not wanting to pursue that.

Maybe when they went to the Pier tonight, Hal would remember the last time—

"Got a minute?" David came in and closed the door behind him. He'd been so quiet or she'd been so pre-occupied she hadn't heard him come in.

"Sure. What's up?" Dana shoved the stack of files to the side and leaned back in her chair, uncomfortable just looking at him. She gestured for David to have a seat, but he remained standing in front of her.

"Nothing. Just wondering if you'd had a chance to talk with Wellesy yet?"

A knot formed in the pit of her stomach. "No, I haven't."

Crossing his arms, he pinned her with steel-gray eyes that looked as hard and cold as the metal. "When do you think you might?"

Her hope that she'd been mistaken dissipated. She'd given David the benefit of the doubt, told herself that she'd read more into their conversation or that she'd misunderstood because she'd been so stressed out. She'd hoped against hope she'd been wrong.

But she wasn't. And she had to deal with it.

"I *don't* think I might. I'm not going to talk to Wellesy. And I'm very uncomfortable that you asked me to do it."

If crimson wasn't the color of David's face before, it was now. But he just stood there, grinding his teeth. Then a peculiar desperate kind of look crossed his face and he stalked out.

She felt ill. By refusing to do what he asked, she'd probably just kissed her career plans goodbye.

And she didn't know what the hell to do about it.

"HOMEWORK FIRST," Logan spouted as Hal dashed up the stairs. "No television, no dolls, or whatever. If you need help, I'm here."

He strolled into the family room, picked up the phone and punched in Remy's cell-phone number. "Yo, buddy."

"Hey. How's it goin'? How's the kid?"

"We're doing okay. Thought I'd check in. Anything I need to do?"

"Not now. We've got a couple guys on the international-trade fraud, including Dante, Brody's on the insurance scam, Gideon's got the feds contract, and you and me are on R and R. It's quieter than a monastery around here. I'll have some things lined up for next week, though. You on?"

"Keep it local and I'm there." Logan's comfort level was at its best when he knew business was set. They had a solid team, many of whom were former colleagues and friends. Dante Marconi, Brody Sinclair and Remy had all grown up in the same neighborhood in South Philly. Logan had met them while visiting his grandmother's that fateful summer and they'd all become fast friends. Like four musketeers, it was all for one and one for all. And though they'd gone their separate ways for a while, they'd remained friends.

More significantly in terms of business, all their agents were experts in their fields. As Remy was fond of saying, they were one badass team.

"Gotcha. By the way, you had a message from your real-estate agent. Said he had something for you. Guess that means you're really gonna do it, huh?"

"Yeah, I need to stick around for a while. He say where the place is?"

"No, but he did say it's a sweet deal and it'll go quick. Woman's husband died and she's selling the place, furniture and all. He wants you to call."

At least something was going right, Logan thought.

"Gideon have an opportunity to work with Dana yet?" Not that he'd have reason to. Corruption in the state's attorney's office wouldn't be something Dana knew about. Her integrity was beyond reproach.

"Nope. Probably better that he doesn't. You never know if she'd somehow put things together, maybe even screw up our gig."

"So, what do we have?"

"Nada. Gideon's gonna get back to me late tonight."

Logan hung up feeling more unsettled than he should. The fact that the real-estate agent had a place lined up was good news, and he should be champing at the bit. It was what he'd wanted in order to spend additional time with his daughter.

So why wasn't he ecstatic?

He stood in the doorway and glanced around the family room, his gaze lighting on the photo of Dana and Hal perched on the baby grand in the corner. It was an old piano, one Dana had purchased and refinished, even though he'd told her to buy a new one.

She was conservative in many ways and took pride in things like saving money, whether she needed to or not. She liked a challenge, and to her, refinishing that old battered piano so the wood shined like a newly lacquered Rolls-Royce, gave her a kind of satisfaction she wouldn't have had otherwise.

He let out a sigh. Everywhere he looked he saw Dana's touch. *And very little of his.* It couldn't be helped. He'd been gone a lot, and when he *was* home, it was more important that he spend his time with Dana and Hal.

That, he realized with sudden clarity, was why he wasn't excited about getting a place of his own. *This* was his home, and dammit, he wanted to stay here.

Was it crazy to think they could try again? They'd been good together in so many ways. And no matter what their differences, they'd always managed to work things out in the bedroom. He smiled at the remembrance. Dana had joked once that they should live in the bedroom, because then they'd never have another fight.

Which seemed to be how their marriage had ended up—one fight, one argument after another. Whether it was about his job or hers, her parents or his, her need to be so damn independent, and his to feel she needed him in some small way.

And nothing had changed. Yeah, it *was* crazy to think they could try again. He pulled out the real-estate agent's card and punched in the number.

"Daddy, I'm done," Hal called from upstairs. "Come and see."

"Be there in a minute, kiddo."

When he finished on the phone, he took one more wistful glance around the room, then headed toward the stairwell.

On the way to Hal's room, he stopped in front of the door to the master bedroom. Why had she said she no longer slept in there? Curious, he reached for the knob, then inched open the door and peered inside.

The shutters were closed, but light shined through the slats, creating an eerie striped effect. When his eyes adjusted, he saw that the room looked exactly as it had when he left. *Odd.* If he was a betting man, he would've wagered a week's salary that Dana had stripped the room clean.

He stepped inside a little farther and noticed their wedding photo still sat on the dresser against the wall. He walked over, picked it up and rubbed a finger on the shiny silver frame. The last real conversation they'd had was after making love in this very room.

A dull ache settled in his chest. Damn, he missed her. He missed her wiseass comments and her laughter, he missed her serious socially conscious side, and all the little things. The way she slept curled into him, the way she sipped coffee holding the mug in both hands, the way she peeled an orange. Hell, he even missed their horrible fights.

Fact was, he missed everything about her and everything they'd had together. He missed their nights together, missed holding her and making love—because it was the one and only time she'd willingly let down all her defenses. The only time he felt that sublime connection—when he felt needed...necessary.

Maybe he should've been more accepting, more communicative. Maybe he should've— Aw hell! All the maybes, would'ves and should'ves in the universe couldn't change the fact that she didn't want to be married to him, possibly not to anyone.

But it *was* puzzling why she hadn't used the bedroom. The room was twice as big as the guest room, the bed more comfortable, and there was even an en suite bath, unusual in these old homes. She'd said she'd changed rooms to be closer to Hallie, but when she'd said it, he hadn't been convinced.

Now he really wondered. He went out, shut the door and made his way toward Hal's room, infused with curiosity. Perhaps he and Dana did have unfinished business.

"See." Hal waved her papers at Logan when he walked into her room. "I'm all done."

He smiled. How much homework could a seven-year-old have? "Great. Let me see."

He looked, and then Hal trilled, "Can we go now? Can I call Chloe and tell her, please, please, please!" Hal bounced up and down on the edge of the bed, her excitement spilling over.

"You can call Chloe. But we're waiting for your mom to come home first."

Hallie stopped bouncing, her face crumpled with disappointment. "What if she doesn't get here in time? What if she's late?"

"Now why would you think that?"

Hal's eyes rounded innocently. She shrugged. "I dunno. I just know she might be late 'cause she's been late before."

This was getting weird. Logan decided first thing in the morning he'd call the doctor. Hal seemed to remember things, yet she didn't. He wanted to know if that was a good sign.

He *needed* to know how long it would be before he would have to leave.

A door slammed downstairs.

"Anybody here?"

"I WANT A HAMBURGER and French fries," Hal announced.

Dana and Logan exchanged glances. Hal's favorite at the fast-food chain had always been chicken nuggets. In her whole life, she'd never ordered a hamburger. Dana shrugged and Logan stepped up to place their orders while Hal picked out a vacant table.

On one side was a bench, sort of a half booth and on the other side were two chairs cemented into the floor, much like those used at the counter in a restaurant. Hal quickly settled on one of the chairs and started spinning around. Dana sat across from her on the booth side and waved Logan over.

So far the evening had been perfect, but remembering the picnic and how that had ended, Dana knew she mustn't get too comfortable. For sure she mustn't get comfortable with their being a family again because it would all end the minute Hal was better and Logan had another job to do. She had to keep that in the forefront of her mind.

Chloe hadn't been able to come along because she'd had to visit with her grandmother, so both Dana and Logan tried extra hard to make sure Hal had a good time.

After visiting the Disney store and riding the Ferris wheel, they'd decided it was time for dinner and ended up at Burger Haven.

"Did we come here lots before?" Hal asked.

"A couple of times." The last time they'd been here as a family was on Hal's fifth birthday. Dana remembered it clearly. Logan had been out of town and was expected back. She'd made plans to celebrate both Hal's birthday and Logan's homecoming quietly at home, but Logan's parents had called. They were in Chicago and wanted to celebrate Hal's birthday.

Hal had then asked to go to Burger Haven, but Andrea Wakefield had insisted on dinner at the Fairmont. It was beyond Dana's comprehension how the woman could think a five-year-old would enjoy spending her birthday in a high-end adult restaurant, but since Logan wasn't home and the Wakefield's had flown into town especially for the occasion, Dana didn't have the heart to tell them to forget it. At least they'd made the effort, and she'd told Hal she'd make it up to her.

Later, at the restaurant with the Wakefields, Dana perused the menu trying desperately to locate something Hallie might eat. When the waiter came over, Andrea looked at Logan's father, the senior Logan Wakefield, and said, "Darling, why don't you order for the girls? It looks like Dana is having a little trouble reading the menu."

Dana's face went hot with anger, and it took a moment before she could respond without snapping. "I was looking for something Hallie might like," she said with saccharine sweetness. "Something other than vichysoisse or steak tartare."

Andrea's face went pale, and after a second she said through pinched lips, "I suppose you're right."

Shocked that she'd agreed, Dana nearly bit her tongue pulling in her retort. She quickly decided to try harder to understand. After all, the Wakefields had had only one child, and no recent experience. And even when Logan was small, they'd hired a nanny to care for him. How could they know the likes and dislikes of a five-year-old?

"Yes," Andrea went on. "I suppose frozen television dinners would blunt a child's tastes." She looked at Hallie. "Hallie dear, your grandfather will order for you."

Hal's eyes went wide, and she looked at Dana in a plea for help. Just as Dana was ready to step in, she saw Logan sauntering toward them. She'd left him a message in case he "happened" to make it back in time.

"Hey, this is a real surprise." He kissed Dana and Hal, shook hands with his father and hugged his mother. "You surprise me, Hal. I had no idea you liked to come to places like this."

Hal wrinkled her nose, then stared at her plate, apparently minding her manners as she'd been taught. If the Wakefields hadn't been there, Hal would've protested loud and clear.

Logan looked at Dana.

"Your mother and father surprised us by coming into town for Hal's birthday and were kind enough to make reservations for dinner." She spread her hands, palms up and shrugged. "So here we are." Dana's tone was so cool icicles could've hung on her words.

But she wasn't about to make waves between Logan and his family. Families were important, no matter how dysfunctional.

"That's great," Logan said as he picked up the menu and held it out.

"Yes, your father was about to order for the girls since they couldn't decide. But now that you're here, sweetheart, you can do the honors."

The girls. It was another one of Andrea's methods to put Dana down without actually saying something she'd object to. Dana ignored the comment. Nothing got Andrea more riled than being ignored.

Still standing, Logan glanced peripherally at the menu and frowned. "But you know, as nice as this place is, I think Hal might prefer something else for dinner. What say we blow this pop stand and head for Burger Haven?"

Hallie giggled so loudly, three-quarters of the mature population in the restaurant turned to stare. Dana suppressed a chuckle of her own. In the end, the Wakefields said they'd stay because they'd made plans to meet a business associate at the hotel in an hour or so.

She should've known. Not likely they would've come to Chicago without calling or knowing if Logan was available.

"Then you won't mind if we head out," Logan said. "We can do something together tomorrow. How's that?"

In the end, they'd had a wonderful evening, just the three of them at Burger Haven. And Dana and Logan had celebrated the occasion later in their usual way. In bed.

Now, watching Logan carry their order to their table, Dana's stomach did a tiny flip. Then he doled out their burgers and sat next to Dana.

Hallie reached for her burger and announced, "I remember this place."

Dana turned so fast to look at Hallie she got a kink in her neck.

"Me, too," Logan said calmly, his eyes alone expressing the excitement he felt. "It was your birthday, and your grandmother and grandfather Wakefield came to visit. Do you remember that, too?"

Hal bit off half a French fry, chewed thoughtfully, then shook her head. After swallowing, she said, "Uh-uh. I remember it from the TV commercial."

Dana's heart sank.

"I forgot I have a grandma and grandpa. Are they, like, all weird like Chloe's grandma?"

Dana looked at Logan. No way was she going to get sucked into that one.

"They love you very much," Logan said. "As do your grandmother and grandfather Marlowe."

Point made. Dana decided long ago she'd not force a grandparent relationship on her parents. If they wanted it, they'd make the effort. And so far, in the seven years since Hal's birth, their effort was underwhelming.

"Chloe's only got one grandma and Chloe said her grandma's very sad 'cause Chloe's daddy is gone. He's dead," she said matter-of-factly. "Chloe showed me her mom and daddy's wedding pictures. Can I see yours, too? And can I show Chloe?"

Dana swallowed a bite of hamburger. How was she going to get around that one? "Sure we have some, but they're probably a little different from Chloe's mom and dad's because we didn't have a big wedding."

Hal looked genuinely disappointed. "Chloe's mom got to wear a white dress with a long, lo-o-ong caboose on it."

Dana snickered. "I think you mean a train. Some wedding dresses have a long train."

"Was yours as long as Chloe's mom's? Hers was really long."

Sliding under the table wasn't an option, Dana thought. The questions were innocent, but unless she lied, she couldn't make their wedding into something it wasn't.

Logan stepped in. "Your mom didn't have a white dress with a long train because we eloped."

Hal's eyes widened again. "What's loped?"

Logan's expression turned very serious and he fixed his gaze on Hal rather than Dana. What would he say? That they'd run away to get married because she was pregnant and he was embarrassed about it? That his mother would've died before she'd have invited all her high-society friends to a wedding between her son and an unworthy slut?

"It means we were so much in love we absolutely couldn't wait for all the frills and fancy stuff. We wanted to be married right away, so we sneaked off to this tiny little chapel in the woods and got married." A beat later he said, "It was very romantic."

Hallie grinned from ear to ear, first at Logan and then

at Dana. "That's even better," she said with glee. "I can't wait to tell Chloe!"

Logan looked at Dana, then said softly, "It was a lot better."

CHAPTER TEN

DANA'S THOUGHTS raced as fast as the car on their way home. How could two people have such opposing views on the same event? She shifted around to see if Hal was asleep yet. In the process, and still sitting sideways, Dana found herself watching Logan in profile.

If ever there was a man with more exquisite features, she didn't know who. It wasn't even that he was so good-looking; it was the way looking at him affected her.

Sometimes he literally took her breath away. She'd never experienced that kind of rush with anyone else. Not before she'd met Logan or since.

From the moment they'd met, she was in lust with him. Love had come a little later, but not much.

"I told Jilly I'd go over for a visit once Hal is in bed. D'you mind?"

Logan glanced over, frowned and then brought his gaze back to the road. "Mind? Why would I mind?"

"Well, I don't want you to think—" She cut herself off, realizing she shouldn't say some things in front of Hal on the off chance she wasn't sleeping soundly. "Oh, never mind." She shook her head, gesturing that they'd talk later.

Later came faster than she'd wanted. Hal had gone to bed immediately, so Dana grabbed the wine she'd purchased after work and was at the door when Logan stopped her.

"So, what was it you were going to say in the car? You didn't want me think what?"

Dana tucked the bottle under her arm and expelled a breath. "It was nothing. Really."

His expression said, *Yeah right.*

"Okay. I didn't want you to think I was taking advantage of the fact that you were here. You know...using you for a baby-sitter while I went out."

"I thought you were only going next door?"

"I am, but still..."

"So how does that translate to your taking advantage? I'm Hal's father. I'm as responsible for taking care of her as you are."

He was right. And it felt good to hear him say it. So why did she feel as if she was imposing on him? It didn't make sense. "Okay, then. I'll be back in an hour or so."

"Enjoy yourself."

He winked and her stomach fluttered, just as it had the first time they'd met. If she'd thought her spirits were uplifted this morning, it was nothing compared to the way she'd felt after hearing Logan describe their wedding. She walked across the front yard to Jillian's feeling a little floaty, as if she'd already guzzled the bottle of wine.

It didn't take long for that feeling to be a fact. After most of the second bottle of wine was gone, Jilly hoisted her glass in the air and said, "Another toast!"

Jillian had also bought a bottle of wine for the evening, and after polishing off the first, both had agreed it would be a shame not to at least sample the other one.

"A toast to what?" Dana asked. They'd already sung the praises of little girls full of sweetness and spice, scorned meddling mothers-in-law, thanked their lucky stars for fulfilling jobs, and lamented the woes of same. What was left?

"To men—can't live with 'em, can't live without 'em."

"Here, here!" Dana clinked her glass against Jilly's. She could relate to *that* one. How she could relate!

When she and Logan were married, all they did was make love or fight. Not exactly one of those happy families she saw on TV reruns all the time.

She was still amazed at how could two people be so incompatible and yet find total fulfillment in one area. Well, at least they'd had something. A little fulfillment was better than none. In fact, just thinking about it brought a low twist of desire.

Dana raised her glass again. "To good sex."

"Here, here!" Jillian grinned like a cat who'd just devoured the pet canary. After a thoughtful moment, she said, "You think you'll ever find a replacement for Logan?"

Still sipping, Dana peered over her wineglass at her friend. She'd never seriously thought about it. In the back of her mind she figured she'd date sooner or later, but find a replacement for Logan? Not possible.

"Not on my agenda at the moment. Besides, he'd hafta be damn good. Why?"

Sitting on the floor, leaning against the couch cushion behind her, Jillian pondered the question with deeper thought than Dana figured was necessary.

"Well," her friend finally said, "I keep getting these vibes that you two should be together..." Her words were a little slow, and Dana realized Jillian had had more than her share of the wine. When her eyes took on a soft nostalgic look, Dana knew it for sure.

"I mean...I'd never seen you two together before, and now when I do, it seems like there's all this energy that kinda zaps between you." She waved a hand, her eyes intense. "Like electricity, an undercurrent, or...or some kind of magnetism...or..." She trailed off, apparently unable to articulate her thoughts. She waved a hand. "You know what I mean?"

Dana couldn't summon up words of denial.

"I can feel it, Dana. I can really feel it." Jilly paused, sighed and drew her tongue over her lips as if they were dry. "Jack and I had that, so maybe that's why I can see it with you two. Really. I think you're too close to see how he affects you. And vice versa."

Dana decided the wine was making her friend far too insightful. Sure, magnetism, she could go with that. An undercurrent of desire, yeah. He affected her that way, too. More than desire? An unquestionable, emphatic yes! He affected her deeply.

But there was no vice versa about the last part, no matter how much she wished it was so.

"Jack is dead and I'll never be able to recapture that feeling again—not with him. But you, you and Logan still have time..." Jilly's eyes suddenly filled with tears.

"Hey, hey, hey..." Dana quickly went to sit at her friend's side and placed an arm around her. "It's okay," she whispered, and then she hugged Jilly and let her cry.

Feeling her friend's loss as if it were her own, Dana suddenly had all she could do not to cry herself.

You and Logan still have time.

Did they?

"ANYTHING IN particular you two were celebrating?" Logan looked askance at Dana as she weaved into the house. "A little tipsy, are we?"

She wasn't as steady on her feet as she would've liked, but it was because she had to squeeze around him through the small hallway leading into the kitchen. She set the nearly empty wine bottle on the island, and chucked the other in the trash.

Jillian hadn't wanted her to leave the bottles there in case her mother-in-law popped in unexpectedly.

"Nope. I am *not* tipsy. Jillian had the lion's share. I...I, on the other hand..." She waved a limp hand in the air, glanced at it, then pulled it down. "Oops, sorry, wrong hand," she said, feeling particularly silly. Then she raised the other hand and waved it.

"Okay, got it. *That,*" she said, "is the other hand." She started to giggle again, then let out a long breath.

Logan stared at her from under furrowed brows. She remembered that look. He obviously didn't appreciate her humor.

"I on the other hand," she went on, "am a model of decorum and sobriety." She could feel another giggle about to erupt.

Logan walked to the cupboard, took out a wineglass and poured the rest of the bottle in it. "You mind if I polish it off?"

"Help yourself, but it won't do you a—a—any good." She came closer and jabbed a finger into his chest. "No good. None whatsoever." Good grief, she sounded like she was trying out for the lead role in *Days of Wine and Roses.*

He pulled back, a whimsical half smile plastered on his face, eyes glinting with amusement. "Do me any good for what?"

She wagged a finger at him. "Oh, I know what you're thinking. I *know* that look." She stepped back, then snared the edge of the island with her right hand. "I know... I know you think I'm just a little bit loose, that my defenses are down." She wagged her finger again. "I know you. Yep, I do."

"Okay, then, you'll know that I'm going to make you some coffee." He walked around her, grabbed the coffeepot and started to fill it with water.

She leaned against the sink next to him, her head angled to see his face.

"Remember that time when Karpinsky..." She started to laugh, cut herself off, then started again. "That time when Karpinsky came into the study room and kinda...sorta...caught us in the ac—" the giggles bubbled up and her eyes started to tear "—and we stuffed the con..."

She was laughing so hard she couldn't finish her sentence, but between bursts of laughter, continued on, "...into the coffeepot, and...and...he went to pour himself..."

Logan started to laugh along with her, and in the next breath they finished the sentence together, "...a cuppa coffee."

Dana laughed so hard her sides hurt, and suddenly she thought if she didn't get to the bathroom really quick, she might wet her pants.

She waved him off and sashayed down the hall. In the bathroom, she took extra time to splash cold water on her face and pull herself together as much as she could. When she finished, she found Logan in the family room stoking the coals of a fire he must've started earlier.

"That feels wonderful."

"Coffee will be done in a minute."

"Great. Thanks." As she watched him at the fire-place, a wave of nostalgia swept over her. She couldn't deny it felt wonderful to have him there, to have some-one to talk to, someone with whom she had a history and who cared about Hallie as much as she did, some-one she lov—

Oh, damn. She stopped the thought in motion. She had to get off that track. She was tired and vulnerable. She'd had too much wine, that was all.

She couldn't allow her old feelings for Logan to blind her. Not if she wanted to maintain an ounce of the self-esteem she'd managed to scrape together during their year apart.

She'd been devastated when their marriage ended. She'd never failed at anything before. Then she'd failed at the most important thing in her life, and it had taken time to get to the place where she felt good about her-self again.

She sat on the soft leather ottoman in front of the hearth, and when Logan finished with the fire, he went to the kitchen and brought back coffee and two cups on a tray.

He placed the tray on the end table, handed her a cup and sat on the floor next to her, his back resting against the side of the ottoman.

"Mmm, this is good," she said, curling the fingers of both hands around the mug. The fire cast an amber tint over everything in the room, including Logan's rug-gedly handsome face. A warm glow flowed through her as she sipped the hot strong brew.

"You remember the first time we had coffee?" he asked.

How could she forget? She'd been dumbstruck that

he'd even been interested. She sipped her coffee, pausing to moisten her lips before she answered, "It was a long time ago."

Logan leaned his head back, gazing up at her. "Yeah. You had one helluva chip on your shoulder back then."

"I beg your pardon." She drew back. "I didn't have anything of the kind."

"Okay, maybe I phrased that wrong. But you definitely had one hell of an attitude."

She smiled. "You mean I didn't fawn all over you. And I was serious about my future, instead of just having a good time?" She took another sip. "If that's what you mean by attitude, then I suppose I'd have to agree."

He laughed. "Yeah, something like that. But I was up for the challenge," he said with a note of pride.

"You were up for a lot of things, and most of it was in a prone position," she quipped back, ignoring the flutter in her stomach. "And talk about attitude! You couldn't stand the fact that I didn't throw myself at your feet."

"Well, yeah. I figured there had to be something wrong with you."

They laughed together and she slid down to sit on the floor next to him. "Speaking of challenges... remember how tough Karpinsky's class was? He was one nasty man."

Logan laughed. "Yeah, but you know, I remember his class the most. I think I learned right then and there what it takes to be a good lawyer."

"I don't think Rob Feldon learned that lesson," she said somberly. Karpinsky had been relentless with Feldon, merciless, for a whole week. Rob had left school only a month into the semester, and later they'd heard he'd had a breakdown and was hospitalized for more than a year.

She'd never forgiven Karpinsky for that and somehow never understood why Logan didn't feel the same.

"Yes, he did," Logan said. "Feldon learned like I did that the law wasn't for me. That was the most important lesson of all."

"But you finished. You saw it through and you still have that knowledge and you could use it in any number of ways."

"Remember Angelina Soltis and Paul Morgenstern?" Logan asked, changing the subject. "Wonder what happened to them?"

She rested her head against the ottoman. "I heard Paul became a hotshot Hollywood entertainment attorney. Angelina Soltis I never heard from again."

"Hmm. Remember when we all went to my parents' place in Boca Raton? You, me, Paul and Angie, Remy and I forget who he was with?"

"Samantha James." Dana couldn't forget that name. She'd had her eye on Logan from the get-go, and that particular weekend, the airhead had done everything she could to get his attention. Logan had all but ignored the woman and spent the entire time with Dana.

That weekend was when Dana realized she was hopelessly in love with Logan Wakefield.

"Oh, yeah. Talk about high maintenance. Remy wasn't happy he'd ended up with her that night. Man, oh man, did I hear about that for weeks afterward."

The fire crackled and snapped as they reminisced about old times and old friends. The fire, the comfortable conversation and delicious coffee made Dana warm and toasty from the inside out. Despite the pressures of law school, they'd had a great time back then, had formed lasting friendships.

It had been the happiest time of her life.

The effects of the wine had dissipated, yet she felt high, half-drunk on nothing but conversation and sitting companionably with Logan in front of the fire. They'd had other times like this in the past, yet somehow, in the past couple of years, she'd blocked even those from her mind, remembering only the problems that seemed to pile up one atop the other until it all seemed insurmountable.

She couldn't help wondering what would've happened if she hadn't gotten pregnant and if his family hadn't been opposed to their marriage. And of course, the even bigger if—if they hadn't been on a collision course of wills.

Mostly she couldn't help wondering if there was a smidgeon of a chance they could go somewhere from here. For the first time in a long time, she felt safe and comfortable, and the only issues of importance were those in this house at this moment in time.

Logan turned to look at her, his eyes sultry and dark.

"This reminds me of sitting on a blanket next to the campfire at the cabin, seeing who could name the most constellations," he said so softly it was almost a whisper. "Remember that?"

How could she forget? But naming constellations wasn't the part she remembered. She remembered desperate kisses, flaming desire and explosive passion. She remembered the way he always held her afterward, and sleeping in his arms.

How had she forgotten all the good things that they'd shared? She hadn't, she realized. The memories were still there; they'd just been locked away to protect her heart.

And now, looking into Logan's eyes and listening to the crackle and snap of the fire, the world suddenly seemed about to combust around her, and she felt almost dizzy with the sensation. Magnetism, Jilly had called it.

Raw lust was more like it, because at that moment she couldn't think of anything more delicious than making love with Logan right this minute, right here, right now, on the floor in front of the fire.

"You remember it," he said huskily. "I know you do."

"I do," she whispered as his mouth closed over hers. She was helpless to resist and she drew her arms up, reveling in the feel of his lips, and kisses so achingly familiar that every muscle in her body trembled with wanting.

She remembered, and the effect was the same. Desire shivered through her. She pulled him closer. He deepened the kiss, his mouth urgent, needy.

This wasn't the answer, she knew. It wasn't the answer to anything except their burning desire and the exquisite joy she felt when they were together...when they made love.

And for tonight, that was enough.

His lips were warm, his hands hot as he unbuttoned her blouse. She pulled his shirt over his head, her pulse racing as she stared at him in the firelight. Slowly he unhitched the front of her bra, then trailed a finger down her neck to the tip of her breast. She was lost in exquisite sensation when a loud crash came from the direction of the kitchen. It sounded like a garbage can tipping over.

Logan sprang to his feet. "Don't move. Stay right there."

Then he was gone. He was fast, quick to move into action. That shouldn't have surprised her considering his line of work, yet it did. Maybe because she'd never been privy to it. His work was top secret and he'd never shared that part of his life with her.

Logan was trained to react to danger, she realized, even though this was probably just another cat or stray dog rummaging through the trash. Their neighborhood was one of the safest in the city.

She pulled her bra together and buttoned her shirt so she could go see what Logan was doing.

In the kitchen, she flipped on the light just as Logan came in from outside.

"What're you doing?" he asked, his voice stern with disapproval. "I thought I said to stay put."

She stiffened, pulled herself up. "Yes, and I heard you. I decided I'd come see what it was for myself."

Exasperation flared in his eyes.

"I was curious."

It took him a second to wind down before he said, "You know what they say about curiosity and the cat. Remember that the next time you decide to do something foolish."

Now what the heck was that all about? It was obviously nothing serious since he was standing in the kitchen ranting at her. And he was obviously miffed about her not doing as he'd said.

"Foolish? If I'm foolish for coming into the room and turning on a light, what does that make you for dashing outside in the dark?" She gave him a once-over, then added, "Half-naked, no less."

He circled the room, his agitation increasing with each orbit.

"You mind telling me why you're in such a state?"

He stopped pacing in the middle of the room, scowling, looking as if he was deciding whether he should answer her or not. Finally he said, "There was someone out there."

She perked up. "You mean walking a dog like before? Or what? Did you see someone?"

Logan snatched a stool from the island, and plunked down. "Someone was out there, on the side near the window. I think someone was trying to break in."

Dana's mouth fell agape. She glanced to the window. "Trying to get into the house? How do you know if no one was there?"

"The trellis under Hallie's window was broken in three places. I think someone tried to climb up and it didn't hold. It looked as if someone attempted to cut the screen on the window to get in." He let out a long breath.

Dana pulled back, her mouth agape again. She got up and headed to the stairs. "I'm going up to check on Hallie. You call the police."

He nodded. "I'll call. But don't wake Hal. I don't want her scared."

She didn't want that, either, but she did want her safe. She waited for a minute as Logan dialed 911, told the police the address and the situation. On her way to Hal's room, she overheard him say he'd seen footprints outside the window before.

Her heart slammed against her ribs. *What?* If he'd seen something before, why the hell hadn't he mentioned it to her? Quickly she checked on Hal who was still fast asleep. Dana went back downstairs, her blood coursing.

"Excuse me," she said when Logan hung up the phone. "Did you just say you saw footprints outside before?"

He ran a hand over his jaw again. A muscle twitched near his left eye. "Yeah, I did. But I thought they were yours because you said you were doing some gardening outside."

"So why did you tell the police something else?"

"I wanted them to hurry."

"I don't think so, Logan. I know you better than that. Now tell me what's going on." He was keeping something from her. She could tell by his expression and the way he avoided looking at her. He might as well have scrawled it on her bathroom mirror in fuchsia lipstick.

Before she knew it, the police were there. One car with two officers. Logan told them what had happened, during which time Dana went up to check on Hallie again. If she woke up and heard all the commotion, she'd be sure to be frightened.

Hal was still sound asleep, and seeing her that way, so precious, so helpless, Dana had an overwhelming need to do something. But what?

Talk to the police, that was what, to find out exactly what they were going to do. She whirled around and practically flew down the stairs, only to see the patrol car pulling away.

"What's going on? Where are they going?" Dana's mind reeled with the possibilities.

"There was no break-in," Logan said. "That's why they left. A broken trellis isn't a high priority on their list of crimes to fight." His exasperation showed in the pinched set of his mouth, in the frown lines across his forehead.

She'd worked enough cases with cops, interviewed and deposed her share of law-enforcement officers to know what he said was true.

"Okay," Logan said, directing her to sit at the kitchen table. "If they're not going to do something, then we will."

"Sure. I'll do anything," she responded. "But what can we do?"

"Tell me again about your cases. What you're working on right now, and if there's anyone anywhere who might want to get even with you."

She shook her head. "No one I can think of offhand. Sure I've put a few sleazebags away, but so have all the other prosecutors on staff."

"How about valuables? Anything in the house that someone might think is worth breaking into the house for?"

"Logan, you know what's here. There's nothing exceptionally expensive, no jewelry, no Rembrandts." She shoved her fingers through her hair, pushing it from her face.

He glanced at her hand. "Your wedding ring—where is it?"

"In the safe-deposit box at the bank." Where else would she keep a rock that was worth more than the vehicle she drove? She'd always felt uncomfortable wearing it and had preferred the plain gold band he'd bought for her when they'd eloped.

He nodded as if that was good. "Okay, what else?" He looked uncomfortable again. "An old boyfriend maybe? A vindictive ex-spouse of a boyfriend? Someone you dumped?"

She shook her head. "No, there's been no one." Which sounded pretty pathetic, so she added, "There hasn't been time, and I'm perfectly fine on my own."

Whatever he was feeling before quickly shifted to discomfort, evident by the way he clenched his jaw. His expression went stone-cold.

"What about you?" she asked.

"Me?"

"Yes, you. Your jobs haven't exactly followed the Dale Carnegie method on how to make friends and influence people. And we both know there could be an old girlfriend or two who could have it in for you." If he could ask, so could she.

Only…she just now realized she really didn't want to know how many women he might have dated or spurned.

"My job isn't a problem. I save people, I don't send them to jail," he said with finality, ignoring the second part of her question altogether.

Then he took a new tack. "How about business associates?" Pacing the room as he spoke, he stopped directly in front of her, his eyes serious as he placed both hands on her upper arms. "Your pro bono work. That's another avenue to explore."

She shook her head. He had good reason to think what he did about her pro bono work. But she didn't have time for that anymore, and the kind of work she was doing now was different. "I think you're forgetting something, Logan."

"Yeah? What's that?"

"Our intruder doesn't have to be someone out to get me or you. It could've been kids, teens out vandalizing, a burglar or a pervert of some kind, someone who goes into homes at night and—'' She stopped, the thought too awful to even verbalize.

''Yeah, could be. Which makes it even harder to deal with. We need to check all leads, can't leave anything to chance.''

Dana folded her arms against her chest, suddenly cold all over. He was right. She turned to head upstairs. ''I'm going to sleep with Hal tonight.''

CHAPTER ELEVEN

LOGAN KNEW WHAT he had to do. He had to get every shred of information he could from Dana, and if he couldn't, he'd get it in his usual way. He wasn't going to take chances. Not where his family was concerned.

He lay in bed with the door open so he could see into Hal's room. He'd insisted Dana leave their door open, too, so he could protect them if necessary. He wished to hell he'd brought his gun with him.

Breathing deeply, he tried to focus, to keep his thoughts from drifting to other nights and other days in this house, days when everything seemed perfect in their little corner of the world. It was an exercise in futility.

Yet where denial didn't work, reality would. What she'd said to him earlier had hit him like a lightning bolt into the past. How many times had he heard her say she didn't need him? Why couldn't he keep that in mind? Why didn't he take her at her word?

Because he loved her. Plain and simple. And he might as well admit it. When he was on a job, it was easier to forget and to keep his mind occupied with other things. But even then, it didn't take away that empty hollow feeling. The feeling that his life was somehow incomplete without her.

Yeah, he was the golden boy, all right. He had everything—except the one thing he wanted most.

In the morning, he wasn't sure if he'd slept at all. The alarm went off, and he poked his head up to see if the ladies were stirring. Hal was sitting up in bed rubbing her eyes. She yawned and stretched, and when she saw him, she waved.

"Hi, Daddy."

Fortunately nothing else had happened during the night, and after Dana and Hal had breakfast and left, he'd set his plan in motion. He'd already alerted Remy that he needed a couple of guys on watch.

"Hey you." He waved back at Hal. "What would you like for breakfast?"

Dana came out from the bathroom swishing a toothbrush in her mouth. She ruffled Hal's already rumpled hair and stopped brushing. "Preferably something healthy," she responded for Hal.

"You got it." He'd have to get Dana alone to tell her what he planned to do, but first things first. He rose, pulled on a pair of jeans and a T-shirt and headed downstairs, trying like crazy not to think about how Dana looked in that skimpy nightshirt.

His blood had stirred at the sight of her. Hell, it always stirred at the sight of her.

Hal came down first, ready for school in a blue sweater, jeans and sneakers. He'd already set a bowl of cereal on the counter along with a glass of juice. Hal gave the setting a cursory glance, then picked up the bowl and transferred it to the table by the window.

"Mom said you make lots of noise when you snore so she had to sleep with me last night," she said matter-of-factly.

"Oh, she did, did she?" He eyed Dana as she came into the room. She wore a light-tan pants suit and a forest-green turtleneck. The colors brought out the red shine in her hair and made her eyes look even greener. "Well, she disturbed me, too, only in another way."

Dana sent him a "cool it buster" look, which quickly turned to surprise at seeing Hal at the table. "Why are you sitting there, honey? I thought you liked sitting at the counter."

Hal shook her head. "I think I like it here better. I like to watch the birds outside."

Dana's face glowed.

Obviously there was more to this seating-arrangement thing than Logan knew.

"Well, then. I'll join you. I like to watch the birds, too." Dana took the mug of coffee Logan handed her. "Thanks," she said, and went to sit near Hal.

Logan grabbed his own cup and joined them. He liked the feeling of being a family again. "Got any idea what kind of bird that one is over there?" He pointed toward a large, crimson-leafed tree.

"That's easy. It's a cardinal." She ate a mouthful of cereal and pointed to the other side. "And that's a sparrow, and over there another sparrow."

Dana smiled. "That's right, honey, like in your book. Did you study your book last night?"

Hal shook her head. "Uh-uh. I memorized them before. They're like the birds at that lake."

A look of sheer excitement flicked across Dana's face, then in the next instant, it switched off. She'd hold back, Logan knew. She wouldn't let her excitement show—just in case she was wrong. But he knew she thought Hal was remembering things.

"At the lake? Do you mean at our cabin?" Dana asked calmly.

Hallie looked puzzled and continued to swing her feet

under the chair. "I can't remember where, but I know those birds were at that lake."

Dana didn't pursue it, apparently not wanting to force the issue, but the shining green eyes that met Logan's brimmed with expectancy.

When they finished eating and Hal went for her coat, Dana asked in a stage whisper, "Did you hear that!" She pressed all ten fingertips to her lips as if to contain her exuberance. "She's remembering. I know she is. That's so wonderful! Isn't it wonderful?"

Logan's chest filled with happiness as much for Dana as for Hallie. He wanted his daughter back, too. And when Dana looked at him with all the hope in the world in her eyes, he had all he could do not to take her into his arms.

"Definitely a step in the right direction," he managed.

"It's more than that. I'm sure of it. When I get to work, I'll call the doctor to see what he says. I think he gets in at nine."

Hal came into the room, pulling on her jacket. "I'm ready now. Can I go get Chloe?"

"Sure," both he and Dana said in sync.

"Bye, Daddy." Hallie skipped over to hug him and he kneeled down, hugging her close. She would be okay. Dana would be okay, too. He wasn't too sure about himself.

As mother and daughter started out the door, he asked Dana, "Let me know what you find out, okay?" Watching them leave, his spirits flagged. There would be a day when he'd have to go. That was the reality, and he didn't even want to think about it.

More than anything he wanted Hal to be the little girl

she was before. He wanted it for Hal and for Dana, even if it meant he'd have to leave.

But first things first. Ensure their safety.

LOGAN PULLED A sweater over his T-shirt, shrugged on a leather jacket and within the half hour drove into his parking space at the corporate offices of Security International.

"Morning, Laine," he greeted the new receptionist minutes later as he whizzed by the front desk. "Remy in yet?"

In his peripheral vision he saw the young woman nod, one hand raised in the air for him to wait. But his family needed protection, and they came first. He charged into his partner's office and found him at his desk.

"Yo. What's happ'ning?" Remy asked, then gestured for Logan to sit.

Logan shook his head. "No thanks, can't stay. Did you get the guys? I want one on Hal and one on Dana. Two at all times."

"Got it. Masters is at the school already. Klienquist is shadowing Dana as we speak."

Logan paced in front of Remy's mahogany desk, feeling not as relieved as he should. Man, he was tense! He pinched the bridge of his nose with two fingers.

"Best surveillance team we've got," Remy said, apparently picking up on Logan's edginess. "What's next?"

"I need names." Logan finally sat in the sleek black leather chair and stretched out both legs. "Can't even get a backgrounder without 'em. What time does Gideon check in?"

Remy glanced at his watch. "Half an hour. What else d'ya need?"

What else? Someone to keep him from murdering the creep stalking his family—if he could find the guy. If that's what it was. "If Gideon can get me a list of Dana's current cases and any others in the past that send up a signal, we can eliminate those that don't fit the M.O."

"You sure that's necessary?"

"Necessary? I don't know. I'm not going to wait till it's necessary. There are too many coincidences for me. If I'm wrong, that's okay. Better safe than sorry."

"I'm with you, buddy, all the way."

"Klienquist know the drill? I haven't had a chance to tell Dana yet. I didn't want to mention it in front of Hal. It might scare her. She doesn't need that on top of everything else."

When Remy gave him a questioning look, Logan added, "Dana will be okay with it."

"You know her better than anyone." Remy shrugged, then asked, "So how come you're going around her on the other stuff?"

"We talked. She can't come up with anything. And knowing her, part of the reason is that she'd feel compromised by giving me information about her clients. If Gideon can get the information, it's less hassle."

"THANKS CHERYL," DANA said as she continued down the hall to her office. She'd had two depositions this morning and already felt drained. However, seeing that Dr. Nero had returned her call sent an extra jolt of energy through her. She'd had a hard time focusing on the interviews because all she could think about was talking with the physician.

The fact that Hallie remembered certain things had to be an indication that her memory was returning. Little by little, it seemed things were coming back to the child.

She stopped for a drink at the fountain, her imagination working overtime on what the doctor would say. When she stood up, she saw the new guy, Gideon, coming out of her office.

"Hi, I'm Dana Marlowe," she said, walking up to him. "Were you looking for me?"

"Ah…yes, I was." He held out his hand. "Gideon Armstrong. New kid on the block." After flashing a one-hundred-watt smile, he added, "But you look busy."

He had a decidedly English accent, and for a second she stood in front of the door, distracted. Finally realizing she hadn't moved to shake his hand, she did so, then motioned for him to follow as she went into her office.

She waited for him sit before she did. "What can I do for you?"

He gave a sheepish grin. "David suggested I work with you on the Lombard case. Thought it might be good for me to jump right in."

That was a one-eighty from what she'd expected him to say. She'd missed the staff meeting when David had introduced him, and she'd been expecting her boss to ask her to take him under her wing, not work with him on her most important case!

"Sure. No problem. But d'you mind if we get started on it a little later?" She glanced at her watch. "Say, eleven? I've got some things to take care of first." The most important of which was asking David what the hell he was thinking.

He held up one massive hand as if in agreement. The man was a tank, yet he wore that designer suit like he'd been born in it. "Absolutely. I'll get out of your hair and when you're ready, give me a call."

"Sure," she said, wondering how he'd ended up in the Cook County P.A.'s office. But there wasn't time to socialize, not right now. "I will," she said, and left it at that. Friendly would have to wait.

When he left, she hurriedly dialed Dr. Nero's office, got him on the line and explained some of the events that had happened. "That's good, isn't it? Does it mean she's getting her memory back?"

"Yes, it's very good," the doctor responded. "However, without examining her, I'm reluctant to give an opinion. Most likely she *is* remembering. That's what we hope for. All the same, it's important not to see things as we want them to be."

She knew what he was going to say. She'd wondered herself if it wasn't wishful thinking on her part and she was reading too much into it.

"Sometimes a patient will read something, hear something on television or even overhear other people talking and then later when he or she remembers it, it's easy to *think* what was heard is the memory returning when, in fact, it's new knowledge."

Dana's heart sank. "Oh."

"Ms. Marlowe, that doesn't mean she *isn't* remembering. Memory returns little by little—that's usually how it happens. I'll know more after the next examination."

"What do you mean, 'usually'?"

"In most amnesia cases, those that aren't organic, that's the usual process in which people remember. It isn't like in the movies where something triggers the memory and suddenly the person remembers everything. It's a gradual process when it happens. Try to be patient. If we're lucky, at some point her memory will be fully restored.''

Disappointment churned inside.

''When is her next appointment?'' the doctor asked.

''Next week. Wednesday,'' she said softly.

''Good. In the meantime, don't lose heart. Continue to do as you're doing, expose her to the familiar and enjoy the fact that you have a healthy child.''

She told him thank-you, then hung up. Yes, she was happy she had a healthy child. There were worse things than not remembering. And if her daughter's memory never returned, she would still be grateful.

So, why did she feel so unhappy?

The phone rang. She hesitated, her hand hovering over the receiver. She didn't want to think about work. She wanted to think about what to do with Hallie, what would be most helpful in restoring her daughter's memory.

When she finally answered, it was a police officer who said they had a suspect in custody—a teenager they'd apprehended breaking into another home in the area, and he'd confessed to burglarizing several others. While they had no absolute proof that he was the same person who'd tried to get into her house, they were ninety-nine percent certain he was and that they'd get a full confession.

Relief washed over her. One less thing to worry about. One less thing for Logan to get all uptight over. She picked up the phone again and punched in the number at home to tell him the good news. When there was no answer, she left a message telling him not to worry, the police had their burglar in custody.

AFTER A DAY scouring files, doing background checks and locating people Dana had prosecuted, Logan eliminated all that he could, and in the end, found himself walking up the steps of a posh home in Lincoln Park. He'd heard the North Side location was one of the hot places to live, but Dana had nixed it as being too trendy.

He glanced at the address Gideon had given him. After following up on Dana's last three cases to no avail, he didn't hold out much hope. This was his last lead, and knowing the facts of the case, he doubted it would cast any light on their stalker.

According to Gideon, the murdered woman had no connection with the mob or Lombard. At least none the police had been able to uncover. By all appearances, she was a schoolteacher who'd gone to lunch with a friend and gotten in the line of fire. Lombard had whacked the wrong person.

Or had he? The murdered woman could've seen or overheard something related to mob business, either there or at another time, and thus signed her own death warrant. It could've been a planned hit to look like an accident. No connection to Dana, though, unless Dana had somehow received the same information.

Information the police didn't have.

Logan rang the bell, and after a few moments with no response, he banged the lion-head door knocker a few times. As he was about to leave, the door cracked open.

"What do you want?" The voice was female, but he couldn't see enough through the one-inch opening to make out her features.

"I'm looking for a Mr. Gerald Peters. Is he here?"

"No," was the reply. Apparently the art of conversation was not one of the woman's social skills.

"How about James, or Carolyn, Mr. Peter's children? Are either of them here?"

A long silence ensued. Finally the small voice said, "No."

Logan stuffed his hands into his jacket pockets, his patience wearing thin. "D'you have any idea when they might return?" He figured the person at the door for a maid, someone who kept to herself—and probably knew everything about everyone in the household. "Or maybe you can answer a couple questions for me? It's important."

Another quick "No."

He pulled a card with his office phone number from a pocket. "Can you give this to Mr. Peters when he comes home and tell him to call me? I'd really appreciate it."

He poked the card through the opening and waited for her to grab it.

"Can I help you?" a man's voice sounded from behind Logan. Turning, Logan saw a fortyish man and a teenage boy coming up the front steps. Mr. Peters and his son, it had to be.

Both looked solemn. Who wouldn't under the circumstances? The man's wife, the boy's mother, had been the victim of a senseless murder.

"I'd like to talk with you for a minute, Mr. Peters. My name is Logan Wakefield. I'm working on a case and I'm hoping you can help." He *hoped* the man bought it and thought he was with the police.

Peters looked at him with unresponsive eyes, his pain over the loss of his wife evident. "Okay, c'mon in, though I don't think I can be of any help." The boy went in first and, at the man's request, Logan followed. The inside of the home was elegant, decorated exquisitely.

"This is my son, James," Mr. Peters introduced the boy who timidly shook Logan's hand. "Carolyn, can you come here, please?"

Within seconds, a teenage girl appeared. Her eyes were red-rimmed and she looked as if she'd been sick. She wasn't much older than the boy, seventeen, maybe, and Logan figured her for the person who'd answered the door.

"This is Mr. Wakefield. He's working on the case and wants to ask some questions." The girl glanced at Logan questioningly, then at her father who said, "Nothing has changed. We told the other officers everything we know."

Logan gestured toward the chair and asked if he could sit. The man nodded and sat on the long white couch with his son on one side and his daughter on the other. He had a need to hold his remaining family close, Logan guessed, or perhaps it was more the need to keep some part of his wife close to his heart.

Mr. Peters straightened and said, "There were witnesses but that man is still on the streets. I don't understand that. How can he be living a normal life when my wife is dead, my children deprived of their moth—" He broke off, his voice quavering.

Logan was reminded how quickly life can change. To avoid causing them any further pain, Logan made his questions quick.

In the end, he came away with nothing—except a burning desire to get his own family together again.

"I GOT AN A IN THE math test," Hallie proudly announced at the dinner table. "And Chloe got a D, so I told her I'd help her learn some stuff."

"That's really nice," Dana said. "It's good to help out a friend."

Hallie made a quick napkin swipe across her mouth. "Chloe didn't like it when I said that and now she's mad at me."

"Really? Why would she be mad when you offered to help?"

Hallie shrugged. "She said I was acting all smarty pants and that she was just as smart as me. Only, she couldn't remember things all the time, and sometimes her numbers were backward."

"I didn't know that. Her mom never said anything about Chloe having trouble in school."

"Her mom doesn't know. And she made me promise not to tell." A look of panic crossed Hal's face. "You won't tell her mom, will you? Oh, please, please, please don't tell. Chloe will be even madder at me if you do."

"Of course not, honey. I won't say anything if you don't want me to. But you know, it might be better for Chloe if her mom knew so she could help her. I'm sure she feels badly about it, doesn't she?"

"Chloe doesn't want help. And she *really* doesn't want her mom to know. She made me promise I won't tell anyone, not her mom or the teacher or any of the kids."

It was a familiar pattern. Dana had learned about dyslexia when she was doing pro bono work and had represented a client whose child needed testing the school wouldn't give.

"Speaking of homework—" Logan looked at Hal with raised eyebrows "—isn't it about that time?"

Hal gave a small pout. "Okay, but can I call Chloe first so I can get her not to be mad at me anymore?"

Both Dana and Logan said, "Sure."

"I called you here earlier today and left you a message," Dana said to Logan after Hal left the room. She'd been annoyed that he hadn't called back and it still niggled at her. She'd wanted to tell him that the police had picked up their burglar, or whatever he was, but she didn't want to do it at the dinner table where the news might scare Hallie. She'd also wanted to tell him what the doctor had said, but again, not in front of Hal.

Apparently whatever he'd been doing was more important than returning her call. Time hadn't changed anything in that respect.

She stood to begin clearing the dinner dishes, reached to collect the plates. Logan rose, gathered the water glasses and carried them to the dishwasher.

"I had some business to attend to. But I picked up a cell phone at the office and gave the school both my cell phone and office numbers."

"Well, I'm glad you finally feel it's okay to venture out. Hal seems to be doing fine, and as long as the school knows where to reach us, I don't think it's a problem." She wanted to say he could've let her know, too, but she didn't. It would serve no purpose.

"Right. As long as one of us is free and available."

She winced. It was obvious *he* didn't feel any qualms about dredging up the past; it was a point he'd brought up often when they were married. He'd maintained if she were in court, she couldn't very well drop everything in the middle and leave if Hal got sick or injured.

As she had on the day she'd fallen at school.

So, okay. He was right. But what else could she do?

She was a single parent doing the best she could with the resources she had. Besides, Logan's job took up twice the time as hers. Triple the time.

"Remy is probably champing at the bit to get you back into action," she added with the realization Logan would be gone soon, and neither one of them ought to get too bothered by their differences. Their situation was temporary.

"Maybe, but I'm going to be taking only local assignments for a while."

She grabbed a plate and shoved it under the faucet for rinsing. "Right. And if I know you, that'll last about as long as it takes for another of those just-gotta-do-it assignments to pop up." She stuck the plate into the dishwasher.

Logan came over, rested his backside against the counter next to her while she jammed another plate into its slot.

"Don't be so quick to judge. I've made some decisions recently, one of which is to stick around and be a real father to Hal. In fact, I've got a town house on the line. Not too far from here. Plus—" he paused, seemingly for effect "—Remy and I are talking about taking on additional staff."

Dana hesitated, uncertain what that meant. "A town house. You mean, so you have a stopping-off place when you're here."

"I mean as a place to live so I can spend time with my daughter. And with extra employees, I'll be around for Hal more often than not."

Dana's pulse raced. Why couldn't he have done that three years ago?

"Speaking of Hal, what did the doctor say?"

"Oh...uh..." Dana fumbled for words, her mind still

sorting out what he'd just told her and how she felt about it. "He said it was normal for her to remember bits and pieces. He said no one actually snaps back in an instant."

"And?"

"He said he couldn't say if she's actually remembering things without examining her. He'll see her on Wednesday, and in the meantime he recommended we keep doing what we're doing. Keep exposing her to the familiar, things she's fond of, places she might remember.

"I've been thinking about that," Logan said. "She mentioned the lake, and it seems that she knows something about it. So I thought it might be a good idea to take a trip to the cabin for the weekend. See if that sparks any memories."

It would spark memories, all right. But those weren't the kind of memories *she* needed. Things were far too confusing as it was.

Still, Logan's pronouncement about sticking around had planted the tiniest seed of hope in her, which instantly grew into a family scene of the three of them together—as she'd always wanted.

Which was stupid. Stupid, stupid, stupid. He hadn't mentioned her in his plans; he hadn't mentioned her at all.

Going to the cabin where some of the most romantic times of their marriage had taken place could only lead to disaster. But that was another selfish notion. This had nothing to do with her and everything to do with Hallie.

If going to the cabin could help her daughter in any way, she had to do it.

"That's probably a good idea."

"*Probably?* Probably nothing! It's a great idea," Logan said. "Hal loved spending time there. And—" he ran a finger down Dana's arm "—so did you, if I remember correctly."

She sucked in a breath. Man, oh, man. She was going to regret this big time. "My feelings aren't important. Hallie's are, and if it'll help her, I'm all for it."

"All right!" Logan exclaimed, and rubbed his hands together. "It's settled, then. Tomorrow's Saturday. We'll pack tonight and leave early in the morning."

When he left to make a phone call, Dana wiped off the counters and the table, trying *not* to think about the last time she and Logan had gone to the cabin. Hal had spent the weekend with Logan's parents, and they'd had the whole weekend to themselves. Her pulse quickened, sending her thoughts in another direction.

Was there any possibility they could give their marriage a second shot? If he was going to stay and buy a town house, was there even the slimmest chance that maybe they… She stopped the thought in motion. It was her fantasy, not his.

Logan came back. "I forgot to tell you. I arranged for a watch on Hal."

Dana stared at him. "A watch?" She blinked. "You mean you're having her followed? Tailed?"

He shrugged. "I think it's necessary. And it'll give us both a little peace of mind."

Dana shook her head, then sighed. "We're still doing it."

Logan looked confused. "Doing what?"

"We're still not connecting," she said impatiently. "Not communicating." She pursed her lips and shook her head again, not caring if her exasperation showed. "I don't know why or how it happens, but it always

does. It's like I'm over here and you're over there.''
She waved her arms in both directions.

Logan crossed his arms. ''Yeah? Not communicating.
You must mean like right now, because I don't have a
clue what you're talking about.''

''Another perfect example.'' She threw her hands up.
''If you'd have called to tell me what you were doing
today, you'd have known there was no need to set up
a watch. I would've told you Detective Andersen called
and told me they have our burglar in custody, a teenager, a kid who's confessed to half a dozen neighborhood
robberies.''

Logan leveled his gaze to hers. ''Oh, no, don't throw
it on me. You could've called to let me know.''

She faced him down, her gaze as steady as his. ''I
did. I just told you that I left a message, but you weren't
here. And apparently you weren't listening to me when
I told you that, either.''

Logan just stood there, until finally he looked down
and shook his head. After a quiet moment, he glanced
at her from under his brows and cracked a sheepish grin.

''How do we always do that?'' Logan asked. ''And
is there anything we can do to fix it?''

She wished there were. Lord, how she wished. But
realistically…? ''Change our basic makeup?'' She
shook her head, too. ''What do you think?''

Logan thought for a moment, then said, ''Maybe not.
But I'd sure like to try.''

CHAPTER TWELVE

LOGAN STOKED THE fire to keep it going. After Hal had gone to bed, Dana rushed out, making a quick run to the store to pick up some items for the cabin. On her way out the door, she'd said she wanted to stop at her neighbor's, too.

She hadn't responded to his comment about trying to change, and it seemed to him that her trip to the store was an escape.

He was still a little bothered that she'd gone out alone. Their burglar had been caught and the police "hoped to get a full confession," she'd said. To him that meant it wasn't a hundred percent sure they had their guy, and he wasn't going to feel at ease until he talked to the police himself.

But if he'd told her that, she'd have thought he was being overprotective or directing her life again. He took comfort in knowing that Klienquist knew what to do. He'd been ready to tell Dana that he'd put security on her, too, but she'd bolted before he had the chance. Just as well. He went into Dana's office, sat in her chair and picked up the phone book to find the number for the local P.D. If he got his reassurance from the police, he'd pull both guys.

Yeah, the cabin was a great idea. One with multiple rewards, not the least of which was they'd be together as a family.

There'd been times in the past couple of days when he'd thought there was a chance, that she'd like things to be different, maybe even try again. The signals were there, but then she'd discount them all with laser-quick speed.

She refused to let down her guard, wouldn't allow herself to depend on anyone. As he saw it, that had been the major roadblock in their marriage—her damn self-sufficiency.

Sure, he knew she'd had to work hard to get where she was, but she'd succeeded. What more did she want?

He'd never been able to figure that one out.

Or maybe it was that he could never figure *any* woman out. God knows they were a species unto their own.

A feeling of futility seeped into his bones. There'd been a time when he'd thought he knew Dana, thought he knew what she wanted. But he'd been wrong. Dead wrong.

He hadn't known what she'd wanted at all. Still didn't.

DANA SAT AT Jillian's kitchen table wondering how to bring up Chloe's problem. She didn't want to betray Hal's confidence or cause a problem between the girls, but she couldn't ignore it, either. She knew too well how feelings of inadequacy could color a child's whole life. Help was available, and she had to make sure Jillian knew it. But first, she had to make sure Jillian knew there was a problem.

"Here you are, ma'am." Jillian set two coffee mugs on the kitchen table. "To what do I owe the pleasure?"

"We're going to the cabin for the weekend. I thought

you'd want to know so you wouldn't think we'd been abducted by aliens.''

Jilly's sky-blue eyes widened, her blond brows sprang up like golden arches. ''Mmm-huh.'' That all-knowing mmm-huh sounded as if Jilly suspected something was going on between Dana and Logan.

''We thought it might help Hal. She's always liked it there, and she seems to remember some things about it.''

The golden brows stayed arched.

''Really. It's true. The doctor said we should keep exposing her to things she liked to do.''

''Uh-huh. But I remember what *you* said about that place—''

''That was a long time ago,'' Dana interrupted. She leaned against the back of the chair, trying to put out of her mind the thoughts that had been spinning in her head ever since Logan had mentioned the cabin and wanting to fix things.

She hadn't been there since the divorce. The place held too many memories. And it was the one place where they'd never allowed their differences to surface; they'd made an unspoken pact. The cabin was sacred.

So were the memories.

''What's there to do up there at this time of the year? Can you still go swimming?''

Dana shook her head. It was easy to forget Jilly had only lived in the state for a year, and since she'd not traveled farther north than Chicago, she wouldn't know. ''No, the lake's too cold. Which is okay, because there are plenty of other things to do.''

Such as long walks in the woods if the weather was okay. Dana remembered those quite well. And she remembered the crystal-clear water of Rainbow Lake, water so clear you could see the pebbles nestled in the white sand at the bottom, water so warm in the summer that two people lying on the shore making love wouldn't even feel the waves washing over them.

"Earth to Dana," Jilly said, waving a hand in front of Dana's face. "So what else is there to do? Come on, spit it out."

"Well, hiking and biking, things like that. You never know what might trigger Hal to remember. And frankly, right now I'm willing to try almost anything."

Her friend's expression shifted. "Sorry, I didn't really mean there was anything more to it, and I'm sorry for joking about something so serious."

Finished with her coffee, Dana shoved the cup away, then reached out to touch her friend's hand. "I didn't think anything of it. Besides, we're good enough friends that I'd expect you to needle me if I'm doing something weird. Or stupid."

"And vice versa," Jilly added with a click of her tongue.

"Speaking of which," Dana went on, "I did want to speak to you about Chloe. Um, I don't want to butt in or anything, but Hal said something today that concerned me."

Jillian gave her one of her impatient c'mon-spit-it-out looks. "Hal said Chloe's having trouble in school, turning her numbers backward and things."

"Oh, jeez. I thought you were going to say something really earth-shattering."

Taken aback, Dana said, "It is. She could have a learning disability. Which can be really horrible for a child. It doesn't have anything to do with intelligence or anythi—"

"Wait." Jillian raised a hand. "I mean earth-shattering as in something I don't already know."

"You know?"

Jillian nodded. "I've noticed things and asked the teacher to watch her. She called me a couple of weeks ago, and we're trying to get her tested so we can figure out a program for her. I didn't want to tell Chloe right away because...because she's so darn precocious. I'd like to get her used to the idea in a positive, gradual way. I'm afraid it'll really bother her."

Dana nodded. "She has to be assured that there's nothing wrong with her, that she's smart and it won't affect how anyone views her."

"Easy to say."

"I know that, too."

"Hey, how come you know so much about it?"

Dana smiled. "One of my first ACLU cases was working with a client who was fighting for her child to be tested. And..." She hesitated, pursed her lips. She'd never told anyone about her own struggles in school and didn't know that she wanted to now, but if it helped... "And because I'd had a tough time in school myself. It was devastating and affected my whole life. I'd just hate for Chloe to feel that way, especially when help is available."

Her friend sagged against the back of the couch. "Wow. Who'da thunk it."

"What?"

"That a brilliant, hotshot attorney like you had ever had any problems whatsoever. Other than the divorce, I mean." Jilly let out a breath and shook her head. "I'm amazed. Can I tell Chloe? I think it will help."

Dana's chest tightened. She'd rather people thought of her as Jilly did, the way she was now, not the way she had been, how she'd had to struggle. She took a deep breath. Her old insecurities were coming out. "Of course. If it'll help Chloe, absolutely. Just make sure she doesn't know Hal said anything."

Jillian's eyes sparkled. "You're a good friend, Dana Marlowe. And I love you to pieces."

Dana's eyes started to get moist. She wasn't used to endearments from friends; hell, she wasn't used to endearments from anyone. Before she made a fool of herself, she asked, "And what about your mother-in-law? Chloe told me she made you unhappy and you went into your room and didn't come out for a long time."

Jillian flapped her hand in dismissal. "Oh, that's nothing. It was a silly emotional reaction on my part. She'll settle down sooner or later."

"I meant what I said about representing you if you need me."

"Thanks, but in all seriousness, I couldn't do anything like that."

Dana frowned. As much as she thought she knew her best friend, she couldn't figure out her reluctance to tell her meddling mother-in-law to take a hike. "I don't know why you feel you can't say something. When someone is that disruptive, why not do something about it? I don't get it, Jilly. That kind of negativity can't be good for you, or Chloe for that matter. What if she bad-mouths you to Chloe?"

Her friend shook her head in vigorous protest. "No. She wouldn't do that. Whatever the wicked witch of the west is or isn't, I know she'd never try to turn Chloe against me."

"And why, may I ask, do you think that?"

Jilly swallowed before she ducked her chin, before

she said softly, "Because we're all she has. And she's all we have."

Dana's confusion must've shown because Jilly quickly added, "I know, I know. It's not a rational thing, and probably hard for someone else to understand." Her friend took a long deep breath, her eyes filled with profound sadness.

"I know I joke a lot and say things about Jack's mom, but..." She fixed her gaze on the table, her words barely audible when she said, "She's Jack's mother, a part of him. Besides Chloe, she's all I have left of him." She paused again, then said, "And Chloe's all Harriet has left of her son. Can you imagine what that must be like for her?"

Dana closed her eyes. Yes, she could. She could easily imagine what it was like to lose someone you love.

"Well, I just keep trying to understand how she feels, and hope someday she'll feel better."

Jilly's logic escaped Dana. But later, on her way home across the front lawn, it hit her, and she realized how different the circumstances between her and Jilly were. When she and Logan first split, Dana had thought it felt very much as though he'd died. But then came that knowing, the continual knowing that he was out in the world somewhere and that he'd never be a part of her life again.

The difference was, no matter what happened, there was no chance that Jack would ever be part of Jilly's life again. Jilly would always love him and wanted to hold on to what little part of him she could.

That fact suddenly seemed significant to Dana's life. Maybe she'd never really get over Logan, either.

Entering the house, Dana resolved to keep a clear head where Logan was concerned. Unlike Jilly, Dana couldn't hold on to something she'd never had. Logan's love. The differences between her and Logan would always be there.

Sure it'd been easy to ignore while they were at school because they'd studied together, complained about the same professors, sang the praises of others, had the same friends. Her world and his were the same back then.

But that wasn't real life. Real life exposed their differences. Differences that made them who they were—and that meant "incompatible" with a capital I.

Water and oil they were. Silk and cotton.

When she saw the light on in the family room, she went in. Logan was squatting in front of the hearth, staring into the fire as if mesmerized by the glow. Her heart skipped a beat at how natural it was to see him there.

"I'm going up to pack," she said. "Then I'll come down and make a list of other things to take. I don't want to pack the food until morning, but if you want, you can get the cooler down from the shelf in the garage."

He turned, his face so utterly handsome in the firelight that she almost stopped just to look at him. Instead, she went upstairs to pack. Passing the master-bedroom door, she had a sudden irresistible urge to open it and look inside.

Lord, she hadn't been in that room for a year. Why did she feel so great a need right now? She reached for the handle, heard a click like the trigger on a gun. Unable to stop herself she inched open the door, then stood with her shoulder braced against the side.

The large four-poster bed rose up in the middle of the room like a monument to their lovemaking. If there was one time she'd truly felt Logan loved her, it was when they were in this very room.

No, it wasn't the raw passion or the unbridled lust that she remembered, although their lovemaking had been charged with all that. It was the pure and wonderful feeling of loving and *being* loved. If Logan had married her out of a sense of duty, it never showed in those moments.

"Looks the same," Logan's husky voice came from behind her. Startled, she jumped, her heart pounding crazily.

He peered over her shoulder. "My favorite room in the house."

Dana's blood thrummed. "I thought I heard something," she lied. "But it was nothing."

"Shame to let such a nice room go to waste."

He placed both hands on her shoulders, and his thumbs started working their magic. Each rhythmic motion chipped away at her protective shell. He was an expert at seduction even when he wasn't doing it consciously; when he did, her strongest resolve melted away as quickly as snowflakes in the sun.

Her insides went all warm and liquid, and it took her a second before she managed, albeit weakly, "The room isn't going to go to waste."

He didn't answer, just kept on massaging, and she could hear his breathing quicken along with her own. If her body had anything to say about it, they'd be headed for that bed in less than a heartbeat. "I'm thinking of renting the room out," she blurted, hoping something would stop both of them from heading down a road that led to nowhere.

His strong fingers stopped moving just long enough

for him to slide his hands down the sides of her arms, after which, he spun her around and pulled her close.

Her senses reeled, her heart fluttered in her chest, and she wanted to kiss him, to feel his lips on hers. She wanted to revel in his embrace and succumb to the sweet forgetfulness of making love.

Because when they made love, nothing else mattered.

"I'll take it," he said. "Whatever it costs." The instant the words escaped his lips, his mouth descended toward hers.

Pulling away, she said, "The price is too high for you, Logan. Besides, I'm going to rent it to Liz."

His hands fell away. He stepped back, his expression incredulous. "Liz? What on earth for?"

He stood there looking at her as if she'd lost her marbles. "She's having a hard time right now, and it would help us both out. It would help her with finances and me...well, she could help with Hallie sometimes."

A muscle in his jaw tightened. "Hallie has parents. If you need help with her, I'll give it. I'm her father."

Dana backed farther into the room, her defenses flaring. She'd only made up the story to keep herself from doing something she knew she'd regret, but now that she thought about it, the idea of Liz moving in seemed to hold greater possibilities. At the least it might keep Logan from knowing how lonely she was at times.

"It would help me a lot to have Liz staying here—in other ways."

Logan followed her into the room, his face a mask of hurt and anger. Then suddenly, he looked around as if something had occurred to him. "I thought you haven't been using the room."

"I...I haven't."

"Then why is it so clean? There's not a speck of dust anywhere."

She waved a hand in dismissal. "Someone comes in once a week to clean. Now, I'd better get packed, or we'll never get out of here early in the morning." With that, she shimmied past him and waited until he came out, too. Then she closed the door once and for all.

The night was long, and Dana couldn't help wondering what Logan really thought. Did he have memories, too? Did he think about the good things in their relationship, or had all that been overshadowed by the fact that he'd *had* to marry her?

Did he ever remember what their relationship had been like before that? What great friends they'd been, how much fun they'd had?

Sure, she knew he'd have no problems with a quick tryst with her. But what then? He'd leave. He'd disappear from her life as he always had, to go off on some job that was always more important than his family.

The problem with Hallie was, she hoped, temporary. The situation with Logan was for sure temporary. But that was not her final thought as she drifted into a fitful sleep some time in the small hours of the morning, still wondering what a visit to the cabin would bring.

LOGAN PULLED THE car into the gas station about thirty miles from their destination, got out and tugged up the collar of his leather jacket against a gust of early-morning wind.

"Old habits die hard," Dana said, poking her head out the window as he gassed up the van. Her voice was low, probably because Hallie was still sleeping in the back seat.

He squinted at her, watching how the wind caught

her hair, how the sun brought out the coppery high-lights.

"And which habit would that be?" he responded, liking the fact that she felt comfortable enough to kid around with him again.

"The way you put gas into the van—the ritual."

"What d'you mean? I'd say filling the tank before we drive thirty miles into the wilderness is a bit of good sense. Not a habit."

"Okay, I'll give you that, but I meant the way you do everything in a certain way, the way you stand with your back to the van, the way you scan the area—that is definitely a habit. And if I remember correctly, the definition of habit is something that's an acquired characteristic and done so often it becomes automatic."

"Ah! The walking dictionary. I forgot." He gave the tank one final shot, then stuffed the pump back into the slot. "What you're forgetting is that I'm trained to do that. When you're trained to do something, it's not a habit. It's a practice."

"Semantics," she sniffed, jutting her chin. "It's a habit because you don't have to do it now. Your practice has become habit."

He eased back into the driver's seat, doubting he'd win that one. It wasn't too often he won much of anything when it came to a debate with Dana. Hell, neither one of them ever seemed to win. With them it was always a standoff.

But right now, winning was the last thing he cared about. He was enjoying the ride. "Okay, I'll give you that one. But only because—"

"You smartass." Dana laughed.

He looked over at her and as he did, he couldn't fathom what had gone wrong between them. He loved the easy way she laughed, her sparkle and energy. She was the one woman who'd been game for most anything he suggested, and her enthusiasm always spilled over to him. He'd loved the way they were together, the way they'd always been.

Damn. How and when had it all changed? Maybe if he could figure that one out...

She sighed, leaned back against the seat and said softly, "Gosh, Logan. I hope this trip will help." She peered over the back of the seat toward where Hallie slept. "I want so desperately for Hallie to remember."

She hadn't said she wanted desperately for Hallie to remember *her,* but he knew that was what she meant. He reached up to trail a finger down her cheek. "I do, too, Dana. I really do."

Yeah, he wanted it. He wanted it for both Hallie and for Dana. Regardless if he had to leave. His needs were not as important as their happiness.

The look in her eyes said she knew he told the truth, and for just a second, he thought she might reach out to him. The fact that she didn't was no surprise, either.

Arriving at the cabin, Logan pulled up near the door to unload. It was nearly noon, and Dana was anxious to make lunch. Hallie had made a point of saying she didn't want to stop to eat because she wanted to see what the cabin was like.

As soon as he turned off the ignition, Hallie bolted outside, her gaze taking everything in like it was the first time she'd ever been there. He watched a smile form as she studied the rustic log cabin, then craned her neck to look skyward at the tall Norway pines surrounding them. She whirled around like a kid in Toyland, and when she spied Rainbow Lake peeking through the trees, her face lit up like the scoreboard at Fenway Park.

"Awesome!" Hallie literally bounced with enthusiasm. "This is gonna be really, really fun," she said, glancing to him, then to Dana and back again.

Dana smiled, watching as Hal started to run toward the lake. But in the next instant, the joy in Dana's eyes shifted to concern. "Hallie," Dana called. "Why don't you wait till we're unpacked? I don't think you should go down alone quite yet."

Hal stopped in her tracks, turned and stood with her feet apart and her hands on her hips. Logan realized this was the very first occasion since she'd come home that Dana had said anything to her that might not be met happily. He couldn't blame her for avoiding contentious issues. The situation was tough enough without getting into discipline, too.

After an uneasy moment, Hallie raised her chin and squinted. "Can you come with me, then?"

Dana's heart tripped at the invitation. It was the first time Hal had voluntarily asked her to do anything. "Sure, I'd love to," she said, trying not to let her emotions get the best of her. It was only one little step, but it felt as if she'd climbed Everest.

"I'll be right back," Dana called to Logan, and grinning from ear to ear, she added, "Do you mind waiting a few minutes before we unload?"

Logan flashed his own happy smile and waved her off. "Not at all. Go ahead. I'll start without you two."

Dana followed Hallie down to the water's edge. It was so quiet she could hear the slurp of water lapping against the rocks on shore. A slight wind rippled the surface of the lake. The sun was warm and bright and glittered off the ripples like tiny fireflies.

"Look, look at all the pretty rocks!" Hallie exclaimed breathlessly as she plunked down on one of the bigger rocks to sit.

Kneeling beside her daughter, Dana reached for a smooth round stone. "We...you and I used to go agate hunting all along this shoreline," she said.

Hallie lifted her gaze to Dana's. "I wish I could remember," she said softly, then reached down and picked up another stone, rubbing it between her thumb and forefinger.

"Oh, sweetheart..." Dana instinctively reached out to put an arm around her little girl. It hadn't occurred to her that Hallie might feel badly about not remembering. Dana had assumed it wouldn't matter, that she couldn't care about something she didn't remember.

"Don't even think about it. It's okay." Dana gave her a squeeze. For not the first time since Hal had come home, Dana couldn't find words. That Hallie had felt comfortable enough to share her feelings with her gave Dana a new burst of hope.

"No, it's not," Hal pouted. "If I remembered stuff, then you and Daddy would feel better, and maybe you'd be like you were before."

Dana pulled back. "Like we were...?" Dread and excitement raced through Dana. "What do you mean, like we were before?"

Hal stood up and started walking back toward the cabin. "Like on those pictures at home—the ones of you and Daddy together, and you looked really happy.

Oh, dear. "What makes you think we're not happy like that now?" She probably shouldn't have asked, and she wasn't sure she wanted to know the answer.

"'Cause in the pictures you and Daddy are always kissing and hugging and stuff. You don't ever do that now."

What could she say to that? Whatever she said, she had to tread carefully. "You know, sometimes people have lots of things to think about. Like work and stuff like that. We get…preoccupied. But that doesn't mean we're not happy. And it certainly doesn't have anything to do with you not remembering. We love you and we'll always love you, whether you remember anything or not."

When Hallie didn't answer, Dana said with a little extra enthusiasm, "So, you stop worrying about me and your daddy. We're happy, especially that you're all right and you're home with us. Nothing else matters, not one little bit. Okay?"

She thought she saw a hint of a smile before Hallie said, "I guess so." And after a brief pause, Hal beamed. "And now you don't have to be thinking about all the work and everything because we're on a vacation." With that, she took off in a sprint toward the cabin.

When both of them reached the cabin, Logan said, "Okay, guys, let's do it to it!" Imitating a commanding officer, he proceeded to give them instructions on what to do with some of the things he'd unloaded from the van.

While they set about their tasks, Hallie skipped around excitedly, firing questions at both Logan and Dana. Could they go on a hike? Could they go for a boat ride? Could they put out food for the birds, and could Logan show her how to make a fire like the cavemen used to do—without matches?

Dana's heart warmed at her daughter's burst of excitement, and she wondered exactly what had happened in the past ten minutes to effect such a change. Hallie was acting more and more like her little girl, even if she didn't know it.

A sudden sense of certainty washed over her. Something good was about to happen. She could feel it in every fiber of her being. This would be a weekend to remember, she was sure of it.

HALLIE HAD GONE to bed an hour before, and after making two cups of coffee, each with a shot of Bailey's Irish Cream, Dana relaxed onto the couch, satisfied and pleasantly tired.

For one whole afternoon she hadn't thought about a thing except having a good time with Hallie, and yes, with Logan, too.

They'd spent the day cleaning up, hiking, collecting agates, and at dusk, they'd had a campfire, made caveman-style. Never mind that Dana had had to give it a little boost with the matches she'd found on the fireplace mantel. Then they'd sat around the campfire, toasting marshmallows while Logan told nonscary ghost stories.

"That'll take the chill off for most of the night," Logan said now, standing the poker back in the rack and then sitting on the floor in front of the couch.

"There's always the electric heat if we need it," she said.

"Yeah. I'm glad we had that put in."

Dana felt the room heat up as the fire in the old stone fireplace caught and held. The cabin was small, one big great room with the kitchen in one corner, and the bedrooms and bath in the back. The furniture was early garage sale, which meant they never worried about theft when they weren't here. Rustic or not, the cabin was warm and inviting.

How had she forgotten how much she'd loved coming up here? In the beginning, she'd thought Logan would hate it. He'd grown up in posh surroundings, attended the best of schools, never having to worry about where the money was coming from or anything else.

She couldn't imagine Logan with his sophisticated tastes liking the rustic ambiance. But having a cabin was something she'd wanted to do ever since she went to Brownie camp when she was ten.

She'd had to talk him into buying the place, but then he'd surprised her, taking to cabin life as if he'd been born in the woods and raised by wolves.

"So tell me," he said out of the blue.

"Tell you what?"

"What happened with you and Hallie down at the lake? She seemed like a different kid when she came back up."

"I wish I knew. In fact, I thought things were going to get worse because she'd said she felt badly about not remembering things."

Logan turned. "Really? She's never said anything like that before—at least not to me."

"It's the first real breakthrough, I think." She paused. "I mean breakthrough in the sense that I feel a bit closer to her than I did."

Logan reached up and placed his hand on hers. "I know it's been tough for you, considering how close you two have been. I'm glad she finally opened up a little."

He meant what he said, Dana knew, and her heart warmed because of it. "That one little thing meant so much. Honestly, Logan, I was beginning to think we'd be strangers forever, that nothing would ever be the same." She pulled in a deep breath, not wanting to let emotion overwhelm her.

"I still don't know if things will ever be the same, though, and sometimes I feel so helpless, so inept. I don't know what to do, how to act or what to say." She bit her lower lip to stop herself from blurting out something she might regret later.

The next thing she knew Logan was on the couch next to her. His eyes met hers with caring and compassion. "I know. It'll be okay. One way or another. I can feel it."

She wanted more than anything to believe he was right. Remembering Hal's earlier comment, she laughed ironically. "She seems to think she's to blame for us not being like we used to be."

"What? Did she remember we're not...together?"

"No, that's what I thought at first, too. But she said she'd seen the pictures in the albums at the house, the ones where you and I were...close. She thought because she didn't see us doing that now, it was her fault. Of course I told her that wasn't the case."

Surprise registered on Logan's face. "You didn't tell her—"

"No, I didn't tell her we're divorced. I don't think she could handle it yet. I said sometimes people get preoccupied with other things like work and that it had nothing to do with her."

"Uh-huh." He studied her face, scrubbing a hand over his chin.

"What? Was I supposed to say something else?"

"No." He paused, his expression thoughtful. "No, I was just thinking that maybe...if we got a little closer, it might help—in more ways than one." He waggled his eyebrows in a Groucho Marx imitation.

She socked him playfully on the arm. "Forget it,

Wakefield. The only thing it'll help is your raging hormones.''

He gave her one of his fake hurt looks. ''Can't hurt. And you'd enjoy it, I know you would.'' His voice had gone all low and husky again. ''Tell me you wouldn't enjoy it.''

He touched her hand, rubbed his thumb and forefinger up her arm, so softly she could barely feel it—on the outside. But on the inside, the nerves under her skin practically ignited.

He was right on that score. He knew her too damned well.

Oddly, she felt him tremble—slightly, not much, but she'd definitely felt it. Was he uncertain, too? For all his sophistication, his innate self-confidence and macho undercover training, could it be that his heart was more vulnerable than she'd thought?

He leaned toward her, reached up to touch her cheek. ''I can't think of anything I'd like better.''

If she'd had even an ounce of resolve before, it melted away in a flash. She wanted to be with him again, for better or for worse, maybe even to see what might happen. She couldn't deny it. *She wanted him.*

The thought gave her pause. Did she still hold out some hope that things could change between them? Did she still think that what pulled them together physically would magically turn to love? God knows, she'd made that mistake before.

But so what? None of this was logical or rational. She knew the difference between lust and love. She also knew that every time she looked at Logan, she longed for things to be different.

She longed for him to love her as she'd loved him.

No—as she *still* loved him.

That was the thought that made her take his hand in hers, to press his fingers against her lips. And the second she did that, she knew without a doubt what would happen next.

CHAPTER THIRTEEN

LOGAN'S LIPS MET hers, warm as summer and soft as velvet. He pulled her close, his need urgent, intense, demanding. She returned his kisses with reckless abandon, and every bit as urgent and demanding as his.

Her body quivered with anticipation and a sudden acute awareness that something was different. Though the motions were familiar, she felt a deeper emotion coming at her in waves, and as he roused her passion, his seemed to grow even stronger.

Between lingering kisses and fiery sensation, they wrestled with buttons, buckles, zippers and shoes. Her senses whirled and skidded, and then he stopped cold. "Wait," he said thickly, tipping his head toward Hal's bedroom.

Of course. They couldn't stay right here. What if Hallie awoke? With her chest heaving, her shirt unbuttoned and hanging half off her shoulders, she nodded in agreement, and the next thing she knew, he'd scooped her up, carried her into the bedroom, gently laid her across the lodgepole bed and locked the door. Then he was back, kissing her, touching her everywhere, peeling off the rest of her clothes, except for her panties.

She fumbled to get his shirt off, making him stop to help. Once he'd shed his shirt, he pushed to his feet, stood beside the bed and stripped completely.

His body was hard, sleek and powerful, and it radi-

ated masculine pheromones. She couldn't wait until
they were body to body, skin to skin, touching, testing,
tasting, drinking each other in until they came together
as one.

Still, for one fraction of a second, she wanted to just
look at him—standing before her, so beautiful and virile, and for some reason, she thought, the tiniest bit
vulnerable. Something *was* different about him tonight,
something about their being together was different. She
didn't know what it was, but the one thing she did know
was that she felt very, very wanted.

He studied her for another fraction of a second, then
reached down to trail a fingertip across the silky slip of
underwear barely covering her. He knew she liked to
wear sexy underwear, that it was her one frivolous in-
dulgence, a secret he'd discovered the first time they'd
been together.

He'd been so shocked, he'd stopped right in the middle of disrobing her, and shaking his head, he'd laughed
out loud.

Then he'd come to her, hard and breathing fire. "I
had you pegged for basic white cotton," he'd said, then
laughed again before kissing her even harder. "Who
would've thought beneath that schoolgirl's jumper and
tights was a Playboy bunny."

"My secret," she'd countered. "And now every time
you see me, you'll know something about this wholesome Midwestern girl that no one else would imagine."

Now, leaning over her, his weight braced on one arm,
he tugged at the elastic, his fingers like hot liquid grazing her skin, sliding lower and lower until he touched
between her legs, igniting a sweet agony of desire. A
desire that needed immediate fulfillment. "Take these
off," he said huskily.

Seconds later, they were in each other's arms, and for one sublime moment, she cherished the way he felt in her embrace. It had been so long. So long since they'd been like this…her joy was so intense she almost wanted to stay in his arms forever.

But there were more important things to attend to. Like kissing his neck and his hard stomach, nibbling on his earlobe and his fingertips. Neither she nor Logan seemed able to get enough of touching and kissing and caressing. He trailed a hot path of kisses to the pulsating hollow of her neck, then downward until he reached her breasts, held both in his hands, then took turns taking the tip of each into his mouth, stroking across the nub until she thought she'd expire.

Or maybe she'd suffocate *him* because she was pulling him so close. It didn't matter. She was a woman possessed.

And right now there was nothing she could think of that held greater pleasure, nothing that could give her such deep emotional satisfaction. She loved him. And for this one moment, she believed he loved her, too.

If he didn't enter her soon, she was sure to implode, she thought, or shatter into a kajillion pieces. He must've sensed her need because he settled between her legs, and as he did, he gazed into her eyes. They knew each other so well, knew what would come next even when it was a total surprise. There was a comfort in that knowing. A comfort that allowed her to let go, and the thought of letting go excited her even more. She knew his mouth would meet hers at the precise moment when they came together, and that she'd raise herself to him for ease of entry. She knew the gentle way he'd ease into her, the way they'd find their tempo and lose all sense of anything but the moment.

Now he was there, and she felt him as she'd never felt him before. Every touch, every movement magnified, her nerves seemed outside her skin, raw and exposed. With near desperation she pulled him to her.

"Please...now," was all she could utter before raising up to meet him, and in that one magnificent moment, they were one.

As if moving to some internal metronome, they rocked in perfect sync, slowly at first, and she reveled in the erotic sensations zapping through her one after the other. The pressure built, their rhythm, their movements faster and faster until her body went taut. She felt as if she were teetering on a precipice, and it wouldn't be long before she'd free-fall into the abyss.

There was no stopping now. The pressure kept building, building, building, and when she thought she couldn't hold off another second, he gave a low guttural moan, setting off a chain of explosions within her.

Afterward, she lay with her head nestled in the crook between his neck and shoulder, and his arm cradled her as he stroked his fingers over her arm and down her back. It was a familiar pattern, a ritual she treasured. Because it was always in this moment that she felt truly loved.

She couldn't think about the future right now. She wanted only to listen to him breathe, to feel his chest rise and fall, to hear his heart go from a rapid staccato rhythm to a slow contented murmur.

Trailing a finger down his stomach, she said, "Just like old times, huh?"

When there was no immediate response, she glanced up to see if he might be asleep.

He gazed deeply into her eyes. "Better," he said huskily. "Much better."

He pulled her to him, his mouth finding hers. She kissed him back and it wasn't long before they were both ready, and they made love again. This time it was slow and easy and filled with the knowledge that at this one finite moment in time, all was perfect with their world.

Almost.

LOGAN AWOKE TO an empty bed. It wasn't surprising as Dana's habit in the past was to rise early, take a quick shower and make breakfast for Hallie. He'd never been much for breakfast, just coffee. But during the time they'd been together since the accident, he'd always seemed to beat Dana to the kitchen in the morning. Probably because he'd been unable to sleep more than a few hours a night.

He kicked the sheets loose at his feet, stretched out and clasped his hands behind his head, savoring a feeling of satisfied completeness. Last night had been like an awakening for him, and he wondered if Dana felt the same. He hoped that she did.

Sex meant something to her, he knew. She'd let him know that many times in the past. She wasn't the kind of person to hop in the sack with anyone just because she needed a release. That was a plus. On the other hand, she'd also let him know that her goals meant something to her, too, and that she intended to do everything she could to reach them. But which, he wondered, meant more? Was it possible the two might co-exist?

Unfortunately he knew the answer to that. From the minute they'd met, she'd worn her independence like a badge of honor. The pregnancy had thrown her off track, and he wondered if maybe the marriage would've

worked if she hadn't been so focused on one thing—or
if they hadn't had a child right away.

God knows it hadn't been planned.

He hadn't found out about the pregnancy until after
he'd already taken the CIA job, a week before they
graduated. Dana hadn't told him right away, she'd said,
because she didn't want it to interfere with his plans.
And she sure as heck didn't want him to feel obligated
to marry her.

He couldn't blame her there. All of his talk about
being free, about not wanting to join the family firm,
certainly sounded as if he didn't want to get married.

She'd never believed his joining the CIA had nothing
to do with her, even though he'd made that decision
well before she became pregnant. To a guy in his early
twenties, the CIA was an exciting way of life, and to
him, a way out of his family obligation.

He remembered the look on her face when he'd
tracked her down after class and announced excitedly,
"I'm in! One last interview, but for all intents and pur-
poses, I'm in!"

He'd been so hyped he couldn't sit still. He'd paced
circles around her as she sat in a chair in the common
area of Harkness Hall. Her green eyes widened, and
after a moment, she'd said, "That's…really great, Logan. What exactly does it mean?"

He stopped his pacing and leaned down, both hands
on the arms of the chair she was sitting in. His eyes
met hers. "It means next month, I'm off for training. Is
that great or what?"

Running her tongue across her lower lip, she been
tentative in her answer. "Sure, that's…really great, Logan. Especially since…well, since it's what you want.

But…'' She faltered midsentence and he thought her eyes seemed to shine a little bit.

Maybe she didn't think getting hired as a special agent for the CIA was as great as he did.

Finally she said, ''I'm happy for you Logan. But…you know I'll miss you.''

Hell, they'd been friends for three years. More than friends. He'd miss her, too, but she'd always talked about her grand plan. After graduation she was going back to Chicago to work in the state prosecutor's office. And from there it was onward and upward—all the way to the state's attorney's job.

The woman was on a mission and nothing was going to stop her.

He'd admired her ambition, admired so many things about her. Her dedication to her goal had made him care about his own future, made him wake up and take control of his life. In fact, if it wasn't for her, he wouldn't have gone anywhere. He'd probably be working for Wakefield and Associates today.

''Hey, I'll miss you, too,'' he'd said. ''But it's only for a couple months. When I'm done, I'll visit you in Chicago like we planned.''

They'd talked about their future plans early on, because even though they'd had a relationship, they'd always known they would go their separate ways after graduation. In fact, she'd been adamant about it. They had agreed, however, to try a long-distance relationship and see where it led. Nothing definite, nothing concrete.

They'd go with the proverbial flow. She, because she had a mission, and he, because he needed a job that mattered. He needed to feel he was doing something honorable and good. If he did nothing, if he followed the path of least resistance and joined his father's firm, he'd never matter in his own eyes.

Dana, he'd thought, had always understood that.

Only at that moment, the way she sat, halfheartedly listening to his excited announcement, it seemed as if it'd all been words in the wind. Because she definitely wasn't happy for him.

She sat there twisting a button on her coat, avoiding his gaze. "Hey." He tipped up her chin with two fingers. "If it weren't for you, I'd be leaving here at the end of the semester to join the family firm. My life would be completely mapped out for me. D'ya know how depressing that would be?"

When nothing was forthcoming from her, he sat on the arm of the chair and forced her to look him. "I mean it. You, of all people know what it's like to go after what you want. I took your cue, Dana." He smiled, figuring he'd given her the ultimate compliment.

"And my going away doesn't change anything else, if that's what's bothering you." He placed a soft kiss on her lips. "I'm still crazy about you."

He hadn't known she was pregnant then, hadn't known it for another three weeks—until one of Dana's friends suggested Logan might want to find out why she was sick every morning.

He remembered the moment as vividly as if it were minutes ago. She was pregnant and she hadn't said a word to him about it.

He'd been furious.

Still, regardless of how it happened, marriage to Dana was something he'd wanted very much. Whether or not she'd been pregnant didn't matter. He'd wanted to live with her, raise a bunch of kids and live happily ever after.

To this day, he wasn't sure he knew what had gone wrong.

Yeah, he had all kinds of theories about what had happened, but now, the only thing he knew for sure was that they'd made a mess of their life together, and that it was their mess, not Hallie's. She was the innocent in all of it, and her parents should've been mature enough to make it work.

Hell, his own parents were about as opposite as two people could get. And while they weren't perfect together, they understood the importance of keeping the family together.

He wasn't very proud of the fact that he'd let his marriage slip away. He should've made the effort. *They* should've made the effort and been more concerned about their daughter than their own fantasies about marriage.

And if he ever had another chance, he intended to take it. Maybe Dana would, too. God knows he loved her.

He'd never stopped.

WATCHING HALLIE skip down to the lakeshore, Dana plucked up her cell phone on the second ring. Logan was still asleep and she didn't want to wake him. "Hello."

"It's about time," her sister chided. "Where in the world are you?" Liz always jumped right into conversation, no pleasantries exchanged.

"Hi, Liz. I'm fine, thanks," Dana needled back.

"Don't be cute, sis. I've been looking all over thunder for you." Her sister sounded frantic. "I've been worried sick that something happened to you or Hallie."

"We're at the cabin, that's all. We decided it might be good for Hal."

After a relieved pause, Liz said, "It might be good for Hal if she had a girl's name. What's going on?"

Liz had never liked Hallie's name. Said it was too boyish. If there was one thing about Liz that Dana admired, it was her honesty. Liz might be a little self-absorbed, but she said what she thought—whether or not the recipient of those thoughts liked it.

Ignoring the comment, Dana answered, "What's going on is a weekend at the cabin. A few quiet days away from the job, away from friends and relatives." She placed special emphasis on the last word.

Liz chuckled on the other end. Their sibling rivalry had long since been dissolved. Liz's perfect childhood, with love and praise coming at her from all directions had come to an abrupt halt when suddenly, the real world expected her to give back a little of what she got.

Apparently Liz thought her whole life would go on exactly as it had, without her ever having to do a thing on her own behalf. She'd hit her peak at about twenty with no effort whatsoever and had been trying to figure out ways to keep it that way ever since. Including marrying Jerrod for his money.

The defining moment for Dana had been when she realized it was their parents' expectations that had separated them. The realization had freed Dana, and from that time on, she and Liz had become closer.

"Okay, okay. I was only wondering what I could do besides the restraining order to keep Jerrod away from me. Every time he comes around I seem to fall into the same old trap. You know how persuasive he can be."

Yes, she knew about traps of that kind. But not when thinking about Jerrod. "Unfortunately there's not much else you can do—not unless he actually does something."

Dana had wondered often what the real cause of her sister's divorce was. But no matter how close they'd become, they weren't close enough for Liz to reveal it was anything other than "irreconcilable differences." Dana suspected Liz's reluctance had something to do with the large amount of alimony she received.

"Has Jerrod done something, Liz? You must tell me if he has."

Liz hesitated. "I…I don't know."

"You don't know? Either he did or he didn't, Liz. And where are you now?"

Another pause. Finally, "I'm at your house. I came by to see you and…I discovered the side window was broken. I thought maybe it was Jerrod because he knew I stayed with you a couple times. I thought it might be his doing."

"What side window, Liz?" An icy fear snaked up Dana's spine. "What about the alarm? Did it go off? Did the police come?"

"There's no alarm now, and no police. But I told Jillian because I thought she might've seen who it was."

"Did she?"

"No."

"So call the police! The longer you wait the colder the trail will be." Why the heck didn't the alarm go off if someone broke into the house?

Liz hesitated. "What if it was him, Dana? What if it was Jerrod? If I call the police, he could be in serious trouble."

Dana couldn't think. If it was Jerrod, maybe he'd been the one who tried the window before thinking Liz was there. But she couldn't imagine Jerrod doing anything of the kind. He'd have come to the door. He'd done that a couple times when Liz stayed with her. But the police had their burglar in custody. And the suspect was a kid, not Jerrod McCaully.

But if the kid was in custody and someone had still tried to get in... Another cold chill shivered through her. That would mean whoever had been trying to break in was still out there.

"I don't give a damn what happens to Jerrod, Liz. This is important. If he's stupid enough to do something like that, he has to know you mean business. If it's someone else, the police need to be notified immediately. Are you in the house, Liz?"

Dana had given Liz a key in case she needed a place to go when Dana wasn't home. She'd never in a million years have thought Jerrod would break in to get to Liz. But if it was him, that would be a relief in itself. Jerrod was preferable to any other alternative.

"No, I'm at Jillian's."

"Well, call the police and then have them call me. I know there's not much anyone can do, because whoever it was is long gone. But it's still necessary. Do it now and call me right back. Okay?"

As Liz clicked off, Dana heard Logan ask, "Call the police about what?" Startled, she clutched the phone to her chest. Logan sidled up next to her, his face serious.

Dana peeked out the window to check on Hallie who was standing on the shore of the lake, practicing the rock-skipping technique Logan had shown her the day before.

"It was Liz. She didn't know we were gone."

"What does she want now?"

He waited, apparently expecting more information.

"She came over to visit and found the side window broken."

Logan's body went taut, and his eyes darkened dangerously. "She see anyone?"

"No, and she didn't go in. She went to Jillian's immediately and called me first thing. She's calling the police now, and I told her to have them call me back."

"Damn."

She nodded in agreement. Letting out a long breath, she sank into one of the wooden kitchen chairs. "That's spooky. Really spooky. Guess I'm glad we're here and not there."

Logan paced before the sink, scrubbed a hand across his chin. "Yeah, I wished to hell I hadn't pulled the guys."

"The guys?" What was he talking about?

He ignored her question and continued pacing from one side of the room to the other, glancing outside at Hal each time he passed the window. "When we decided to come up here, I didn't think it was necessary to keep them on."

"Them? You had more than one?"

"Yeah, I had one on you, too," he said absently. "But that was before I knew the police had the guy in custody."

Okay, she could go with that. She was all for protecting Hallie, and even herself if necessary. Still, she wished he'd told her. "It's probably Jerrod trying to find Liz, that's all. He's not going to hurt anyone."

"You know that for sure? How can you know that?"

"How do I know it's Jerrod? Or how do I know he wouldn't hurt us?"

"Both. You don't know either one with certainty, do you?"

No, she didn't know for sure it was Jerrod. But it made sense. And she didn't understand why Logan seemed to think it was such a big deal. Perhaps he'd forgotten what a geek Jerrod was.

"Liz is calling the police as we speak. And since we're here and not there, we have nothing to worry about. Right?"

Logan nodded, yet he still paced.

"And if you're worried about Jerrod, can't you call your security guys and have them go back to the house?"

"If I'd known about Jerrod before, I would've kept the guys on. Now we don't know who it was or why. Besides, domestic situations are often the most volatile. People get all crazy when their lives are ripped apart."

She knew that, based on many of her own cases. But Jerrod was a gentle man, laid back. She couldn't imagine him getting crazy over anything. Liz had gotten an order of protection because one time he'd gotten drunk and unruly, but it had been an isolated incident.

What bothered Dana the most was that she sensed Logan was keeping something from her, that it wasn't just Jerrod he was worried about. She had to ask.

"Why didn't you tell me you had me tailed? Do you know something I don't?"

When he didn't respond immediately, her annoyance kicked up a notch. Still, she tried not to think about the fact that he'd done it again—that he'd taken care of things without so much as a consult. It didn't matter. *Let it slide.*

But try as she might to stay with logic, it didn't work.

"You should have told me."

Logan pinched the bridge of his nose and shrugged. He mumbled something about it not being a big deal, then went to the window again and stood with his back to her.

He *was* keeping something from her!

Blood thrummed through her veins, and her nerves stretched tighter. "If you were that concerned, the least you could've done was consult with me."

His spine went rigid, and his fingers tightened on the window ledge.

If he'd just talk to her, for crying out loud. If he'd just once act like her opinion mattered. *So much for thinking things could ever change.*

They were acting exactly like before. She'd press and press for him to talk to her, confide in her like any normal husband, and finally, he *might* give in a little. But only a little. Why did it have to be so damn hard?

Just when she was about to press the issue, she saw his shoulders relax. Then he turned and said, "I'm sorry things got screwed up, and sorry I didn't find the time to talk to you about it. I didn't tell you because I didn't want to say anything in front of Hallie. Then I learned from you that the police had a suspect in custody and when I found out from them he'd confessed, I released the men. We came up here after that, and I forgot about it. That's it. No big deal."

He glanced out at Hal again. A beat later, he added, "It's the nature of my business, Dana. I don't talk about my business with anyone except my partners. It wasn't personal. I thought you knew that."

She was taken by surprise at the apology, and words failed her. She tried to gather her thoughts. He'd said he was sorry. She was happy he was looking out for them, happy he cared that much. And he'd actually explained something to her about his business. Not a monumental feat, but it was more than he'd ever done before.

He turned toward the door. "I'm going to see what Hal wants to do this afternoon."

Dana followed him as far as the deck where she sank down on the wooden swing. Both Logan and Hallie remained within sight, Logan on a log near the shore, Hallie lying on her tummy across the dock, apparently watching the minnows swimming in the glassy water below. He hadn't said he was worried about anything else, so why should she think he was?

Especially since the cabin was buried deep in the woods, and the road was a maze; even the few people who knew where the cabin was had trouble finding it. Jerrod had never been invited to visit, and she doubted he could find it even if he had. She also knew, even if Logan didn't, Jerrod would never hurt either her or Hallie, even if he was crazy enough to try to get in their house to find Liz. Which she now had to believe was true since it'd happened again.

Minutes later Logan left Hallie playing by the shore and came up to sit next to Dana on the narrow swing. "So, what do you think we should do now, Sherlock? Or is that shylock?" Dana teased, trying for light-hearted.

She'd been on an emotional seesaw from the minute Hallie'd had the accident, worrying about everything from her daughter to her job. She needed a mental rest.

She wanted, for just a little while, to feel as if there were no intrusions in their life. That she and Logan and Hallie were together again, a family, and that nothing else mattered. Because in truth, nothing else did. Not even her job.

What had all her hard work gotten her? Her parents

hadn't changed their attitude toward her because she'd excelled in school or in her career. Her financial success hadn't changed Logan's mother's opinion of her, and being a damn good attorney didn't make Logan love her.

And on top of that, her hard work couldn't change what might happen in her career, since she'd refused on principle to do as David had asked. Right now she wanted to forget about all of it.

Logan shrugged and winked. "I'll think on it and let you know." And for the next few minutes, with their bodies touching at the shoulder, elbow, hip and knee, they swung in silence.

For once, she didn't feel a compelling need to talk and, instead, felt a strange sense of comfort in quietly swinging together, without saying a word. Then he took her hand in his and held it against his thigh while the swing rocked forward and back, forward and back.

Soon an incredible longing filled her. A longing not rooted in the physical passion that had been their mainstay, but something much deeper than that.

It was a longing of the soul. A need for love of a kind she'd never had—from the one person she knew would never give it.

The thought made her breath catch. She fought for some sort of detachment, a way to blot out everything she and Logan had been to each other, or at least what he'd been to her. If she could think of him as a friend...

A futile effort, that, because in her heart she knew she could never feel mere friendship toward Logan Wakefield.

He brought out the passion in her. He was her weakness, her fatal flaw. She needed him. She needed for him to love her.

Damn.

Her self-sufficiency was the one thing in her whole life that had given her confidence. And her saving grace was that she'd always had a goal. If she focused on that, she could obliterate all the improbable thoughts that invaded her brain in her weaker moments.

Thoughts about not being good enough, smart enough or pretty enough. Thoughts about love and marriage and happily-ever-after. None of which could ever be between her and Logan.

Not between two people so different it was almost as though they were different species.

Logan's mother had certainly made her opinion known, telling Dana that she'd ruined Logan's life, that he'd had plans to marry some debutante. As usual, Dana had shored her reserves, determined to prove herself, to show Logan's family that she was worthy of their son.

Once again, she'd escaped into the comfortable world of achievement. A place where no one could touch her and she knew she could hold her own.

To no avail, of course. Nothing she'd ever done during their marriage had changed the woman's belief that Logan had married beneath him. No career success, no awards or salary increases had swayed Andrea Wakefield's opinion.

With sudden clarity it dawned on Dana that though she'd lived her life trying to prove herself to others, all she'd proved was that she was an achiever. Deep down she was still that lonely, needy little girl.

The thought was sobering. Had it all been for naught? She glanced to the shore where Hallie was playing and felt a sudden need to get as close to her daughter as she possibly could.

Logan must've read her thoughts, because he said,

"How about we go down and skip stones with Hal?" He rubbed his thumb across Dana's palm before he stood and pulled her up by the hand with him.

The familiarity, the tenderness in his touch and in his voice sent a crazy hopeful feeling surging through her. There *was* something different about Logan, both last night and today, something she couldn't define. Whatever it was gave her hope that being together meant more to him than she'd thought.

Was it possible that they could build something between them? Something deeper than passion, than sex?

Could she be happy with whatever it was?

Could Logan?

Was he willing to try?

CHAPTER FOURTEEN

LOGAN PACED THE wooden deck, shifting the cell phone to his other ear as he listened for Remy to pick up. He kept one eye on the door watching for Dana and Hallie to come out. After skipping stones and a mother-daughter canoe ride, they'd decided they wanted to go for a hike, which prompted Dana and Hal to come in to change into their hiking gear. He took the opportunity to catch up on business.

"Yo," Remy answered.

"Got your page. What's up?" Logan sat in the swing.

"Babies, that's what."

"Babies? Plural?" Logan heard heavy breathing on the other end of the phone, as if Remy had just finished a workout. Logan had accused his buddy once of being addicted to exercise, which Remy thought ludicrous. A guy can't be addicted to something that's good for him, Remy had said, and if it feels good and can't hurt you, why not keep doing it?

Famous last words, which Logan had no qualms about reminding Remy of after Crystal became pregnant.

"Twins. A boy and girl."

Logan cracked a wide smile. He couldn't imagine Remy parenting one baby much less two. Yet hearing the happiness in his partner's voice, Logan felt the excitement as if it were his own. "Hey, congratulations, buddy. That's great. How's Crystal?"

"Happy. Beautiful. But that's not what why I paged you." Remy paused. "Gideon call you yet?"

"No. Why?"

"Said he was gonna be on the horn right after he tied up a couple loose ends. Just thought I'd give you a heads up so you didn't go somewhere you couldn't be reached."

"Did he say what it's about?" Logan ran a hand through his hair. Gideon had done some checking for him on Dana's cases. Maybe he had something concrete to go on.

"He's got a lead. He knows something's goin' down, and he said he had to talk to you. That's all I got. He's checking in at eleven hundred hours. We'll keep you posted."

"Great. Can you contact Masters and Klienquist? Tell 'em to be on alert."

"Sure. What's up?"

"Precautionary measure. That's all. Let me know ASAP, okay?"

"Got it."

Logan clicked off the phone and pocketed it. *A lead.* Good news, he hoped.

Just then, Hallie flung open the cabin door. "Ta-da!" she stretched out her arms and pivoted to show off her new hiking duds. She wore blue jeans, a red sweatshirt with a white turtleneck underneath, hiking boots and a purple backpack.

"Pretty spiffy, kiddo."

Hallie beamed from ear to ear at his compliment, then plopped down next to him on the swing. She seemed happier during this trip to the cabin than at any time since she'd come home from the hospital. "Better tell your mother to get on the stick or it'll be sundown before we get out of here."

Just then Dana sauntered out wearing a matching outfit, minus the purple backpack. Hallie popped up and ran over to Dana. She took Dana's hand and the two of them struck a pose, like mother-and-daughter models in a magazine.

Picture perfect they were. Just looking at them made his chest puff up. "Wait right there, both of you." He dashed inside and came out with the disposable camera Dana had purchased, and then lined them up for a photo.

Yeah, picture perfect. After two shots, Hallie complained that that was enough, and after the third, she stomped over to Logan and held out her hand.

"What?" he asked.

She plucked the camera from his fingers. "You go over there." She waved a hand toward the side of the deck facing the woods, then turned to Dana. "You, too. Now *I'm* going to take a picture of both of you."

Logan was pleased to see she'd become a little more assertive, more like her old self—and, he had to laugh, like her mother. Which was reason enough to obey the order. Dana joined him at the designated spot, and he draped an arm loosely across her shoulders.

Dana looked up at him and Hallie clicked off a shot or two, during which he felt Dana reach up and close her hand over his. Standing only an inch or so apart, he got a heady whiff of freshly shampooed hair, and was reminded of the first time they met.

He lowered his gaze to settle on her mouth. Damn, she had a great mouth. He'd like to— Dana must've known what was on his mind because she swiveled around and elbowed him in the ribs.

She still held his right hand, so he closed the small gap between them and caught her around the waist with his other arm. He pulled her tightly against him. It wouldn't take long before she'd know he was ready for a repeat of last night.

Hallie happily clicked off another photo, then waving them to look at the camera for another, she suddenly stopped. "Look, there's something moving back there." She gestured at the woods behind them.

Logan grabbed both Dana and Hallie, and in a split second had them shoved flat against the deck with his body as cover. He reached up and tried the door to the cabin. Locked. Dana had already locked it.

"Daaddee, you're squishing me," Hallie's muffled cry came from somewhere under his chin. He could feel her wriggling to get out, but he held her and Dana firmly as he looked over his shoulder, his gaze scanning the woods.

"Hold on a minute."

Nothing.

He moved away a little to give them air, but still kept them covered. "What did you see?" he demanded of Hallie.

Hallie's eyes grew round and her bottom lip quivered. "A...a deer. I think it was a deer cause it was brown."

Relief flooded through him.

"Deers can't hurt us, can they, Daddy?"

His chest heaved as adrenaline still pumped through his body. "Not usually, kiddo."

"Did you think that one was dangerous?"

It took all his willpower not to laugh. "No, honey, I

didn't. But since you didn't say it was a deer, I thought it could be something else. A…bear, maybe.''

He glanced at Dana, who was lying directly under him. She gave him one of her arched-eyebrow looks as if to say, *Yeah, right.*

''I was…uh…just being cautious.''

He got to his feet and held out a hand to each to help them up. He retreated a step, shoved his hands in his pockets and shrugged. ''Training kicked in,'' he said under his breath to Dana.

''Overtraining, I'd say.''

He shrugged again. ''It comes in handy when I need it.''

''Can we go hiking now?'' Hallie chimed in impatiently. ''I wanna go to that place by the hill and find agates.''

LOGAN SAT ON THE top step of the deck waiting for a call from Gideon or Remy. After they'd returned from their hike, they'd had supper, lit a fire, played a couple games of crazy eights, and then Dana went off to help Hallie take a bath and get ready for bed.

Logan had never found out if Hal had actually remembered something about the place where they'd gone rock hunting. When he'd asked her a couple questions, her response had been a shrug and ''I don't remember it.''

The doctor had said the last time they spoke, that Hal probably wouldn't even *know* if she remembered. That she might feel a familiarity, but that might be as far as it would go. Or one minute she might think something was totally new to her, and the next she'd act like she'd known it all along.

Like tonight when she'd asked Dana to read her a

story before bed. Bedtime reading had been a ritual for Dana and Hal practically from the day Hal was born. Even when their daughter was a baby, Dana had read to her. When Hallie had asked him to read a story last night, he knew Dana had been hurt by it. He didn't understand the reason for this latest change, but he was pleased nonetheless. Because every time Hal didn't remember her mom, every time she asked him to do something her mother had usually done, he could see the toll it took on Dana.

Dana never complained, but he saw every little wince, the quick straightening of her shoulders, the way her mouth thinned, the hurt that switched off as quickly as it appeared. She'd be damned before she'd let anyone know she was vulnerable.

But today Hal had seemed to want to be close to her mom. She'd held Dana's hand during the hike and kept asking her questions about everything under the sun. "Where did you live when you were little? Did you like to skip rope and play with dolls? Did you and Daddy want me to be a girl or a boy before I was born?"

The questions had gone on and on, and he might as well have stayed at the cabin. He'd finally taken the opportunity to lag behind and call Remy to get the scoop on Gideon.

At the same time, he felt guilty for not telling Dana what he was doing. He was torn. Gideon had a job to do for the company that was quite separate from what Logan had asked him to do as a favor. He didn't want Gideon to put the other job in jeopardy because of it, nor did he want the man to put *himself* in danger.

When Remy had said he hadn't heard from their agent, Logan was concerned. If Gideon didn't make

contact, he'd better find a way to get in touch with him
himself.

As DANA FINISHED reading the last page of *Little House
on The Prairie,* she saw that Hal had fallen asleep. She
closed the book and sat quietly watching her precious
child. Hal's cheeks were pink from being outside most
of the day, and she smelled like bubble bath, all sweet
and innocent.

Lord, it felt wonderful to be even a bit closer to her
little girl. The closeness told her they *could* forge a new
relationship if Hal's memory didn't return. It was just
the encouragement Dana needed to keep up her brave
front. Today they'd made a mountain of progress, and
she prayed each day would get better.

After tucking Hallie in, Dana placed a soft kiss on
her baby's forehead. As she left the room, she gently
pulled the door shut behind her, then stood with her
back against the wood, savoring the moment.

After a few moments, she realized the lights in the
living room were off and it was dark. She moved into
the room and saw the fire had nearly sputtered out; all
that was left was a low glow under a pile of ash. She
flicked on a lamp by the couch. Maybe Logan had gone
out for more wood.

One glance at the full log bin next to the hearth told
her she was wrong. Then she caught a glimpse of Logan
outside the window, pacing the deck.

Logan never paced unless something was wrong.
When he made another pass, she saw he was on his cell
phone.

He did have a business to take care of, after all, so
maybe he was getting ready to go back to it. The
thought gave her pause, and she realized how much

she'd miss him when he did. Realized she didn't want him to go away again.

But what she wanted wasn't necessarily what Logan wanted. She snatched up a log and tossed it onto the grate in the fireplace. If he wanted to go, he'd go. And that would be that.

She tossed some crumpled newspaper, then another log, and the fire was quickly renewed. Soon it was too warm to stand near. She peeled off her sweatshirt and went to the kitchen to make a drink. Cider, maybe. Warm apple cider with a little brandy sounded good, and Logan, she remembered, liked it, too.

As she filled the pot, she heard the door creak open. She looked up to see Logan standing in the open doorway, his hair windblown and his face reddened from the brisk autumn air. He kept his hand on the knob as if he didn't know whether to come in or go back out. When a gust of wind blew leaves inside, he quickly shut and locked the door.

He stood for a second scratching the stubble on his chin. He hadn't shaved today and with his dark windblown hair, he looked dangerous and sexy.

But something was wrong. She knew it. She grabbed the two mugs and walked over. "Here, drink this. It'll warm you."

He stared at the mug she'd pressed into his hand and then looked back up at her. "Thanks," he said absently.

"C'mon. Sit in front of the fire." Dana tugged on the sleeve of his leather jacket. He followed, but instead of sitting, he stood by the fireplace, where he rested one hand on the mantel.

"You're right, that's a better spot for warming up." She dropped onto the well-worn couch, then tucked the corners of the plaid blanket under the threadbare cushions and waited. When he didn't move and just stood there sipping his drink, apparently pondering, she finally asked, "Business problems?"

It was presumptuous, she realized. He could have other problems besides business. Problems with a woman. A girlfriend.

The thought caught her off guard. But as quickly as it came, she discarded it. Logan wasn't the type to be with two women at one time. At least he'd never been before.

She had no reason to believe anything different of him now. He was a man with utmost integrity. It was one of the qualities that had drawn her to him.

"I guess you could say that." He turned to face her. "One of our guys has...uh...disappeared."

"You mean he ditched the job?"

He took a sip from the mug, then set it on the mantel. "I don't think so. More like he's missing in action."

Dana knew Logan and Remy's business could be risky. She didn't know exactly how risky, since the two men had been in business less than a year when she and Logan had divorced.

"Missing in action covers a lot of territory. It sounds ominous." He was being evasive again. "If you don't want to tell me, Logan, just say so. But don't tell me a little bit and then expect me not to ask questions."

He came over, shrugging off his jacket on the way. He sat next to her and leaned forward, elbows on his knees, his eyes dark as midnight and more serious than she'd seen in a long time. "We had a guy on a job who was supposed to report in hours ago. He hasn't. We don't know what's happened." He let out a frustrated breath. "Damn. It wasn't even a dangerous job."

For the second time today, he'd opened up about his

work. She barely knew how to react. If it wasn't dangerous, then why was he so worried? "Maybe his car broke down, or he got sick," she offered feebly.

"He'd make contact if that were the case."

"Well, maybe he's just not reliable."

"Yeah, except that we don't hire unreliable people. We hire only the absolute best." He proceeded to systematically crack one knuckle after the other. Dana winced at the sound.

"Is there anything you can do?"

Logan shook his head. A long silence followed. Then a faint ringing interrupted the quiet. Logan launched to his feet and pulled the cell phone from his jacket pocket, answering it on his way out the door.

Okay. Guess that's a private conversation! Nothing she hadn't experienced before, she told herself. She should be used to it.

When they'd been married, he'd had a whole other life, one she couldn't share. She'd never been able to talk to him about his job or how his day had gone because it was all covert secret-agent stuff, and talking about it could put his family at risk. She understood that, appreciated the concern. But the lack of sharing, coupled with his frequent absences, had taken its toll.

When Logan was gone, the only thing she'd had to focus on besides Hallie was her job. When he'd accused her of caring more about her job than her family, she'd felt stung. When she'd told him her reasons, told him how shut out from his life she'd felt, they'd wound up arguing. One day the argument had escalated into a bitter fight, and all her feelings about his job and his being away had come spilling out. She'd said she'd rather be single than have a husband who was never there.

She'd been stunned when Logan had said fine, he'd

leave. Just like that! He'd barely given it a second thought, which truly cemented her belief that he'd never wanted to marry her in the first place.

Devastated, she'd gone through the motions of working out the divorce settlement. Then she did the only thing she could do—she'd focused on the things that made up the rest of her life. The things she cared most about. Hallie—and her job.

Watching him now, she felt as if they were actors in an old movie on perpetual rerun. She got up to stoke the fire, and as she did, she saw him stop short.

He stood completely still, listening or talking, she couldn't tell which, and then he finally sat down heavily on the porch swing.

A few minutes later he came back in, pocketing the phone on the way. Still agitated when he stopped in front of her, he said, "Sit down. We need to talk."

She sat. Waiting, a knot formed in her gut. He was going to leave. That was what this was about. Whether it had to do with his missing agent or another assignment, it didn't matter. He was going to leave just as he always had. She'd been dreaming to think anything might change.

"Okay. What's on your mind?"

"There's a problem."

"Well, that's obvious. So spit it out, Logan. You don't have to candy-coat anything for me."

He looked hesitant, then sat beside her. "Okay," he said solemnly. "We…I mean, SISI has an agent working a case and he's in possession of information that might be a tie-in with the break-in at the house."

"Our house?" she asked, aghast. "You mean someone trying to get back at you?"

He shook his head and leaned forward, elbows on his knees.

"Well, what?" she demanded. "What could your company possibly be working on that would tie in with the break-in at our house if it isn't related to you?"

Logan let out a long breath. "One of our agents, the guy who went missing, who is no longer missing, by the way, got wind that someone in the P.A.'s office is working to get the Lombard case tossed out. They figure you're sure to get a conviction and want you off the case to make sure of it."

Dana's back stiffened. "Run that by me again. Someone in my office?" She couldn't imagine. Lombard was their biggest case, and their department could only benefit by a conviction, whether it was Lombard or Leonetti. "What purpose would that serve?"

Logan shrugged. "I don't know. Maybe they figure if you're off the case, they'll get a prosecutor with less experience and he could easily make the kind of mistake that'd get the case thrown out."

She shook her head. "I don't understand. No one in my office would do that. And how would a break-in get me off the case, anyway?" Unless… "Oh, God. Are you thinking someone wants to take me out of commission for a while? But that doesn't make sense when all they'd need to do is somehow get David to take me off the case—"

Logan held up a hand in a time-out gesture. "Hold on a minute, okay? You're going too fast."

She couldn't hold on. Her brain swirled with questions and as she thought of one, she answered it with another. The new guy, Gideon Armstrong, he could be involved. He was supposed to work with her… But how could he have gotten David to agree to that? *David.* Was

David involved? No, he wanted a conviction so badly
he'd even asked her to talk to Judge Wellesy... Oh,
man.

No... No way. That couldn't be. Or could it? If she
talked to Wellesy, she'd get thrown off the case and
then Armstrong would take over, and with little time to
prepare, he'd probably lose the case. Or if Armstrong
was getting a payoff, he'd lose it willingly. But how
would that tie in with the break-in? And why on earth
would David get involved with anything? He had the
attorney general's job practically in his pocket.

She remembered David's response wasn't exactly
positive when she'd told him she wouldn't talk to Wellesy. But after that, he'd hadn't said a word, and she
figured he'd accepted her decision and decided to forget
about it.

And how did Logan know anything? She'd never
even told him what cases she was working on, and he'd
been out of the country till a week and a half ago.

"How'd you know I was working the Lombard
case?"

He hesitated, deflected his gaze. Then he shrugged.
"Everyone knows that, don't they? It's been on the
news, in the papers..."

That was reasonable, but when Logan finally looked
at her, she saw the truth in his eyes.

She stood up, her stomach churning. "Tell me the
truth, Logan. How did you know? Did you talk to someone in my office?" She positively throbbed with anger
and it was an effort to keep her voice low. "Did you?"

He stood up to face her, his muscles tensed in that
attitudinal way she knew so well. He hated to be chal-
lenged.

"Okay, yes. I was discreet and got some information

because I wanted to make sure you and Hallie were protected.''

''You talked to someone in *my* office about one of *my* cases? Who did you talk to, Logan?''

He looked at her, then he shook his head. ''Don't worry, your job isn't in jeopardy. I was concerned about my family, so I got some information, that's all.''

God! She couldn't believe this. She stalked from one side of the small room to the other. If he'd talked to the wrong people...if they thought she was giving out confidential information... ''Do you know what you've done?'' Hell, she'd be lucky if she had a job cleaning toilets in the P.A.'s office when she returned, much less make a bid for state's attorney.

The irony of it all was that no matter what she did, she was screwed. If Logan was right, it had to be David. And she couldn't confront David because she had no proof. She realized now that David had made sure of that. And if she confronted him, anyway, he'd take her off the case. Which, again, if what Logan said was true, was exactly what someone wanted. Lastly, if she went ahead with prosecuting Lombard, she or Hal could be in danger.

''What I've done is try to look out for my family.''

''And you didn't think to talk to me about it? Didn't think you'd mess up my job and everything I've ever worked for?''

''Dammit, Dana. I don't give a rat's ass about your job,'' Logan shouted. ''I was trying to help.''

She whirled around. ''Help? Help me get fired? Help me lose all credibility? Good God, Logan, spare me from your good intentions. I don't need your help. And I've had all the protection I can take.''

Her thoughts shotgunned as she circled the room,

high-octane adrenaline shooting through her. Her chest heaved when she said, "When we get back to the house tomorrow, I want you to leave."

Logan stalked toward the front door and yanked it open. "Fine. Just fine." His words were punctuated by the sharp bang of the door behind him.

CHAPTER FIFTEEN

IT WAS JUST A BAD dream, Hallie thought. The voices weren't real. She stretched out and then curled into a little ball and snuggled under the covers again to go back to sleep. But then she heard the voices again, like people talking really loud.

Loud voices were scary at night, and she sat up in bed and scrubbed her eyes with her knuckles. The voices stopped and she was glad, but now she had to pee really bad.

It was dark, but with the night-light on, she could see just enough to go to the bathroom, so she swung her legs off the bed. Then she heard the loud voices again and thought maybe it was the television. Was there a TV at the cabin? She couldn't remember.

She gripped the doorknob and turned it slowly. Maybe her mommy would let her sleep with her. Mommies let kids do that if they had bad dreams or got scared, and she remembered from the last time how nice it was to sleep with her mommy.

Hallie hurried to the bathroom across the hall because her feet were cold, but then she heard the voices again. They sounded louder and louder, like hollering. Her tummy started to hurt because she knew something bad happened when there was hollering.

Daddies went away.

Her tummy started to hurt more, and she wanted to

go back to her bed and sleep really hard so the mad voices would stop. On her way back to her room, she saw Mommy and Daddy standing in the living room waving their arms.

Their faces looked really mad.

"I want you to leave," Mommy said to Daddy. Hallie covered her ears with her hands and tried to hum. If she couldn't hear them, then maybe nothing bad would happen. Maybe her daddy wouldn't go away again.

But even with her ears covered she could still see them. Tears sprang to her eyes and her nose started running and her tummy hurt so awful she didn't know what to do. She ran back into her room and stood by the door, but the tears started rolling down her cheeks. She tried make them stop by putting her hands over her mouth and she swallowed hard again and again.

If she cried too loudly, they'd hear her, and she couldn't let them hear her. She wasn't supposed to listen either. Her teacher said that wasn't nice and if her daddy knew she listened he'd think she was bad and he'd go away. But she didn't know what to do so they couldn't hear her. And she had to do something.

She just had to.

DANA BIT HER lower lip and watched Logan stalk across the deck again. The second he'd walked out that door her heart plummeted. She'd been overwhelmed by regret, and she felt incredibly alone—more alone than she ever had.

In that single moment, she suddenly understood what she'd lost. More important, she understood what they'd had together: the history, the camaraderie, the caring, the great sex. They had a child. They'd been a family. Maybe not the perfect family, but still, what they'd had for a while was more than some people ever did.

It was definitely more than she had now.

How could she throw it all away for some fantasy of what love should be? Sure, when she was a kid full of hopes and dreams, she'd fantasized that she'd marry someone who filled all her empty places. The man she married would adore her; he'd love her just because she was who she was.

She'd known for a long time that the driving force behind all her achievements was the sad relationship she'd had with her parents. When she'd eventually learned they hadn't wanted another child after Liz, unless it was a boy, it made all the sense in the world.

No wonder she'd taken second place all her life. But knowing the reason had never made it more palatable, just easier to stop blaming herself. Even so, she'd never stopped hoping she'd find that one person who would love her just because.

But Logan had never been the man to fulfill her fantasy. It wasn't his fault. His life had been molded differently from hers, and it had made him who he was.

That was the reality, and since the divorce, she'd tried damned hard to accept it.

Then Logan had come back, moved in and stoked up those little-girl hopes and dreams all over again. How foolish *was* she? She couldn't change Logan's feelings any more than she could her parents'. When would she realize that?

But beyond her own selfish needs, Hallie needed a family. *She* needed a family. And she knew right then that no matter what, she wanted Logan to stay. She knew she'd be willing to accept less than the fantasy if there was some way to make it work.

But what she could accept and what Logan could were two different things. After a few soul-searching moments, Dana knew she had to ask. She had to ask him if there was any chance for them.

She loved him and she loved Hallie. She had to risk her ego and her pride—even if he turned her down.

Just then the door opened and Logan tramped back inside. Her heart thudded wildly. Now what?

They stood for a tentative moment, each one staring at the other, waiting, assessing. Then they both spoke at once. "I'm sorry."

A second later Logan took her hand and gently led her to the couch, where he pulled her down beside him. "We need to talk, and not about either of our jobs."

Her pulse raced in anticipation. Had he come to the same conclusion as she had? God she hoped so.

"Dana," Logan said, "first of all, I take back what I just said. I do need to talk about your job. But the only reason I'm saying anything is because I know how much your job means to you, and I want you to know it's not in jeopardy. What I'm going to tell you must remain confidential. Okay?"

She nodded, wanting only to talk about them, to know if they still had a chance.

"SISI had an undercover guy in the state's attorney's office."

Her mouth fell open. "What?"

"Please don't ask for details. It was the guy who went missing. But that's all cleared up and we got what we needed. I promise you'll hear the rest soon enough. I can't tell you anything else right now, but just know that your job is safe. I didn't talk to anyone other than our guy."

"My job…" She tossed her head and laughed wryly.

"My job isn't as important as you think. Is there something else?"

He nodded. Then he cleared his throat and looked into her eyes again. "What we have between us goes deep, Dana. But something happens when we're together. Something neither of us seems able to control. And if we ever want Hallie to have a normal life, we're going to have to figure it out or bury it. We need to get on with our lives."

Her heart skittered, then felt as if it might stop completely. He wanted to try again. Oh, God. He wanted it, too!

"Wh-what…" she stammered, feeling so elated she could barely squeak out the words. "What can we do?"

He ran a hand through his hair, seeming frustrated. "I don't know—not exactly. Maybe we need to know why you strive so hard…why you have to be so self-sufficient that you don't need anyone."

Dana felt her chin quiver. "Don't need anyone? Oh, Logan." She shook her head. "Knowing me as you do, how can you even say that?"

"How? Because whenever I try to help, you let me know in no uncertain terms that you don't need anyone. You pride yourself on doing every single thing yourself and doing it better than anyone." He gave a sad ironic laugh. "And I gotta tell you, you've succeeded in spades."

She didn't know what to say. Her self-sufficiency was the one thing she thought he *did* like about her. If he didn't like that, what else did she have left?

He went on, "I guess if that's all it takes to make you happy, I shouldn't say anything, because then you've accomplished your goal in everything. All I know is that never needing anyone would make me feel lonely as hell.''

Truly confused, she said, ''Logan, you're the one who wanted freedom. You're the one who wanted to live dangerously, to take chances with your life, no matter how much it bothered me, no matter how much you were away or how much it interfered with our life. When I merely mentioned—in a moment of extreme frustration, I might add—that I'd rather be single than married to someone who was never there, you practically sprinted out the door.''

''Dana—'' now it was his turn to shake his head in disbelief ''—I wanted you to need me. For years, I needed something from you that said, 'I fill that space in your life that no one else could possibly fill.' I left because you wanted me to, and because you made me feel…unnecessary. Do you have any idea how hard it is for me to admit that?''

She stared at him in shock. How in the world could he ever think she found him unnecessary? He couldn't possibly be that blind, could he? He had to know how very much she needed him, how much she loved him.

''I…I wouldn't have married you if I thought you were unnecessary,'' she said. ''And unless I've gotten the wrong signals all these years, there's no way you wanted me to be a clinging vine.''

He gave a small wry laugh. ''There's a hell of a lotta room between clinging vine and being a world unto yourself. But y'know…'' His expression shifted to one of resolution. ''Y'know, I don't think it's a solvable problem, or rather, one we have to solve. What I really want, for Hallie's sake, is to learn how to work together. Hallie needs a support system. She needs both her parents, and I don't think we can do that if we're constantly dredging up the past. I want to do whatever is necessary to get Hallie better, and in the meantime I won't bother you with anything else."

Dana felt as if all the blood had suddenly been drained from her body. Weary and battle-scarred, she stood up and shakily held out her hand.

"Okay, let's have a truce. We're going to help Hallie and keep our personal feelings out of it. Now I'm going to bed. If you want, I'll get some blankets and sleep on the couch."

"I'll sleep on the couch," he said softly. "I'll tell Hallie I had to keep the fire stoked during the night."

Dana nodded. "I'll get the blankets." A bleak hopelessness consumed her as she plodded toward the bedroom, trying not to cry, trying not to fall apart, trying to give herself some reason to take another step. Hal. She had Hal.

She went to her daughter's bedroom door to make sure she was covered up. It could get darn cool before morning, and she didn't want her little girl to catch cold.

Logan punched the couch pillow. This wasn't a satisfactory solution, but for now, it would have to do.

"Logan!" Dana shrieked from the bedroom. He heard another shriek, then Dana calling "Hallie! Omigod, Logan, come quick."

He was there in a flash.

"She's gone!" Dana's voice verged on hysteria. She dashed to the open window. "Hallie," she called out, then spun around, her eyes darting every which way. "She's…she's just gone."

Dana and Logan began searching every nook and cranny in every room and closet in the house. Finished, they charged outside. Dana continued calling Hallie's name as they rounded the corner next to the window in Hal's bedroom.

The screen lay on the ground with a long slice down the middle. The damp earth was deeply gouged with footprints. Dana let out a long guttural moan and swayed on her feet.

"Steady," Logan said, using both hands to prop her up, then with one arm around her, he directed her toward the cabin door. "C'mon. Let's go inside."

"No!" Dana dug her heels into the soil as he urged her forward. "We have to look for her. Those aren't her footprints. They're too large. Someone took her."

"We don't know that," Logan said, all his senses on red alert. He knew, first and foremost, that he had to get Dana inside.

"First thing we need to do," he went on, "is get help on the way. And we have to be extremely careful so we don't mess up the evidence."

"Evidence…" Dana uttered as they went inside. She sat on a kitchen chair, put her arms on the table and laid her head on top. Logan retrieved his cell phone and punched in 911.

The nearest town was some little burg about twenty miles away. He knew there'd be only one sheriff, who may or may not be trained in abductions. But if nothing else, he could order a roadblock on the main road.

The dispatcher, if the slug who answered really *was* one, took directions and said someone would be on the way. Next Logan called Remy to get a team together. Upon hearing the problem, his partner instantly switched into action mode. They'd be at the cabin within the hour. Before if possible.

Logan hung up and glanced to Dana, "Okay, I'm going to ask you a couple of things before we start the search. Time is of the essence in cases like this, and so is maintaining the integrity of the evidence. Organization is critical.''

To which, Dana spat out. ''Dammit, Logan. I don't care about evidence or organization. I care about finding Hallie.''

''We both do, and if we go about it right, our chances of finding her unharmed will be much greater. If she's been—'' His throat seized up and he couldn't get the words out. He'd done this dozens of times with parents of kidnapped children and spouses of corporate kidnap victims, and in the past, he could only imagine the terror those families had gone through.

Now he knew.

''If someone kidnapped her,'' Logan continued, ''he'll no doubt contact us regarding a ransom. Remy's getting a team here within the hour and he has staff working on profiles.''

Dana covered her mouth with her hand and sagged into one of the wooden kitchen chairs. Finally she managed, ''Why would anyone want to kidnap Hallie? What possible reason could anyone have? It isn't like…'' Her voice trailed off, as if she'd realized there were many reasons someone would kidnap Hallie, and she couldn't possibly vocalize them.

Logan knew what those reasons were. Money, for one. His family had money out the kazoo. His enemies, for two. Yeah, there were two or three people who might want to get even with him—if they ever found out who he was. There were also a few hundred criminals who might want to get even with the prosecutor who'd ended their crime careers, and there was Lombard's connection with the mob.

There was another he didn't even want to think about.

A pedophile, or a serial killer. Hell, there was even Jerrod, his Milquetoast-like former brother-in-law—who knew what lay beneath that mild exterior? All were possibilities.

But Logan quickly narrowed the field. Jerrod was out—unless he had a motive. The most likely scenario was that whoever wanted Dana off the case had found a way to keep her busy. That meant Lombard or the guy he worked for. Which everyone knew was Salvatore Leonetti.

"What about Jerrod?" Logan asked just to be sure.

Dana stared at him. "Jerrod?"

"Yes. Didn't Liz tell you Jerrod had been stalking her? And wasn't she supposed to call the police?"

Dana nodded. "She thought maybe Jerrod was the one who broke into the house looking for her. And she did say she was going to call the police."

He went to her, squatted down and took her hand in his. "Do you think Jerrod would do something like this to get back at you for giving Liz a place to stay?"

"No. I don't think he would take Hallie. I really don't."

Logan held her eyes, hoping it had a steadying effect. Yeah. Jerrod was out. While he might break in, he really didn't have a motive to kidnap Hal. "It's critical that you listen to me and do as I say. Okay?"

Dana drew herself up, then pushed to her feet. "Okay, you're the expert, what do we do now?"

"I'm going to ask you to do some things you might not like. Here's the plan. First of all, someone must stay here in case we get a ransom demand."

"But…how would…"

"If there's a kidnapper involved, he'd figure out how to contact us. A rock through the window with a note on it, a call on the cell phone, I don't know. *Someone* must stay here for that, and also to answer questions if the police or the SISI team arrives. That someone would be you," he said.

She didn't exactly glare at him, but he couldn't tell if she accepted his directives, either. He doubted there'd be a ransom demand if the mob was involved, but he had to consider the possibility.

"I'll go out to see if I can find a trail," he continued. "I know what to look for and I know what not to disturb."

"Okay. And what should I do besides sit here and wait?"

His heart went out to her, especially because he knew what it had taken for her to agree. She had to agree to do nothing, a concept totally foreign to her.

"That's it sweetheart. You wait for the help, and I'll let you know the minute I pick up a trail of any kind. Tell the guys when they arrive that I'm using the Plan A. They'll know what direction I went and what to do from there."

The last thing Dana wanted to do was sit and wait—especially alone. But Logan was right, she knew. It was the first time she'd seen him in action on a job, and for the first time, she realized how incredibly difficult his job must be.

For him, lives were continually at stake, and he was the expert. She couldn't imagine living with that burden day in and day out, couldn't imagine the toll it would take. Yet he did it with absolute professionalism and certainty.

If anyone could get the job done, it was Logan. She trusted him implicitly. "Okay, I'll do as you say. But please promise me you'll let me help if I can."

He reached out, tipped her face up with two fingers under her chin and looked into her eyes. His pain-filled gaze was full of compassion.

"Absolutely," he said. "I need your help. I'm sorry if I seem to be running the show, but I know what I'm doing and it has nothing to do with anything except finding our daughter. It has to be this way."

"Go," she urged. "Please find our little girl."

Watching him leave, she swallowed down the bile that climbed the back of her throat. Her hands were shaking, her head throbbed and her stomach was twisted into one huge painful knot. She'd never felt so totally helpless.

Despite that, she had utter confidence that Logan would do everything he could to find Hallie.

The next thirty minutes seemed an eternity. Again she checked the bedrooms, the bathroom, the closets, searching everywhere for some kind of clue. What had happened and when? How long had Hallie been gone?

It couldn't be more than an hour or so, because Hal hadn't been in bed that long before Dana had gone to check. Maybe an hour and a half at the most.

When the cell phone rang, Dana darted for it, then hesitated, unable to breathe for second. Oh, God. What if it was the kidnapper? What if he was going to give her an ultimatum? Frantic, she flipped open the phone. She was shaking so hard she couldn't find her voice, then finally croaked out, "Who is this?"

Someone answered on the other end, but the loud noises in the background drowned out the voice. Finally she realized it was Remy. "We're in the chopper over Fern Creek. We're gonna need coordinates to land. I can't get Logan on this phone."

Remy said he had a couple of cars waiting for them

to land, so he needed specifics to get to the cabin from that spot. Dana gave Remy what directions she could, feeling some comfort that the SISI team of experts would be here soon. She wasn't alone. They weren't alone. And with additional people looking, surely they'd find Hallie soon. But why couldn't he make contact with Logan?

For the first time in a very long time, Dana said a prayer. She'd give up everything in the world that she'd once found dear—if only she had her little girl back again and Logan was safe.

With nothing to do except worry, she went to the kitchen and made a pot of coffee. She stoked the fire and then took her cup into Hallie's room. The bedcovers were half on the floor, and for the first time, she noticed that Hal's backpack was gone.

That was strange. She hurried to the closet and rummaged through everything. No backpack. She tried to remember what else Hal had brought to the cabin so she'd know what else might be missing.

Pooka. Where was Pooka? She couldn't find the stuffed animal anywhere, either. Which brought a dozen other questions to mind.

How likely was it that a kidnapper would pack a backpack and make sure the victim's favorite stuffed animal was along? Not much, she'd guess.

Had Hallie run away? Good God! Was that even a possibility? Dana couldn't imagine. Not in the middle of the night in the middle of the woods. Hallie would never do such a thing. And they'd been having a wonderful time from the minute they'd arrived at the cabin.

Still, the backpack was gone, along with Hal's favorite stuffed animal. That had to mean something. Oh, no! Maybe she'd heard them arguing? But would that scare her enough to run away? It didn't seem likely, especially this late at night. And yet...

Odd as it was, the possibility sparked a tiny bit of hope in Dana. If for some reason Hal had decided to run away, that relieved her of worry that someone might hurt her. But the thought of her little girl lost and alone in the woods was almost as frightening.

God, she wished Logan would call.

A loud banging on the door made her jump a foot in the air. She sprinted from the bedroom to answer it.

A rumpled mound of a man said, "Sheriff Beuler, ma'am." He looked as if he'd just awakened and had been sleeping in his uniform. Tipping his hat to the back of his head, he said, "Is this the place with the missing child?"

"Yes. Thank God you're here. C'mon in." Dana peered over his shoulder for others.

"There's no one here but me, ma'am. Couldn't round up anyone on such late notice. Everyone must've gone into town to the movies or something. I figured I'd come get the information to see what we had to do." He stepped inside.

Dana's heart sank again. Even so, one more person looking was better than nothing.

"You mind telling me what happened?"

"I went to check on my daughter before I went to bed and she was gone. The window was open and we found footprints—big ones—outside and the screen looked like it'd been sliced. Hallie's father is out looking for her now."

The man rubbed his chin, then said, "Uh-huh."

"We have other help coming, too. An investigation team." Her thoughts seemed disjointed and she had the

oddest feeling that this man would be no help whatsoever.

"Help, huh? An investigation team. Uh-huh. Sounds
good." He crossed the room, his gaze moving from the
fireplace to the closet to the kitchen window.

Dana's patience wore thin. "I'm sorry Mr...Sheriff.
I've got to find my husb—Hallie's father. I need someone to stay here in case the team comes to tell them
that—" She stopped midsentence because he wasn't
even listening.

"Oh, hell." She found some paper on the kitchen
table and scribbled, "Tell the team Plan A." She went
over to him, shoved the paper into his palm and headed
for the door, grabbing her coat as she went.

On her way out, the headlights of a car beamed out
of the blackness. Remy. Relief flooded through her, and
she stood on the top step waiting for the car to reach
her. No, two cars.

As soon as they pulled in, eight doors flew open and
six men piled out, three from each car. Remy unfolded
himself from the driver's side of the first vehicle. Another surge of relief swept through her as she ran to
him. "Thank God, you're here!"

Remy gave her a quick hug. He was dressed in his
pickle fatigues and she realized his mode, like Logan's,
was pure professional. "Plan A," she blurted. "Logan
said to tell you he was using Plan A."

He nodded, then tipped his head toward the sheriff's
vehicle. Dana shook her head. "Forget it. He's inside,
probably taking a nap."

"You hear anything?" Remy asked. "Any calls?"

Dana shook her head. "Nothing."

He gestured to his men, who must've known what he

meant, since they spread out in a circle around the cabin.

"Can I come with you?" Dana asked. She needed to do something. On a peripheral thought, she glanced again at one of Remy's men, a tall black man making his way into the woods. He looked awfully familiar.

Frowning, Remy eyed her suspiciously. "What'd Logan tell you to do?"

"Okay, okay." She raised her hands. "He said I should stay in case a call comes in." She sighed. "I know he's right. But I can't stand doing nothing."

Remy gave her a concerned look. "Understandable. However, in a situation like this, it's critical to follow instructions, like my team." He gave his men another gesture and they instantly fanned out into the woods. "Gotta go." And with that, he started in another direction.

"Wait, Remy. When I was in Hal's room a few minutes ago, I noticed her backpack was missing, and so was her favorite stuffed animal. You know that ratty little rabbit she's had since she was born? I thought it might mean she's run away."

He nodded. "She have reason to run away?"

"She could have heard us raising our voices. I don't really think that would be a reason…" After a thoughtful moment, she added, "But Hallie hasn't been herself lately. Still, I can't imagine a kidnapper taking her backpack."

"The thing is—" Remy gave her a quick sympathetic smile "—a familiar object will sometimes help keep a child quiet." He waited as if gauging her reaction. "Logan said there were footprints."

Dana's hope that Hal hadn't been abducted deflated.

"We'll find her," Remy assured her, and then he was off.

LOGAN'S NERVES WERE taut as he followed the footpath coming up from the lake. There was a full moon and the beam of his flashlight was strong. He'd found no other prints or evidence that someone might've gone toward the lake. He'd heard the chopper a while back; the team would be in action any minute.

A noise. A snap on his right. He flicked the light in that direction. An animal scuttled through the dense underbrush.

He stopped for a second, deciding which way to take. The path toward the highway, or the overgrown path that led to the nearest cabin a mile away?

He chose the path toward the highway. More likely a kidnapper would head in that direction, to a car.

He tried to get a take on what kind of job this was. The pattern didn't fit that of a professional, and that was not a good sign. Professionals wanted money; they were willing to negotiate. Amateurs tended to panic, were more volatile, more prone to violence. The percentage of successful negotiations with kidnappers dropped dramatically with the amateurs.

The fact that break-ins had happened in both places he and Dana owned ruled out a random act. And whoever was involved was as inept as Lombard had been. In which case, he feared the worst. He had to focus, follow the plan, not think about a terrified little girl— his little girl—out there somewhere.

He started toward the highway and within seconds, he heard Remy's signal. Relief flooded him. He'd never been so glad to know his buddy was there.

More noise, shouting, and then the crack of gunshots.

Sprinting in the direction he'd heard the shooting, Logan saw a dark form crashing through the underbrush—and heading directly toward him.

With extreme stealth he slipped behind a tree and waited, his heart slamming against his ribs. Then, as the guy approached, Logan drew his hand back, jumped out and delivered a chop to his throat.

The guy doubled over, fell to his knees. Logan could kill a man that way, but he'd gone light because the guy was alone, which meant if he *was* the kidnapper, they'd need him to find Hal.

The guy curled into a ball, writhing in pain on the ground. Seconds later Remy was at Logan's side. He poked the guy in the ribs with his boot and whacked Logan on the shoulder. "Hey, bro. This the dude you're lookin' for?"

"Hey, Rem." Logan grabbed the writhing form by the scruff of his coat, noticing that it was a long brownish job like an old army coat—like the one worn by the old guy who'd been hanging out at the school yard. His anger peaked, colors exploding in his head. He jerked the suspect to a semistanding position.

A balaclava covered the guy's face, and when Remy reached out to yank it off, the guy retched and then vomited right through the knitted fabric. Remy let go.

Logan dropped the suspect to the ground and said, "You better have some goddamn good answers when you're done, or you'll wish you'd died, instead of puking your guts out. And if you've harmed one hair of my daughter's head, you'll wish you were dead a thousand times over."

When the guy stopped retching, Remy reached down and pulled off the balaclava.

Logan shone the beam of his flashlight on their captive's face. "What the hell…"

CHAPTER SIXTEEN

DANA PACED the deck in front of the cabin, waiting for news of any kind. The sheriff had gone, supposedly to recruit a couple of volunteers to form his own search party. So Dana waited, listening for any little noise, for the phone to ring. For Logan to come back with their little girl.

If only the kidnappers would call! At least then she might be able to speak with Hallie, to know she was okay.

Thank God Logan had been with her. She clasped her hands in front of her and prayed that he'd find Hallie, all the while blaming herself for what had happened.

If she'd expected too much, worked too many hours or placed greater importance on things other than on those she loved, she vowed to change. In the past two weeks she'd lost her daughter not once, but twice. And if she could get her back safe and sound, she'd never again try to be all things to all people.

The Superwoman syndrome, Logan had called it once. No wonder he'd thought she didn't need him; she'd never once let him think she did. Of course, she hadn't known it herself, because she was too damn busy thinking she could do it all.

And she couldn't.

Another horrible thought descended on her. If Logan, the man she'd loved more than anything, didn't think she needed him, then how could her own daughter feel needed and loved? How many times after Logan had gone had Hallie asked what would happen if she did something really bad?

Did Hallie blame Dana for her daddy's leaving?

Dana's throat closed. Tears began to flow.

Logan had been right about her. One hundred percent right. But if he didn't love her, anyway, what difference did it make? Would he have stayed in the marriage without love if he'd known she needed him?

She hauled in a deep breath. It didn't matter. It was too late for her and Logan. But she *would* make things right with her daughter—if she had another chance.

A noise sounded in the woods in front of her, then on her left, more noise like cracking twigs and voices. Logan? Hallie? It had to be. Dana's heart rushed. Had he found Hallie? She prayed he had.

Four men came thrashing out of the woods, and then she saw Logan and Remy, holding up a man in a long brown coat between them. As they got closer, Dana did a double take.

The guy was slight, his dirty-blond hair pulled back in a ponytail. On second look, she realized it wasn't a man at all. It was a young woman. A teenager.

What on earth was she doing out here at night alone in the woods? As they came closer, the teenager looked familiar, yet Dana couldn't place her.

She didn't care. She only wanted to know about Hallie.

Dana ran down the steps toward them. "Did you find her? Did you find Hallie?"

Logan shook his head. "Ask her."

"What are you talking about, Logan?"

"She said she wants to talk to you. She won't talk

to anyone but you. She said that you're the reason her mother's murderer is out on bail.''

Dana's blood pumped erratically. "What does that have to do with Hallie? Did you find Hallie?" Her voice rose a decibel with every word, and she knew she sounded hysterical.

She didn't give a damn. All she cared about was getting her daughter back. Then Dana smelled a foul odor coming from the girl and put a hand over her nose.

"She threw up," Logan said. "I thought she was a guy and knocked her flat."

Dana's head swam. "Will you please tell me what's going on?"

"It's your fault," the girl spit out. "My mom is dead and she's never coming back. And you let that man get out of prison and he'll never have to pay for what he did."

Instantly it became clear—the girl was the daughter of the woman Lombard had killed. "I'm sorry about that. But bail is a court procedure, decided by the judge. It's not anything I can control." Her patience at breaking point, Dana demanded, "What does this have to do with my daughter?"

The girl's face contorted with hatred. "You don't know what it feels like to lose someone you love. I wanted you to know what that feels like."

Panic of another kind seized Dana. She looked helplessly at Logan, then back at the girl. "What's going on? Where the hell is Hallie? Did you hurt Hallie?"

"I wasn't going to hurt her or anything," the girl said, almost as if she had no idea why Dana was so upset. "I only wanted to take her away for a little while so you'd see how it feels, and then...and then maybe you'd make them put that man back in jail. That's all. That's all I wanted to do." She started crying.

"You took Hallie!" Dana shrieked, shaking with anger. "You've been stalking her, trying to get into our house to kidnap her, so I'd see what it's *like?*" Dana was filled, suddenly, with horror and rage. She grabbed the girl's coat and started shaking her. "You tell me where she is, damn you!"

Logan reached for Dana and pried her away, then put his arms around her. The girl started sobbing, and Logan whispered in Dana's ear, "Appease her. Say something to make her want to tell us where Hallie is."

Appease her. Oh, God. Yes. Okay. If that's what I have to do, I will.

Dana drew in a long gulp of air, and Logan released her. She faced the distraught teenager. "I understand," she said, summoning calm from some deep part of her. "And I do know how it feels now. And I promise to do everything in my power to put that man back in jail—for life. I promise you that."

She waited a second, assessing the girl's reaction. When she looked the least bit receptive, Dana said, "But we need to know where Hallie is so *you* won't get into any trouble. Can you please tell me where you took her?"

The girl sniffled as mucus ran down from her nose to her lip. Dana reached in her pocket for a tissue and handed it to her. Remy released one of the girl's arms, and she wiped her nose and mouth and started talking at the same time. "I...I didn't take her. I came to the cabin and she was climbing out the window. She said she was running away, so I told her I'd help her. See, that way I wasn't doing anything wrong and you'd still know what it feels like," the girl said almost proudly.

Dana was livid, her stomach roiled and she was ready to shake the girl again, but she said, her voice still calm, "I do know that now. I really know what it feels like...so can you tell me how you helped her? Where did you take her?"

The girl pointed. "I took her to the boathouse down at that next cabin."

"You left her there," Logan interjected, "alone?"

The girl nodded. Dana turned to run, but Logan caught her arm. "The car. It'll be faster."

Remy nodded toward his vehicle. "Keys are in the ignition."

Leaving the teenager in Remy's care, Logan and Dana climbed into the black car, and before Dana's door was even shut, Logan hit the gas. As they careered down the road, they passed what looked like a car in the ditch, but there was no time to check it out, and they sped on until they screeched to a stop at the cabin a mile down the road.

It was dark. Apparently the owners hadn't come up for the weekend. They both hit the ground running toward the boathouse. Dana crashed through the brush, stumbling on rocks, ripping her jeans and cutting her ankle in the process. Out of breath, they reached the boathouse and tried the door.

Locked.

It didn't matter because a split second later, Logan kicked it down. Frantic, Logan cut through the dark with his flashlight.

At first the beam of his flashlight revealed nothing, and pure unadulterated fear shot through Dana.

And then she heard a soft whimpering sound. Logan shined the light toward the sound and came upon a pile of blankets in the corner.

Rushing over, Dana lifted the blankets. "Oh, Hallie. Thank God." She pulled her daughter to her.

Then Hallie spotted Logan. Her eyes went wide and she shrieked, "Daddy, Daddy! You didn't leave!"

Logan reached and took her from Dana's arms. "I'm right here, sweetheart. Why did you think I left?"

"'Cause I heard you and Mommy shouting, and then Mommy told you to leave—just like before.

Logan and Dana exchanged horrified glances.

"But...why would you run away?" Dana asked, her heart pounding.

Hallie shrugged. "I was scared. I didn't want you and Daddy to hear me crying, 'cause then you'd think I was bad and Daddy would leave for sure."

Dear God. Dana's heart wrenched. Hallie had heard them fighting. She tried to remember what they'd said, what damage they might've done.

"I don't want you to go, Daddy." Hallie started to cry. "I want you to stay."

Dana tried to hold back her tears, but they flooded down her cheeks, anyway. They'd found her little girl and she was okay.

Hallie sniffled, then looked at Dana. "Don't cry," she said. "I wasn't *that* scared. That nice lady gave me her hat and coat to keep me warm until we got here, and then she gave me the blanket. She said we could play a hide-and-seek game and that if I would hide, you and Daddy would come and find me later. And you did, just like she said. I tried not to be scared, Mommy, but she didn't come back, and I got a little scared, anyway."

Mommy. Hallie called her Mommy. "Oh, sweetie," Dana said, gulping down her tears. "It's okay to be scared and it's okay to say so, too. We were so worried that something had happened to you and, oh..."

Dana couldn't imprison her deep sob. She wept openly with relief. Her daughter was safe.

Hal reached out to Dana and said, "Please don't cry, Mommy. It makes me really sad. I didn't want Daddy to leave again, that's all."

The implication of Hal's words hit Dana full force. Her knees shook, and she grabbed onto Logan's arm so she wouldn't fall. Leave again, she'd said. Leave *again!*

Had Hal heard the fight before their breakup a year ago? Had she heard Dana tell Logan she'd rather be single and he might as well leave? No wonder she'd blocked her mother out of her life. She'd thought her mommy had sent her daddy away.

Dana swiped at her eyes with the sleeve of her jacket. Despite all that, Hallie had called her *Mommy.* She remembered. Her little girl remembered.

Logan drew Dana closer, pulling her into the circle of his arms with Hallie. "Everything is going to be fine," he said. "Now let's go back so we can tell everyone to stop worrying."

Hallie reached a chubby hand up and patted Dana's cheek, smoothing away her tears. "It's okay, Mommy. Daddy said everything's going to be okay."

ONCE THEY WERE back at the cabin and Hallie was asleep, it took an hour for them to straighten out the rest of the details. The sheriff had taken the girl, Carolyn, into custody while they were with Hal at the boathouse. Apparently, by saying she had to give Dana urgent information on the case, she'd cleverly gotten information from Jillian that they'd gone to the cabin and then had been smart enough to get public information from the assessor's office that gave her the exact location. The car they'd seen in the ditch was hers.

Gideon, Dana learned, worked for SISI. The company had been hired by the FBI to do an independent investigation to uncover major corruption in the county government, including the state's attorney's office. The mafia had tentacles reaching far into the judicial system, from jury tampering to payoffs. Top-secret stuff, the details of which would be disclosed later.

David, she discovered, had only recently been involved. He'd been indiscreet in his private life and was being blackmailed by the mob, who threatened to expose him and ruin his bid for attorney general if he didn't get Lombard's case thrown out.

When his plan to lose the Lombard case fell through, Leonetti ordered a hit on Lombard. Gideon had gotten wind of what was coming down through his moles and placed Lombard in protective custody until the trial, which was why he'd disappeared for a while.

Apparently Lombard wasn't quite as stupid as he seemed and said he'd cut a deal—information against Leonetti for a reduced sentence in a secured prison. Leonetti was arrested immediately.

The fact that Dana had refused to talk to Wellesy was, apparently, what started the chain reaction.

Her job was secure. Her bid for state's attorney would be clear. If she took on the Leonetti case and the state won, which was pretty certain, considering the evidence, it was a walk in the park. The problem was, she wasn't sure she wanted it anymore. It was a decision she'd have to make, but the last thing on her mind right now.

She was tired. Damn tired. When everyone was gone, Dana and Logan slept with Hal between them for the rest of the night. Dana didn't know how she could possibly explain to Hal that it was better for her parents to live apart.

God knows, it wasn't what she wanted, but Logan hadn't said anything further on the subject since Hallie had gone missing. She suspected he'd wait until they were back at home and alone, where Hal couldn't possibly hear their conversation.

What was there left to say, anyway?

The next morning, Hal was no worse for wear. She'd become the same little girl she'd always been and seemed to remember most everything. She talked about going over to Chloe's the minute she got home.

Dana was grateful the child had such resiliency, but as far as she and Logan went, she was stymied. Logan acted as if nothing had happened, going through the breakfast motions as he always had. He kidded with Hal, teased Dana about her hard-cooked soft-boiled eggs, and then he'd said he had some calls to return.

His calls apparently done, he came back in and stood behind her while she finished up the breakfast dishes. Hal had gone down to the lake for one last rock hunt before they left for home.

"The town house is almost a done deal," Logan said. "And I'd like to sit down and talk the first chance we get…about shared custody."

Dana swallowed around the lump that had formed in her throat. She'd thought she was braced for anything, but she'd been wrong. If she'd felt alone before, it was nothing compared to how she felt now. "Fine," she said, "I'll go pack." She went into the bedroom and closed the door.

For the next twenty minutes, she lay quietly across the bed. What did she expect? That suddenly all the hurt and pain would go away? That because Hal had remembered, everything would be the same? After all they'd been through, she didn't see how that could ever be. Logan had made his intentions clear.

She loved him. She'd never stopped loving him. If she thought she had no more tears, she was wrong, and for the first time since she was a child, she allowed tears of regret to flow freely.

There came a point when all the tears were gone, so she dabbed her eyes and finished packing. The least she could do is hold on to her dignity. It was all she had left.

When she came out, Logan was standing at the fireplace, one arm against the mantel, and she stopped in the hallway to look at him. He seemed so solid and strong, from the inside out.

She wished she had a fraction of that strength.

But the truth was, no matter how strong she'd looked, it was a facade.

Right then, in admitting to herself that she wasn't as strong as she thought, she felt infused with a strange sense of resolve. It felt good to admit she needed him, and she felt stronger for being able to do it. For the first time, she realized that needing to be loved wasn't a weakness at all.

If only she'd had that realization when it might've made a difference! Logan might not have loved her as she wanted, but at least they might've had a chance. She took a deep breath. It was time to get on with her life.

Then Logan turned, and what she saw wrenched at her heart. His eyes were distressed, his skin pale, and she realized that he'd been just as scared as she was about Hal's disappearance. How had she missed that? How had she so totally missed that?

Because he was the strong one, that was how. He'd always been the easy-going, devil-may-care kind of guy who pulled his strength from a bottomless well. She realized now that, it wasn't bottomless. He needed something from her, too. In that flash of enlightenment, her heart ached for all the lost time, the lost hopes and dreams.

Suddenly she saw that he had tears in his eyes. She rushed forward, desperate to give him any comfort she could, the comfort he'd given her without a second's thought.

When she reached him, she touched his arm and said, "Logan, come sit with me for a minute. Please?"

He did as she asked, but he seemed so withdrawn, so defeated. She couldn't bear to see him that way.

"I know this won't matter now, but I really need to tell you this." Her throat clogged. She cleared it and then went on.

"I struggled all my life to be important in my family's eyes. I guess I believed that my achievements would make them love me as I wanted them to. Then somewhere along the way, that drive to achieve became who I am."

She closed her eyes and took a breath. "I never intended to make you feel unnecessary to my life. You were so strong, and I felt so inadequate. All I ever wanted was to matter to somebody without having to be perfect.

"When I met you, Logan, I fell in love." She drew in another deep breath, willing herself to go on, to get it out once and for all. "I knew you only married me because I was pregnant. I knew you had your life planned, but I hoped so much that maybe you'd learn to love me.''

She looked down, twisted the hem of her shirt. Her voice, she knew, was as shaky as her hands. ''Don't ever feel the failure of our marriage was your fault. It was mine. I needed too much, and because I needed too much, I hid it from you.'' She turned her tear-filled gaze to him. ''And I'm sorry. So very sorry.''

She paused and straightened her shoulders. ''So. Let me know what you want to do about Hallie and we'll work out whatever arrang—''

Logan placed a silencing finger over Dana's lips. ''That's what you thought?''

She frowned. ''Is what, what I thought?''

''That I didn't love you? You thought I married you only because you were pregnant?''

''That wasn't too hard to figure out.''

Logan shook his head incredulously, then gave her a broad white smile. ''Oh, Dana, Dana, I can't believe this. How could you *not* know how much I admired you, your intelligence, your wit, your charge-ahead, torpedoes-be-damned attitude? Getting pregnant just speeded things up a bit.''

Admire. He'd said admire, not love.

She gave a wry laugh. Who was he kidding? ''Speeded up? Logan, it changed your whole life. Don't you think I know you'd planned to marry someone else? Someone who fit into your world—someone...of your class?''

He stared at her, then nodded as if finally understanding. ''Ah! My mother. Right?''

''I didn't say that.''

''You didn't have to.'' He laughed. ''Man, oh, man. Yeah, my folks had things planned, even a girl they thought would be perfect for me. But I nixed that the minute I met you.'' He pressed his lips together, then went on. ''Dana, you do know where my mother was born and raised, don't you?''

Dana nodded. ''In Philadelphia.''

''You know the neighborhood, don't you?''

''Your mother said it was near where Grace Kelly grew up. I've only been to Independence Hall.''

''South Philadelphia,'' Logan said. ''Not near Grace Kelly's at all. Little Italy to be exact, near Remy's old stomping grounds.''

''I've never been there, either. What's it like?''

Logan laughed again. ''It isn't Nob Hill, that's what. Row housing. Lots of tenements. Some of it nice, some of it not. Whatever it is, it's not where my mother wanted her roots to be. My mother is a snob, Dana. She wanted to escape a life she considered beneath her. She could never see that her past is part of who she is.

''She'll probably never change. But y'know what? That's okay. I don't need her to change to live my life as I want.'' He grinned. ''We are who we are, you and me. And *you* are the woman I fell in love with.''

Dana felt a little dizzy. *Love?* He'd said love.

He reached out and held both her hands in his. ''Yes, I admired your achievements, even your damned independence. But I cared about those things because *you* cared about them. I cared about them for you, not for myself.'' His voice quavered and he had to clear his throat.

''This—'' he tapped her chest ''—this in here is who I love. I love your tenderness, your warmth and your ability to sometimes make me feel ten feet tall. I love you, Dana. And you know what?''

He kept looking directly into her eyes. "You know what?" he repeated.

She bit her lip and shook her head, afraid to say anything, because the tears welling behind her eyes would surely flood everything.

"I've loved you from the start, and I've never stopped."

Stunned, she couldn't move, couldn't say a word.

He loved her. Her heart soared and suddenly *she* was the one who felt ten feet tall.

She wanted to sing and dance and laugh and cry all at the same time. But she only gave an awkward little laugh and blinked back her tears of happiness.

"We're really a pair, aren't we," she said in a shaky voice between sniffles. "What are we going to do now?"

Logan's radiant smile held all the hope and love that filled her own heart. "I'd like to take my family home, Dana. I'd like to take my family home for good, to live with you and make love with you for the rest of our lives, for better or for worse. I want to show you I love you in a million different ways—and I want you to open the door to that damn bedroom of ours."

His mouth came within a breath of hers. "Can you handle all that? Because what I want most of all is to marry you again, Dana. Will you marry me?"

The ache and swell of emotion filled her chest, cutting off her air supply, and the only words she could find the second before her lips met his were, "Yes. Oh, yes. Definitely yes."

EPILOGUE

The next spring

HALLIE SKIPPED OVER to where Dana stood in front of the mirror. "You look beautiful, Mommy. Even if you don't have one of those really long train things." Then Hal examined her own reflection.

"Well, thank you, sweetheart." Dana adjusted one of the pink tea roses threaded through her daughter's hair. "You look beautiful, too. You and Chloe will steal the show, believe me."

Chloe peered into the guest bedroom from the open door. "I think your dress is even better'n the ones I saw in all those magazines, too."

"That's because your mom helped pick it out," Dana said. The two little girls wore matching pink taffeta dresses with tiny embroidered roses all over. The theme was carried through to their baskets, brimming with shell-pink tea roses to match those in their hair.

Dana's stomach fluttered. For one fleeting moment, she wished she hadn't agreed to do this. She rather liked the romantic notion of eloping as they had the first time. But Logan had insisted they do the whole shebang since they hadn't done it before. So they'd compromised on a small wedding in their backyard with family and

friends, no giving away the bride, and no receiving line
or gifts.

Both sets of parents had been invited and, surpris-
ingly, both had come. Remy and Crystal were there with
the babies, and Hal had been completely charmed by
them. Dante, Gideon and Brody, SISI's permanent staff
were there, too, but none had come with girlfriends or
dates. Earlier Dana had noticed that all the men had
seemed interested in talking with Jillian and the only
other single woman there—her sister, Liz. She was sure
Logan would set them straight on that one, if they didn't
find out for themselves first. Of course, Liz could be
irresistible when she wanted...

"Okay, girls," Jillian said, swooping into the room
amid a flutter of apple-green satin. "Time for you to
go with Auntie Liz so your mom can finish getting
ready."

When the girls had gone, Jilly scurried around the
room, checking Dana's dress, shoes, veil and flowers.
"Okay, no need to be nervous, everything is taken care
of. The guests are arriving and, omigosh, I know I'm
forgetting something."

"I'm not the one who's nervous, Jilly. At least I
wasn't until you came in. Will you just go sit somewhere and relax? Please."

"Okay, but there's only a few minutes before we
need to go. Here, let me check your hair. I missed a
couple strands..."

"My hair is fine." Dana waved her friend away.
"Everything is fine," she said sweetly. "Why don't you
go out and wait with the girls, and I'll be there in a
few."

Jilly frowned. "You sure?"

"I'm sure." Smiling, Dana gently pushed Jilly toward the door. "Really, I'm all set. I just need a minute. Okay?"

When she was alone, Dana glanced at her reflection again. Everything *was* fine. And every day since Logan had asked her to marry him again, she'd awakened in this room filled with wonder at how things had turned out.

She'd gone back to work, cut a deal with Lombard and hoped to get a conviction on Leonetti. She had everyone urging her to take on the state's attorney job. Oddly, even realizing that was what she'd worked so hard for, she'd finally decided against it. Her career, while fulfilling and important to her, would never take priority over her family. And the job required more time than she wanted to give it right now.

For she and Logan had found a whole new level for their relationship. He was working locally and she wanted to spend more time with him and Hal. And— she touched her fingertips to her stomach—there were other considerations in the future.

No, they hadn't opened that bedroom door yet, deciding to wait until their wedding night.

Tonight.

The sound of music interrupted her reverie. *It was time.*

Oh, Lord. If she wasn't nervous before, she was now. She smoothed the front of her strapless, off-white satin gown and moistened her lips with the tip of her tongue. *This is it, Dana. It's now or never.*

As she took one last deep breath, she heard a light knock on the door behind her. She turned to see Andrea Wakefield standing in the doorway.

The woman's face was pink, as if she was either hot or angry about something. Dana hoped she wasn't going to spoil the moment. After listening to Logan talk about his mother's background, Dana had decided he was right. Andrea Wakefield didn't need to change for them to be happy together, any more than her own parents had to change. She'd vowed to make the best of it. Regardless.

Now she wasn't sure. "Yes, Andrea. What is it?"

Logan's mother looked as she wanted to say or do something, but seemed riveted to the spot and couldn't spit it out. Finally she stuck out a hand in which she held a small velvet box. "I'd like you to have this," she said. Her words weren't warm, but they weren't filled with their usual disdain, either.

The music played more loudly, and Dana knew her cue was coming. She had to leave. The man she loved was waiting under the arbor of flowers they'd had built in the yard.

But this seemed important to Andrea.

Dana reached out, and Andrea put the box in her hand. "It's something old...to wear today."

Her hands shaking, Dana opened the box. A simple diamond pendant sparkled at her from against the black velvet inside.

"It was my mother's."

"It's beautiful," Dana whispered as tears filled her eyes. She swallowed hard. "Can you help me put it on?"

Andrea nodded. "I'd be happy to, Dana."

When that was done, Dana turned around and gave Andrea a hug. The first ever. "Thank you," she said. "Thank you for the gift of your wonderful son."

*   *   *   *   *

Turn the page to read a fascinating interview with Linda Style, as she discusses her experiences in the world of writing and publishing.

Don't miss this—especially if you're interested in writing, too!

INTERVIEW WITH LINDA STYLE ON WRITING AND PUBLISHING

Linda, tell us first why you write. And more specifically, what drew you to romance fiction?

Why do I write? Curiosity, maybe. Or perhaps it's because I have something to say? I'm in a continual discovery mode, learning about people, their lives and careers. I'm fascinated by what makes people tick, and through the examination of my characters, their conflicts, goals, values and beliefs, I discover more and more. What I learn and what I have to say about it comes out through my stories and my characters. Why I write romance is an easier question. I was drawn to the uplifting nature of romance. I like to write about fallible people who learn and grow and are rewarded for doing the right thing. I was drawn to romance because love and relationships are the very essence of our lives. Romance fiction is about people overcoming great odds to find love and happiness; it gives readers hope. I hope my stories will do that, too.

How long have you been writing? And how long did it take to get published?

I feel as if I've always been a writer, and from my earliest memories on, I wrote in diaries, journals, and scribbled out new endings to novels that didn't turn out the way I wanted. (I was always into happy endings.) I was published in nonfiction long before I started writing romance fiction. It took about five years and five books from when I first started writing romance to get published in the genre.

Your background includes working as a journalist, a photographer and in social services. (Have we missed any?) How do these other jobs and experiences relate to your writing career?

Yes, you missed a few. I've also worked as a human-rights advocate, an internal investigator and a management consultant, all for the state of Arizona's Department of Behavioral Health. With the exception of journalist and photographer, all my jobs were in the social services/behavioral health field. When I look at the different positions I've held, I see a pattern, and it all harks back to that curiosity factor I mentioned in my first answer. The same curiosity, the need to discover what makes people tick, is what led me to those jobs and to writing. After twenty years in social services, I've been exposed to the human experience from all angles, from homeless shelters to the governor's office. Working intimately with people from all walks of life allows me to draw on my experiences to deepen my stories, my characters and their conflicts.

The question everyone asks a writer is: where do you get your ideas? How would you answer that? (What for instance sparked the idea for this book?)

My ideas are from life. It's as simple as that. Ideas are everywhere—a tiny story in a newspaper, something someone says, a situation that sparks another idea, and then I build on it, using my own life experience and whatever research is necessary. My imagination takes it in many different directions until I settle on one main idea. For example, I watched a special on brain injuries, and that sparked an idea for my current book. An article on corporate kidnappings in a magazine sparked an interest and my research in top-secret private investigation companies, and since I've worked with internal investigations and with the law as the manager for the state of Arizona's Office of Grievance and Appeals, I came up with Dana and Logan's story. The emotional parts come from within me.

For you, does a book start with a plot premise or with a character or a place or something else?

All of the above. Any one of those elements can come first, but whatever it is, I decide all three before I ever start writing. Most of the time, I'll get the spark of an idea for a story, which I toss around to see if it goes anywhere. If it does, before I do anything else I decide what characters would best fit; what personality types would make this story most interesting. Place can be first, last or somewhere in between, and sometimes the plot dictates where it will be set. To me, character development is most critical and I focus on that before I start that first chapter. Right now I have the beginnings of a story that I developed because I'd visited Charleston, South Carolina, and fell in love with the area. In that book, place came first, but usually it's a combination of all three.

Describe a day in your life as a writer.

Would "flat butt" cover it? That's from sitting at my

computer all day, every day. It's the only way writing will happen. Aside from that, I start early—5:00 a.m. or even before. I do e-mail, go for a mile walk, have coffee and sometimes breakfast (usually at my computer) and if I have time, take care of other business. Whatever I'm doing stops at 8:00 a.m. when I start writing. I work through lunch sometimes, depending on what needs to be done. I work all day, every day, whether it's writing, research or promotion.

Linda, do you think it's difficult for a writer to keep a sense of balance in her life (between the demands of writing and her personal life)? More difficult than with other occupations? How do *you* manage it?

It's very difficult to keep a sense of balance between writing and one's personal life. I believe the reason for that is not only due to the demands of writing, deadlines, promotion and producing more work, but because I love what I do. When you love what you do, it's all too easy to do it "all" the time. While I felt a great deal of satisfaction from my other jobs, I viewed them differently; they weren't jobs I could do all the time. From my perspective, it's more difficult for me as a writer to "make" time for other things. Then there's the problem with working from home. Not too many people see that in the same way as working out of the home, so there are many intrusions. I manage by using an answering machine and taking vacations. That's the fun part. I can take vacations when I want—as long as I'm not on a deadline. Of course, vacations are research, too—and I can do more fun stuff, like taking photographs. In essence, even when on vacation, I'm still working.

What books and writers have been important influences on you?

That's tough. There are some authors I read for pure pleasure because I love the way they put words on paper. And there are others whose storytelling abilities amaze me. One of my all-time favorite books is *To Kill a Mockingbird* by Harper Lee. I read that book years ago, but it's stayed with me. I felt the same way about *Exodus* and *Trinity* by Leon Uris. Romance writers include Debbie Macomber, Jan Freed, Susan Elizabeth Phillips, Suzanne Brockmann, Kathleen Korbel, Sherryl Woods and far too many others to name.

Being a published writer: Has it been what you expected—or different?

By the time I sold *Her Sister's Secret,* I'd learned a lot. I'd joined RWA, attended conferences, writers' workshops, met with editors and agents and learned everything I could about the business of writing, so I haven't been surprised by too much. I was realistic going into it, and knew I had to be disciplined if I wanted to succeed. The only difference I've found is that everything takes more time than I thought it would, so being organized is critical.

What is your favorite part of the writing and publishing process?

I really love it all. But there's nothing like taking the germ of an idea and developing it into a story. There's a special excitement when it all comes together and you start writing. Seeing the final product in book form is pretty thrilling, too. But as far as creativity is concerned, it's the actual writing process that excites me, including revisions.

In both of your books, you've established a strong sense of place; in *Her Sister's Secret,* it was the Arizona landscape, the small town, the B and B, while in this story it's the house and cabin shared by the family.

I mentioned in one of the previous questions that I write because I have something to say, and I think this question relates to that. When I pick a setting, it's usually because that place speaks to me emotionally. I have a feel for it and I know my characters will, too. It would be difficult for me to write about a place I didn't care about. On the other hand, I find so many places fascinating that I'll never be able to write about all of them. I've spent a great deal of time traveling—to more than fifteen different countries, from Australia to Turkey, and almost every state in the U.S. When a particular region and its people strike a chord in me, I must write about it. I don't travel just to see the scenery—I want to know about the people, how they live and how they feel about their lives, and I hope to convey those emotions and that sense of place in my books. In my first book, *Her Sister's Secret,* I wrote about Arizona because it's my adopted state, and I have a special affinity for everything Arizonan. However, my roots are in the Midwest, where I grew up, and I have deep-seated feelings for that part of the country, too, especially the old, substantial homes, and cabins in the woods. I spent my early years in those old homes and had cabins of my own in both the Midwest and in Arizona. Consequently, I have a special feeling about those, too, and wanted to share such feelings with readers in *Daddy in the House.*

Do you like to hear from readers? What kinds of things have readers told you and how have they affected you?

I love to hear from readers! I can be reached by e-mail at LindaStyle@LindaStyle.com, or at my Web site at www.LindaStyle.com, or by mail at P.O. Box 2292, Mesa, AZ 85214-2292. I've had wonderful responses from readers, some who've said my book gave them hope, and that they were moved to laughter and tears and were entertained, as well. I felt ten feet tall hearing that. My hope is always that my stories, besides being a good read, will touch readers' emotions in some way, and maybe illuminate the human condition a little. It's wonderful to know that I've done just that.

Finally, what advice would you give novice and as-yet-unpublished writers?

Read what you want to write. Learn your craft and keep writing. Do whatever you can to pursue your dream and don't give up. Never give up! The most inspiring words I've ever heard came from one of my sons when he told me that I've shown him by example that dreams can come true—if you want the dream enough to work hard and keep trying. When I think about that, I know I've given my children something really solid and good.

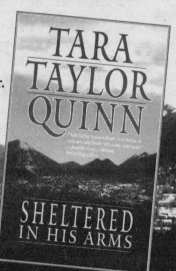

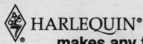

Special Deliveries

Experience the joy of parenthood,
delivered by two of your favorite Harlequin authors

Janice Kaiser
THIS CHILD IS MINE

Pain can be the midwife of joy…
That's what Lina's fortune cookie tells her.

Beverly Barton
CAMERON

What's in a name?
Everything, if it's all you've got to offer.

Coming April 2001
By Request 2

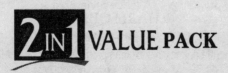

2 IN 1 VALUE PACK

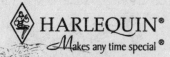

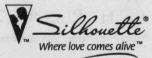